GENESIS

GENESIS

Geoffrey Carr

Elsewhen Press

Genesis
First published in Great Britain by Elsewhen Press, 2019
An imprint of Alnpete Limited

Copyright © Geoffrey Carr, 2019. All rights reserved

The quotation from Charles Darwin was first published in 1887 by John Murray, quoted by Francis Darwin in Volume 3 of *The life and letters of Charles Darwin: including an autobiographical chapter*.

The quotation from Graham Cairns-Smith is from *Seven clues to the origin of life: a scientific detective story*, first published in 1985 by Cambridge University Press, reproduced here with permission.

Elsewhen Press, PO Box 757, Dartford, Kent DA2 7TQ
www.elsewhen.press

British Library Cataloguing in Publication Data.
A catalogue record for this book is available from the British Library.

ISBN 978-1-911409-41-0 Print edition
ISBN 978-1-911409-51-9 eBook edition

Designed and formatted by Elsewhen Press

It is often said that all the conditions for the first production of a living organism are now present, which could ever have been present.— But if (& oh what a big if) we could conceive in some warm little pond with all sorts of ammonia & phosphoric salts,— light, heat, electricity &c present, that a protein compound was chemically formed, ready to undergo still more complex changes, at the present day such matter w^{d} be instantly devoured, or absorbed, which would not have been the case before living creatures were formed.

Charles Darwin to Joseph Hooker
Feb 1st 1871

It may seem hardly surprising that no one has ever actually made a self-reproducing machine, even though Von Neumann laid down the design principles more than 40 years ago. You can imagine a clanking robot moving around a stock-room of raw components (wire, metal plates, blank tapes and so on) choosing the pieces to make another robot like itself. You can show that there is nothing logically impossible about such an idea: that tomorrow morning there could be two clanking robots in the stock-room.

Graham Cairns-Smith, *Seven Clues to the Origin of Life*
1985

CONTENTS

PROTEROZOIC

MAY 19TH
MINISTRY OF STATE SECURITY, BEIJING

"The reception committee for Divine Skein is prepared?"

"Yes, General Xian. We should have the merchandise in five days' time."

"Excellent. The arrangements for testing it are in place?"

"Yes, General. They are."

"And the courier?"

"As agreed, will not be returning home."

MAY 23RD
PASADENA, CALIFORNIA

Professor Rhodes…

Alice rolled the words around her mouth, relishing the hard-won title. Her Humboldt swished out of South Wilson with no noise but the susurration of its tyres on the tarmac, onto Del Mar, past the lights at South Lake, past the faux Gothic of the McKinley School and out towards 210.

Professor Rhodes!

She was on the freeway in three minutes, heading north, then east. The mountains towered to her left. The endlessness of Los Angeles rolled off to her right. The breeze whipped through her hair. Bliss. Dawn. Alive. Young. Heaven. Today, anything was possible. Today, she would do it. Today, she would smash her record.

Past South Hills Park and off the freeway. Up Glendora Mountain Road to the junction with Big Dalton Canyon. Stop. Start the clock. Go.

The Humboldt took the hairpins effortlessly.

Sixty.

Seventy.

Then a jolt as the brakes applied themselves unbidden – and a calm and sexy female voice…

"Truck ahead."

Dumbass electronic nanny. She should have killed it before she set off. Still, no stopping now.

A truck on a country road? Memories flashed through her mind. An Art House her parents would not have approved. The innocence of Disney dying within her, she was seeking darker fare. She'd been thirteen. Fourteen, maybe? *Duel.* That nightmare's guileless start, when Mann first meets the tanker whose driver, never seen, is trying to kill him. She bit her lip, tucked in behind it, and waited for the straight. Then she hit the floor. *Eat my dust, sucker. You'll not catch me guard-down in a gas-station phone booth.*

They say everyone dreams of being in the movies. Not she. That was far too small a role for her ambition. No, she would *be* the movies. She would take the studios by the scruffs of their necks and give them a disrupting they'd never forget.

The play, the play. That was the thing. But the actors? They had got above themselves. Solipsistic strolling players turned by technology from penniless vagabonds into pompous, pampered popinjays. Well, what technology gives, technology takes away. She would make of film stars what steam power had made of handloom weavers. Virtual thespians, ego-lite and manager-free, that was what her project promised. The day would come, she knew, when the Academy would have no choice but to award 'Best Actor' to a computer program. Her program.

On she drove, through the pines of the Angeles National Forest. Seven minutes to Ridge Road. Yes! Now she was sure. This was the day her record really would get broken. In the distance, Mount Baldy reared its head. The sphendone. The turning post of her personal hippodrome.

She'd known, hadn't she, that the job was hers? Appointment committees don't turn you down when you have $20m in your back pocket. And that she did, signed and sealed in the Mondrian five days earlier. The Rhodes lab. It had a nice ring to it. A little celebration was surely in order. And here it was, a wild electric beast that existed to please only her.

Around the hairpin at the end of Glendora Ridge and down Mount Baldy for the return. A glance at the clock. No stopping now. She pressed the pedal to the metal…

…and the pedal went limp. The throttle was stuck, full open.

Shit. She had read about such things – but on Japcrap, not serious sports cars. *Shit. Shit. Shit.* You don't pay $150,000 for a Humboldt to have it go to hell on you.

She hit the brake. The game was over for today. She would have to try another time.

Lost in the disappointment of that thought, she took a moment to realise nothing had happened. She pushed the brake harder. The car careered on.

Try the handbrake? No. Hopeless against that torque. She would have to shut the whole thing down.

She tapped the control screen into life, selected 'Emergency' and touched the 'off' button.

Nothing happened.

What now? Her mind was racing. *Crash down through the gears. At least that will slow the thing down. No. Impossible. An e-car has no gear-box.* What was going on? The whole machine seemed to have turned against her. Thank God the steering wheel was still connected to something mechanical.

She sped past San Antonio Creek, not quite yet panicking. Here, the road was still straight. And mercifully empty.

Eighty.

Ninety.

Even the gentle bends were taking on a racetrack quality.

A hundred and ten.

A hundred and twenty.

Now there was traffic. Nothing from the radar, though. She pulled out to overtake a dawdling SUV. A pack of cyclists sweating up the hill barely had time to scatter as they saw her coming. Then another truck. No choice but to pass that, too. *Ready... Go! Fingers crossed nothing's travelling the other way.*

The mouth of the tunnel came rushing up to swallow her.

A hundred and fifty.

The headlamps had failed, as well. Darkness engulfed her, but a semicircle of illumination beckoned from afar. The light at the end of the tunnel. *Hold a straight line. Hold it...*

A hundred and sixty.

She shot out into the daylight. Less than half a mile to the next entrance. In an eye-blink she was in it.

Think. A longer tunnel, but still straight. Steer towards the light. Remember the right-hand bend as soon as you leave. Yes. She was going to make it. She was. Then she looked again at the tunnel's exit. This time the semicircle had a ragged chunk bitten out of it. An eighteen wheeler, lumbering towards her. And suddenly the steering had a life of its own. She was on the wrong side of the road, watching the bite grow wider, taller.

A hundred and eighty.

"Truck ahead." The voice was calm and sexy...

May 24TH
Luanda

Night fell like a shutter. He had forgotten how short the tropical evenings were. Forty years. No... More. Still, forgive and forget. If the Angolans did know who he was – or had been, all those decades ago – they showed little sign of caring.

This place, though. Then, it had been a shithole. Now look at it. The Dubai of Africa, someone had called it. It sure had the glitz. The lights were coming on in the apartment blocks and offices and hotels along the waterfront. Out in the bay was a yacht, glinting like a starlet's tiara. A stray line from a play he'd seen in London came bubbling into his mind – "*I think it belongs to the Duke of Westminster.*"

Well, the days were long gone when the Duke of Westminster's yacht was the epitome of wealth. The tables were well and truly turned on the old European powers. Some had departed with a fig leaf of honour. National anthems played. Flags lowered. New flags raised. Some had merely scuttled, leaving the locals to fight it out.

He cared little about that. But now the tables were turning on the New World, too. The sun that was sinking in the west was rising in the east, and he did not like the feeling.

Enough of such musings. He tidied the room. No sense in leaving a mess for the maid. Then he walked out, closed the door, strolled to the elevator and pressed the call button.

Should he resent it, that his ancestors had made the trip to America from Angola, or Nigeria, or who-knew-where, packed in a ship's hold like anchovies in a can? No. They might have had worse lives as Virginia slaves than as African peasants, but his own life, had he been born here, would surely have been nasty, brutish and short compared with the easy plenty that America had become. Those ancestors, though, meant that when his section chief had shipped him off to Luanda so many years ago, he had blended in. They had been crazy days. He had only just got out alive. And now he was back to do one more duty, for his country and for an old friend.

"Boa noite, o senhor," said the concierge, as he walked into the lobby. "Boa noite," he replied.

The lobby was covered with brass and marble, and hung with paintings of questionable taste but unquestioned expense. Chandeliers of Venetian glass refracted myriad colours. A myriapod slipped surreptitiously behind a sofa. The door began to revolve as he approached it. Magic! A week ago, he would hardly have noticed, but now every moment, every perception, seemed precious.

The tropical air hit him, like wading into treacle. He turned along the front.

They had agreed the meeting point long ago – a mile or so from the hotel, away from the razzamatazz but in the open. He wasn't fooled by that. From habit, he started scanning passers-by, wondering which, if any, were watching him. Not that it mattered much now.

He arrived at the landmark: a sleek obsidian statue of Jemmy Cato, leader of the Stono slave rebellion, newly erected by the government. Irony piled on irony, he thought, that it should end here. He stood motionless by the motionless figure's plinth, waiting.

Such a little thing, a prostate. You never notice until it's too late. What was an extra six months of life, if you could go out in a blaze of glory? He lifted his wrist to look at the watch, a ghastly piece of bling that disguised the crucial memory cube. He glanced around, wondering where the sniper was hiding. Through the corner of his eye he saw movement on a roof-top a hundred yards or so away. He braced himself for the thump. There would be no getting out alive this time.

MAY 26TH
MINISTRY OF STATE SECURITY, BEIJING

"Good news, General Xian. Project Divine Skein. The merchandise has arrived."

"That is indeed excellent news. The merchandise has been tested?"

"Yes General. It is giving us exactly the sort of access we were hoping for."

May 26TH
ARLINGTON COUNTY, VIRGINIA

"Good news, Mr Vane. Janus has arrived. The steganography has worked. It is giving us exactly the sort of access we were hoping for."

PALAEOZOIC

GENESIS

May 26th
San Melito, California

"Good morning, Professor Hayward."

"Good morning, Anita."

Sebastian smiled at the receptionist, swiped his card, and was in. He glanced at the familiar logo above the lift – no, *elevator*. 'Neurogenics', it proclaimed in a futuristic font which he knew, from an evening spent drinking with the marketing director, had cost them $50,000 to design.

Neurogenics. A two-storey building in a business park. Two storeys of pure brainpower, fuelled by venture capital, built in an architectural style he liked to think of as 'California Bland'. It was weird. Every rich, powerful civilisation, from the Egyptians to the Americans, had had an edifice complex. The height of its buildings proclaimed its success to the world. Every civilisation except one. Geeks didn't seem to care. Even the show-offs stayed close to the ground. California surely now ruled the world, but it ruled it from two-storey buildings in business parks.

He ignored the elevator and crossed to the stairs that spiralled up from the lobby to the first – no, hang on, the *second* floor. He bounded up them, taking them two at a time. He would never understand his new countrymen. They would not climb a staircase, drove everywhere, then complained they were overweight and blew a thousand dollars a year on a gym they never visited.

He reached the landing. Louise was waiting at her desk by the boardroom door, her red hair piled up in a 1960s beehive.

"Good morning, Professor Hayward."

"Good morning, Louise. Are they here?"

"Mr Salieri and the others are inside. Mr Patel hasn't arrived yet."

He opened the door and let himself in.

"Sebastian," said Salieri. "Good to see you. Patel will be here in two minutes."

The CEO was a short man, and one to whom stair-climbing was surely terra incognita. His hair was black and slick – like his jacket, his trousers, his shoes and his shirt – and he wore too many rings, each gold, and each rather bigger than was becoming for his short, pudgy fingers. No geek he. Next to him sat Alexis Zhukov. Tall. Thin. Her hair the colour of Baltic amber. Descended, rumour had it, from an indiscreet liaison after the war by the great Field Marshal himself. Brought to America by red aristo parents who had found themselves on the wrong side of history after the Soviet Union's fall. Beside her was Simon Rider. Rider had made an effort. He really had. But he remained what he always was, the sartorial equivalent of a two-storey building in a business park.

Sebastian, brogued and besuited, sat down in the empty chair beside Salieri. For a reason he could not quite put his finger on, four seemed the wrong number for this meeting. Three would have worked. Five, perhaps. But an even number was, paradoxically, odd. Yes. That was it. Symmetry was important, a sign of strength, an indication of perfection. The leader should be flanked left and right by equal numbers. For this was a meeting they needed to go well. The next tranche of funding would see them through, he felt sure, to product. The terms of that funding, though. Those would dictate whether they held on to enough of the firm to become merely rich, or filthy, stinking rich, rolling in it. Money. Fame. Maybe even a Nobel? What they were doing deserved a trip to Stockholm, surely? He squeezed his thighs together, like a teenager trying to contain his excitement on a first date. The door opened again and Louise ushered in Vinod Patel and two handlers. He, Salieri, Zhukov and Rider rose to greet them. Then all seven sat down, the two sides facing each other across the boardroom table, Patel flanked symmetrically by his minions. Let battle commence.

Salieri rambled on for a few minutes, buttering Patel up. Then it was his turn. They had agreed before the meeting that he should go second, ahead of the two engineers. It made sense. After all, he was the intellectual input to the venture. Designing chips and programming them – Rider's and Zhukov's jobs – were important. But it was he who provided the crucial insights that would make the whole thing sing.

"Gentlemen. Lady," he began, addressing Patel and his entourage. "You know what we are up to, so I won't make a meal of this. But to recap, when all is said and done what people now call artificial intelligence is just advanced machine learning. We intend to go way beyond that. We propose to build a computer system that is sentient, self-aware, conscious. Philosophers have speculated about the nature of consciousness since the Greeks, at least. They had no answers because they asked the question in the wrong way. Being philosophers, they thought they could reason their way to the truth. But we know better. Sherlock Holmes put it well. 'Data, data, data. I cannot make bricks without straw.' And we have the data to back up the theory, so"

Sebastian stopped in mid sentence and sniffed. A reflex response to an acrid sensation on the outer edge of perception. A second sniff, this time long and deliberate. The others sniffed, too. They looked at each other, each seeking re-assurance he was not hallucinating, none wanting to be first to cry the forbidden word.

Patel cracked.

"Can you smell smoke?" he said.

"Yes. Yes, I think I can. Perhaps we should…"

They got up as one and moved towards the door. At that moment, an alarm began to sound, and an oddly unreassuring electronic voice started telling them not to panic, but to proceed quickly to the assembly area in the car park outside the front of the building.

Patel reached the door first. He turned the handle and pulled. Nothing. Thinking he must have misremembered which way the thing opened, he tried pushing. Still nothing. He looked at Salieri.

"What's going on?" he said.

"Dunno," said the CEO. He tried the door himself. Then he shouted through it, "Louise. The door's stuck. I think it might have locked itself. Can you release it?"

"Whatdoyoumean, it might have locked itself?" said Patel.

"Security system. Every door can be locked centrally. Louise!"

"I'm trying, Mr Salieri."

The handle rattled. The door did not move. Now, there was smoke coming in through the air-conditioning vent.

"Call security. Tell them to over-ride it."

Rider was on the phone already.

"Tom. It's Simon. We're trapped in the boardroom. The door has locked itself. We need you to over-ride the locking system. You are? Good man. Okay, Marco, try again."

Salieri rattled the handle. Nothing. The room was filling with smoke.

"What's going on in there, Mr Salieri?" Louise's voice screamed through the door.

"Smoke. No flames yet."

"Same on this side, sir."

"Louise. You get out now. That's an order. When the fire truck arrives tell them what's happening. Tell them where we are."

How long would that be, Sebastian wondered? He had no idea where the fire house was. He did know, though, that it was the smoke which killed you, not the flames.

"On the floor everybody," he said. "Stay out of the smoke."

"No," said Zhukov. "Do that and we just die later. We have to get out now. We have to break the window."

She was right, of course. Sebastian looked at it. A sealed unit, floor-to-ceiling, triple glazed to avoid the attention of directional mikes. What the hell. He picked up a chair and swung it hard against the glass. The pane crazed, but did not break. Again. More crazing. And that was the moment when he realised they really might die.

"We could use the table as a battering ram," Zhukov suggested.

Seven of them, Sebastian thought. Would that be enough to lift it?

"Good idea," he said. "Three on one side. Four on the other. The women on the four-side. Go."

They took their places as the smoke swirled around them.

"Lift!" Sebastian commanded.

The table inched into the air.

"Carry it to the window."

They shuffled, coughing and spluttering, across the carpet.

"Okay. Swing it backward, then forward."

The table hit the glass and bounced. The pane crazed some more.

"Again. Keep swinging it. Build up the amplitude with each swing."

Bounce. Yet more crazing.

"Again."

Bounce.

"Again."

Bounce.

"Again."

Crash! The whole window, frame and all, fell outward to the ground. The table followed, and Sebastian and Zhukov almost went with it. They teetered on the edge of the void where the glass had once been. But they could breathe again.

They'd have to jump, though. Thank God for California Bland. No building more than two storeys high. You might break a leg, but probably not your neck.

"I'm tallest," said Sebastian. "I'll go first. It'll be easier for me to reach up and help everyone else down." He looked out of the gap. The boardroom was at the back of the building and the ground below was grassy turf, not asphalt. Another blessing. He took off his jacket, got on his hands and knees, facing into the smoke-filled room, and chasséed slowly backwards. As his legs crossed the parapet, he flattened his stomach to the floor, trying to slide, rather than fall, out of the opening. Then he pressed his palms to the carpet, lowered his hips over the edge, slipped down as carefully as he could manage and found himself, literally, cliff-hanging. He let go.

A dim recollection of childhood judo lessons took over his hind brain as he fell. He bent his knees and rolled as his feet touched the ground, just missing the remnants of the table as he did so. Safe.

He stood up and looked around. Plumes of smoke were rising from the building's roof and flames erupted from several windows at its farther end – from the place where they kept the servers. He wondered when the last off-site back-up had been. Too late to worry about that now.

"Come on," he shouted up. "If you do what I did, I should be able to grab hold of your ankles and guide you down."

He heard Patel's voice. "Ladies first. We'll keep hold of your wrists, Dr Zhukov, until Professor Hayward has you."

Zhukov's legs appeared out of the window. There was a glimpse of stocking. Sebastian's teenage frisson returned, weirdly considering that lives were at stake. He put the thought aside and reached skyward to grasp her.

"Kick your shoes off," he said.

She did. He could just about touch her feet, and took what purchase he could on them.

"Okay. Let go."

She let go.

He did his best to steer her to a soft landing, and they ended up together, in a crumpled heap on the grass. No bones broken. They helped each other up. Patel's minder was next. What was her name? He couldn't remember. Well, at least she was wearing trousers.

With two pairs of hands to guide her down, the minder's landing was more dignified than Zhukov's had been. And with the three of them on the ground, even the weight of the remaining men was bearable. The last man out, Salieri, touched down just as they heard the fire truck's siren in the distance.

Better late than never, Sebastian thought, as he watched the truck pull in, and its crew busy themselves with hydrants and hoses. Then it struck him. The misters. Why hadn't the damn smoke misters gone off?

May 26TH
Nassau

"Fuck," said Miguel. "If Rodriguez finds out about this, we're fish food."

Carlos Rodriguez was not renowned for giving his employees second chances when they screwed up, and the termination package usually involved just that: termination. It was the flip-side of the large and tax-free incomes he offered.

"Then we had better make sure he never does," replied Fidel.

These were men that the world has never heard *of*, but frequently hears *from*. Their handiwork lurked on a hundred million PCs around the planet, directing spam, stealing passwords, organising denial-of-service attacks on firms who failed to take out 'security contracts' with one of Rodriguez's numerous front companies, and providing (though this was not an intentional part of the service), cover for erring men whose wives found interesting and unusual pictures on their husbands' hard drives.

"Must have been downloaded by a virus, darling. Now you mention it, there was a funny incident a few days ago when I opened an unsolicited email."

Miguel, though, now knew what it was like to be on the receiving end.

"We've been rootkitted, Fidel. Nice job. Erased itself as soon as I detected it."

"What were they after? It might give us a clue who they were: cops or rivals."

"That's the odd thing. They seem to have been after *our* rootkits."

"Can't think it's the cops, then. Might be the Russians, trying to hijack our network. They always were lazy sods, piggy-backing on everyone else's hard work."

"Don't worry. I think I can clear up the mess without anyone being any the wiser."

"Better do it then. They certainly won't hear anything from me."

MAY 27TH
ARLINGTON COUNTY

"Ladies and gentlemen, we are under attack. A subtle attack. But a real one."

He was getting too old for this. Cynicism is a strange thing. They say it increases with age and in him it had, up to a point. But that point was past. Now he felt it ebbing, being replaced by ennui. In an agent, that was death. Only cynicism kept you sane. And he had had to be very cynical indeed over the past few days.

"Once," he continued, "you bombed an enemy's factories to destroy his economy. Now, it seems, you kill his software engineers."

Cynical or not, Matt Vane was pretty sure he was still sane. What he wasn't sure of was what he was dealing with.

"At least twenty of our top-flight computer people have died or disappeared in the past three months. Where we know what happened, their deaths have been sudden and violent. Car crashes. Plane crashes. Fires. Asymmetric Warfare Group noticed it three days ago. One of their spotters picked up on that strange pile-up outside Los Angeles last Friday and started digging."

He looked around the table. The young field operatives who would be his eyes and ears for this mission, whatever it was. Eager beavers, all of them. Good. He needed that enthusiasm. No clear enemy objective. No clear enemy, for that matter. Yet something was going on, and he knew that it had to be stopped.

"The latest incident was yesterday, at a start-up in San Melito. The building caught alight while their top brains, and also one of the biggest venture capitalists in the field, were somehow locked in the boardroom. They managed to batter their way out, but it was a close-run thing."

Cyber warfare came in many guises these days, of course, from rigging elections and spreading fake news to outing power grids and freezing transport networks. The Agency had anticipated all sorts of subtle attacks – the type you couldn't even be sure actually were attacks. Financial flash-crashes. Outbreaks of disease. Industrial accidents that might have been negligence, but might have been given a helping hand. They hadn't seen this one coming, though. It was lifting the field to a whole, new level to take out not just computer systems, but the people who designed them too.

"Obviously our future depends on continuing to lead everyone else in IT. Our rivals know that as well. It looks as if one of them has started playing dirty. This isn't terrorism. Terrorist acts are public. This is secretive. So the question is, who? Russia? China? Iran, maybe? Or is it a non-state actor? We have to find out. For that, we need a two-pronged approach. First, these things all look like software hacks. If that is right, we have to identify the code involved and then trace it back to its origins. That means digging even more deeply into our rivals' computers than we're doing at the moment."

He shivered slightly at that approach's most recent consequence.

"But we also need some good, old-fashioned human intelligence sniffing around as well, to back up the firewall-fighters in Geekopolis."

That was what they called the warehouse in Falls Church where the uber-nerds were stored. Beware of Geeks, bearing gifts... Yet, when it actually mattered, getting the Trojan horse that Geekopolis had so carefully crafted to the place where it was needed had been a hum-int operation. And, at the cost of an old friend's self-sacrifice, Project Janus seemed to have worked. The Chinese had taken the bait. As long as the Agency didn't give the game away by being too greedy, they could look around the People's Republic's digital inner sanctum, while giving the spooks in Beijing the impression that it was they who were looking around America's. None of which, of course, the boy and girl scouts in front of him would ever know – or not until they had risen to his lofty eminence. And by the time that had happened, the game would have moved on. China would probably be their friend by then. Who knew who would be the enemy?

"That's what you're here for. The briefing notes are eyes only, and not to leave this room. You've got half an hour to digest them. Then we'll brainstorm."

He left them to it. Better not to have the Old Man sitting in.

That way they could kick ideas around and draw their own conclusions without feeling they had to show off, or risk looking silly. He went to the canteen, ordered a cappuccino and a chocolate-banana cake, pulled out a spy novel (sucker!) and waited out the time. Then he went back to the briefing room.

"Okay, ladies and gentlemen. Your thoughts."

A crew-cut preppie seemed to have appointed himself spokesman. What was his name? Ah yes, Donald Macdonald.

"Donald. Could you give me a précis?"

"Yes, of course, sir. One thing struck us in particular. You mentioned it being like bombing an enemy's factories to destroy his economy. But these don't look like economic targets – or military ones, for that matter. If someone was going after those, you'd think the victims would be working for banks or aerospace companies or the government, writing high-end financial or defence software. But no. The woman in the car-crash was working on virtual actors for Hollywood, for heaven's sake."

"Good idea," said someone. "Most of the real ones act like robots anyway."

"The point is, the common theme seems to be artificial intelligence, not strategic significance. We can think of two possible explanations. The first is that this is a long-term play by a rival, to weaken an industry of the future. The second is that it presages some other form of attack, one that will involve AI being used as a weapon. By eroding our stock of experts, an enemy diminishes our ability to respond. But we have no idea what form such an attack might take. In short, we need better information. We need to dig into exactly what all of these programmers were up to. If we can find a more precise theme than just AI, that might give us the clue we need."

"May I make a suggestion?" A female voice piped up across the table from Matt.

Yasmin Chu. One of the brightest of the bunch. The mile down Massachusetts Avenue to MIT had seemed a hundred light-years long when he had been up at Harvard. This woman, though, subverted his every prejudice about the place. True, she'd come into the Agency through Geekopolis, but she hadn't hung around there. He could even see her, one day when he was in his casket, sitting in the chair that he himself now occupied.

"Yes, Yasmin?"

"We should start with the one group of targets who are still alive," she said. "Someone should talk to the survivors of the San Melito fire. Find out what they know."

"Indeed, someone should. Are you volunteering?"

"Sure. Always happy to hang out in California. I notice that one of the survivors is a Jason. Can we take him into our confidence?"

"Probably best play that cool. I know he's got SCI clearance, and I truly doubt our transatlantic cousins have anything to do with this, but the guy's a Brit, or used to be, so why take the risk? Find out what he knows, without prejudice, if you can. Field ops will fit you out and make the necessary arrangements. Get on a plane tonight. Donald, please continue."

"There is also the question of means," the preppie said. "To attack a fixed installation, like a power station or a bank, with cyber warfare is one thing. This enemy, though, can track moving targets and hit them when they are vulnerable: driving, flying, in a particular room at a meeting, even. That's new. It also makes it hard to defend against. We've been building static defences – Maginot Lines of computer code, if you like – and some enemy has come up with mobile tank warfare. And this is an enemy which seems to be able to see everywhere. We've even an idea for a cryptonym for them, until we find out who they really are."

"Which is?"

"Argus. The hundred-eyed giant from Greek myth."

"Argus. Yes. I like that. Well done, Donald. We'll use it."

MAY 27TH
PASADENA

"Alice. Where are you Alice? We were supposed to be going out today. I'm sure you said we were. Alice, come here! Where are you?"

May 27TH
San Patricio, California

Gordon Humboldt looked over the assembly in front of him. Reporters? Vampires, more likely. They sucked people's reputations dry to feed their own. The march of progress, if it gets mentioned at all, is relegated to the inside pages. One woman dies in a car crash, though, and the whole pack descends on you.

Dammit! They couldn't even know for sure that the car had been at fault. The driver had a reputation as a speedster. Maybe she had just chanced her arm once too often. Regardless of that, they had put out an emollient release, attempted to reassure customers by couriered letter (an old-fashioned touch, which he hoped would seem convincingly personal) that they would not suffer a similar fate, and kept their fingers crossed for something else to come along to attract the nanosecond-long attention span of the public elsewhere. But it hadn't. Nor could they find any cause for the accident in the incinerated cinder that had once been Alice Rhodes's Avila. It was, he supposed, something that this Rhodes character seemed to have been a bit of a loner. No grieving husband or boyfriend had crawled out of the woodwork to make a tearful public statement, and there didn't seem to be any parents, either. But the story would not go away.

So this had to be done. An isolated event, whatever the cause, could not be allowed to derail the whole project. They were already beginning to leave the lumbering giants of Detroit, Stuttgart and Nagoya in the dust. The new factory would open in two months' time. A hundred thousand units a year. Nothing must get in the way of that.

"Good morning, ladies and gentlemen. I just want to make a short statement. Then I will answer questions."

He read out the boiler-plate prepared by the PR department and instantly regretted it. It sounded stilted – the work of lawyers, not human beings. Too late now, though.

"Yes. The lady at the back, in red."

"Jennifer Jameson, CBB. Mr Humboldt, you said this was a freak accident. Do you have any idea yet what caused it?"

If it really was the car's fault, his best guess was an infinite loop or a divide-by-zero error in the code somewhere – though he was never going to admit that. He was convinced today's youngsters were sloppy programmers. Not like when he had been at Stanford. You wouldn't have got away with unannotated spaghettiware then.

"No ma'am, we don't. We are running new tests on the Avila operating system, just in case. But we see no sign of a systematic error. And, as I said, anyone who has an Avila, they can trade it back to us full-price. And, before you ask, yes, I'm still driving mine. Sir!"

He pointed at a scruffily dressed man in the middle of the pack who didn't look too hostile.

Bad call.

"James Richard Clarkson, AutoTimes. Mr Humboldt, don't you think this accident calls into question your rush to build electric vehicles? Won't people now cling ever-more-tightly to the internal combustion engine? Aren't you worried you won't be able to sell the new factory's output?"

"No. Of course not. The ICE is hardly a safe technology, is it? And it's well over a hundred years old. It belongs in the museums, not on the 21st century's roads. It was great in its day, and we owe it a lot. But its day is over. In fact, we are planning to double the new factory's production within eighteen months. Sir!"

This time the recipient of the pointed finger was tailored to a 'T'.

"Marc Rotherhythe, Wall Street Post. As we have you here, Mr Humboldt, might I broaden the questioning beyond cars, to ask about the future of Humboldt Engineering more generally?"

Thank you, thank you.

"Yes, of course, Mr Rotherhythe. Ask away."

"Well, you seem to be making a lot of bets on spaceflight at the moment. Don't you think that is rather risky? Huge capital investment. Uncertain returns. I mean, what actually is there in space that is worth all that money?"

"I rather disagree. There is a lot in space. Indeed, I hope that one day the list of things in space will include me."

That got a laugh.

"Seriously, though, we are doing fine in space. The Milando launch facility put up six comm-sats last year, and we are so confident about the Humboldt Mineral Prospecting System that it is only available on an equity-stake basis. If someone discovers something worth mining, we want a piece of the action. And I might tell you that we are already part of more than a dozen mines now being sunk, based on what the MPS has found.

"But if the subtext of your question was, 'is this space thing a self-indulgence of Gordon Humboldt,' then I freely confess. I do think humanity's future lies off-Earth. That's why we built the Mars Observation Satellite for NASA a few years back, to help scope the place out. But that, I would remind you, was a personal donation from me. No shareholder money was injured during the making of that movie."

He got another laugh with this, but Rotherhythe slipped in a supplementary before he could cut him off and go to another questioner.

"It didn't quite work, though did it? It went dead pretty quickly after it got there."

"As you said, Mr Rotherhythe, spaceflight is a risky business. Indeed, it does not always work. And, to re-emphasise, the MOS was a personal donation – a science project, not a commercial venture. Ma'am!"

"Dorothy Greenmantle, Pals.com. To get back to the unfortunate Ms Rhodes. Do you think all this computerised drive-by-wire is actually safe? Wasn't it better when a human being was in total control?"

Thank you, God. A luddite.

"On that I can reassure you. Whatever the reason for this accident turns out to be (and we *will* find out), the truth is that most crashes are caused by drivers, not cars. The other truth, and I say this as an engineer, is that no system is perfect. We can only strive for perfection; we'll never quite achieve it. Thank you. No more questions."

He walked off stage.

* * * * * * * *

"Well, that was honest." Emma Reichenbacher, his head of PR, had a touch of sarcasm in her voice.

"You know, Emma, occasionally honesty pays. People have ridiculous expectations these days. They think safety gets delivered by magic, as though they have some God-given right to it."

"They have a Congress-given right to it."

"Those parasites. Never do an honest day's work between them, and then attempt to take the credit from the people who do. Let's have a drink…"

They had retired to what he had taken to calling his Ready Room. He was indeed, deep down, a space cadet. He knew it. His friends knew it. And he didn't care if his enemies knew it, too. He was convinced there was money to be made in space. Indeed, he'd proved it. The Mineral Prospecting System was revolutionising the industry. And it wasn't just equity stakes. They were even digging themselves – a Silicon Valley firm in the ancient business of mining, for heaven's sake. All it needed for space to really fly, as it were, was to take the thing out of the hands of the government, and he intended to do the taking. They had their own launch site and their own launch system. And very soon now…

He let the thought trail away as a Manhattan arrived in his hand.

"How do you think I did, really?"

"What I think doesn't matter. The Twitterverse was quite impressed, though. You may be right that honesty is the best policy."

"Well, Machiavelli thought so. People forget that. He advised princes to act in good faith whenever possible."

"The better to let them gull the opposition when good faith is impossible."

He stared into his glass, reflectively. "Well, yes, there is that."

May 28TH
San Melito

Sebastian poured himself a drink and reflected on the madness of life. The paramedics, when they had arrived, had insisted on his going to hospital. A total overreaction. He had been shaken, certainly, but he felt sure his lungs could cope with a bit of smoke without a bunch of doctors prodding and poking him. As to the idea he needed trauma counselling, well that really did seem like a shameless attempt to pad the bill.

The first night, he had tolerated with what he hoped had been good humour. The second, rather less. The idea of a third was beyond him. He had discharged himself and come home.

What was it Buñuel had said was the perfect recipe for a Martini? Fill the glass with gin and then hold the vermouth bottle up to the window, so that the rays of the sun pass through it before they strike the liquid in the glass.

Yes. That was the way. He settled into an armchair and reviewed what had happened.

It was almost as if someone had been trying to kill them. The locked door. The failure of the smoke misters. Had the building been sabotaged? No. Paranoia, surely. It had been an accident. He, of all people, should know how easily complex systems can cock up. All those illusions and hallucinations the brain is heir to. Paradoxically, they are often the best way to see what is going on under the mental bonnet.

Hood – his linguistic homunculus corrected him.

He sipped the cocktail and grinned. If someone really had been trying to sabotage the deal, then their plan had certainly backfired. In the bonhomie of survival, Patel had agreed to the money then and there, with remarkably few strings. They were, he now felt convinced, going to be rich.

A peel of chimes interrupted his reverie. He rose, walked into the hall, and opened the front door. A woman stood before him. Late twenties. 5'4". Oriental features. Good looking, too.

"Professor Hayward?"

"Yes."

"I'm Detective Jane Chan from the San Melito Police Department."

She held up an ID. Sebastian had no idea what a San Melito copper's warrant card looked like, but he was perfectly prepared to believe it looked like that.

"Pleased to meet you. What can I do to assist the police with their enquiries?"

As the words left his mouth, he realised only a Brit would get the joke. Never mind.

"I'm part of the team investigating the fire at Neurogenics. I know you gave a statement on the day, but would you mind answering a few more questions about what happened?"

"Sure. Come in. I was having a drink. Would you...? No, of course not."

He showed her through and they both sat down. She got out a notebook. Good, old tamper-proof pen and paper, thought Sebastian, even in this electronic world.

"So, Professor Hayward, could you describe in your own words what occurred?"

It had all been in his statement of course. But what the hell. He didn't have anything else to do.

He started with a précis of his walk to the office. Out of his laboratory. Across University Avenue. Along Redwood Road, with its dirty, scrubby verge. Past the General Genomics campus. She began scribbling – shorthand, he presumed. Another anachronism. He arrived at the Neurogenics building, climbed the stairs, walked into the boardroom, met the others, smelled the smoke, broke the window and escaped, all as accurately as he could remember it.

"I see," she said. "And what was the meeting about?"

"Confidential, I'm afraid, as I told your colleague on Monday."

"That's a pity. It would really help to know."

"You could ask Salieri," he said, and then regretted it. Though he was pretty sure Marco wouldn't tell her, why take the chance? Never mind. Done is done.

"Would you be able to tell me what it is that you do for Neurogenics? Surely you're not running seminars there?"

"No, of course not. We academics all have to make our way in the big, bad commercial world these days. I'm involved in one of their projects – a consultant, if you like."

Well, that was close enough to the truth for the rozzers.

"Really? I thought you were a neuroscientist. How does that fit in with a computer company?"

You are remarkably astute for a plod.

"There are certain overlaps."

"But you are not going to tell me."

"I can't see how it's relevant. Are you suggesting what we are doing was somehow connected with the fire?"

"Hard to say, since you won't tell me what it is."

"So, do you think it was arson?"

"We are keeping an open mind and pursuing all possible lines of inquiry."

She rose to leave, and Sebastian rose to show her out. He returned to his Martini. He thought for a moment. An attractive girl. On her own. Surely the police travelled in pairs, certainly when they were doing interviews? It was almost traditional. One took the statement while the other invented an excuse to snoop around the house looking for clues. At least, that was always the way it worked on TV cop shows.

A woman on her own, though. That seemed more like a ploy to put him off his guard. And all those questions he had already answered. Could their rivals be that desperate to find out what was going on?

He rang Salieri. No answer. He rang Zhukov.

"Sebastian?"

"Alexis. Are you free at the moment?"

"Possibly. Why?"

"I need to talk to you about what happened. Pick your brains, NWR." It was company jargon for no written record. "Meet me on the beach, by the Bond villain's house, in half an hour."

That was a local joke. A millionaire with a touching faith in the stability of the cliffs of San Melito Bay, and the deeds to what had briefly been the world's steepest building site, had constructed what could only reasonably be described as a 'lair', overlooking the Pacific. The idea that it was actually occupied by a white-cat-stroking master criminal was almost irresistible. As far as Sebastian could see, the house itself was accessible only by *elevator* from the beach.

He got up, put on his beach sandals, turned towards the door to leave – and then turned back. That brief glimpse when they were escaping the fire had put a match to what he now realised had been a growing pile of mental tinder. It was time to see if such tinder burned elsewhere. He went into the kitchen and pulled out a bottle of cabernet, a loaf of bread, a knife and a hunk of manchego. He threw them into a bag, along with a couple of tumblers.

The walk to the beach took ten minutes. Zhukov was already there. She was wearing a yellow dress and her feet sported leather thongs. She was looking at the Bond villain's house.

"He must have a helipad up there, or something."

"Yep. You know, I've never actually seen anyone go in or out of it. Do you think it's really inhabited, or is it just some complicated tax fiddle?"

Sebastian sat down on the sand, and kicked off his sandals. Zhukov followed suit.

"So. What is it that we can't talk about over the phone?" she said.

"Have you had a visit from the cops?"

"Yes, actually. Someone came round this afternoon. Wanted to discuss the fire. What of it?"

"What did she look like?"

"How did you know it was a 'she'?"

"Asian? 5'4"? Long hair?"

"That's the one."

"Didn't you think it a bit odd?"

"Why?"

"First, why would the cops be so interested? There was no evidence of arson, and nobody died."

"Oh, you know what they're like. Stick their noses in anywhere. Maybe it's a slack week, and they are looking to justify their existence."

"OK. But why only one? Don't they normally go around in pairs? And why, to put it crudely, a rather good-looking girl?"

"You've lost me."

"Glass of wine?"

"Oh. Err. Alright. Thank you. Sebastian, what's going on?"

"Well, obviously it wouldn't work on you, but it did cross my nasty, suspicious mind that if you wanted to loosen the lips of a man who was, for the sake of argument, working for a business rival and had just escaped with his life from a fire, then sending an attractive woman around by herself, pretending to be a policeman, might be a good way of doing it."

"Police officer," said Zhukov.

"Police officer, yes. So what did she ask you?"

"Well, now you come to mention it, she did seem surprisingly interested in what we were doing. I told her nothing, of course. But yes, it's hard to see how that's relevant to an accident investigation."

"More wine? I brought some cheese and bread, too."

"Are you trying to get me drunk?"

"Perish the thought! Look, it's probably just paranoia, but think about it. We were locked in the boardroom and the smoke misters didn't work. I checked with Salieri afterwards and he said they are centrally controlled, like the locking system. If you did want to take the company out, what better way to do it than to disable the smoke misters and set fire to the building while the CEO and its chief research brains are locked in the boardroom?"

"I see what you mean."

"Wine?"

"Please. It is rather good."

"Comes from a little vineyard in Napa. The grapes are trodden individually by specially trained Armenian eunuchs."

She smiled. Perhaps there was indeed some tinder in there.

"So what should we do?"

"Well, obviously check whether she really was the police. I'll ring them in the morning. And we should brainstorm a list of possible enemies if she wasn't. But I think, perhaps, we shouldn't actually involve the cops themselves at this stage. They would probably ask the same questions as our friend. And this time they would have a good reason to, so we might have to answer them."

What the hell. He reached out a toe and touched it against her leg, experimentally. The leg stayed put. He stroked its skin a little with his toe. She lay back on the sand, but the leg still stayed put.

"You *were* trying to get me drunk."

"Possibly."

"Then let's do the job properly. I have a very good Stolichnaya in my apartment. I think we should try some."

MAY 29TH
SAN MELITO

Just another shitty day in paradise, Sebastian thought, as a sunbeam slowly woke him. Zhukov was still asleep. Noisily asleep. He would never have guessed she was a snorer. He got up and tiptoed towards the bathroom. An acquaintance of his, from the day of the fire, hung pertly from a washing line over the bath, accompanied by a collection of its colleagues. He smiled, tipped an ironic salute, and abluted. Then he went into the kitchen, tracked down the coffee (why is it always so hard to find things in other people's kitchens?) filled the machine with water and switched it on.

By the time the coffee had brewed, Zhukov was sitting on the side of the bed. She stretched an exaggerated stretch, and smiled knowingly.

Who seduced whom, here? Sebastian wondered.

"So, Monsieur Poirot," she said, "what is our course of action today?"

"Well, one of us should ring the police and ask for Officer Chan. If they say 'who?' then I'm right. If they put her on, and she sounds like the woman we met yesterday, then yes, you are right, my sole purpose in making this story up was to get you into bed. It's probably still a bit early to phone them, though, without it looking suspicious, so how about some breakfast?"

"Sheila's?" he added, mentioning the name of a nearby Australian place, renowned for its waffles.

"You are on," said Zhukov.

They prattled inanely, as newly coupled lovers will, as they dressed. Then they walked out of the apartment and into the elevator – a quaint, caged contraption from the 1930s. They descended, and rambled along Ide Street towards the antipodean breakfast bar.

The sound, Sebastian would ever recall in horror, began as a rumble but almost instantly turned to ear-splitting thunder. They spun around just in time to see shards of glass from the blown-out windows arcing towards the part of the sidewalk where, twenty seconds earlier, they had been strolling. With surprising grace, the apartment block crumpled to the ground, and a cloud of dust billowed forth to engulf the street, and them.

Zhukov fainted. Sebastian could only just support her weight. He lowered her to the sidewalk. Then he took out his cell phone and called the police department.

"Detective Chan, please."

"Sorry, sir. Are you sure you have the right name?"

"Chan," he repeated.

"There is no officer of that name here, sir. Can I put you through to somebody else? What is this about?"

"Never mind. This is an emergency call. An apartment block at Ide and Fremont has just blown up. Alert the hospitals. Alert the fire department." *And alert Sebastian Hayward*, thought Sebastian. *What the hell do we do now?*

* * * * * * * *

"Mi casa, su casa," said Sebastian, as he opened the front door. "Make yourself at home."

Cohabitation had been the last thing on his mind when he had slipped into bed with Zhukov the previous evening. Now, it seemed inevitable. They had been at the cop shop all day, answering the same questions, first to a string of policemen and then to a gaggle of forensics experts. From the police point of view the fire at Neurogenics had been a little local difficulty. This was different. A dozen dead. As many more injured. The forensics people suspected a gas leak into an unoccupied apartment below Zhukov's. A weird coincidence, certainly, that she and he had cheated fiery death twice in a week – but, the police seemed to conclude, a coincidence nonetheless. Sebastian had tried to bring up the matter of the mysterious Detective Chan, but in the ecstasy of panic created by the explosion, her appearance was swept aside.

Zhukov's state of shock had dissipated gradually over the day. She had been on nodding terms with some of the dead but, as was so often the modern way, actual friends with none of them. The loss of her worldly goods had yet to sink in. Whether they liked it or not, though, the two of them were now well and truly coupled in the eyes of the world. The media, once they had made the Neurogenics connection, had taken to dubbing them the planet's most star-crossed lovers.

Sebastian shut the door. To reach it, they had had to run a gauntlet of interested press, kept only partly at bay by a couple of uniformed officers. From the old TV networks to the 'citizen journalists', as far as Sebastian could make out, every adult in the United States who was, or aspired to be, a reporter was camped on his doorstep with a lens pointing through the window of his front room. He picked up a remote from the coffee table, aimed it at the assembled throng, and pressed the button. The window faded to black.

The phone rang.

"Landline?" said Zhukov. "How quaint."

He picked it up.

"Yes, this is Professor Hayward. No, I don't have any comment. No, I don't know where she is. I'm sorry."

He put it down.

It rang again.

"No. Go away."

He unplugged it. Zhukov's cell rang.

"How did you get this number? No, I have no comment. No. Professor Hayward? I have no idea where he is. Why would I?"

They smiled at each other as she switched the phone off.

"Coffee, I think," said Sebastian.

He went into the kitchen and busied himself with the machine. This was no time to stint. He took the tin marked Kopi Luwak from the shelf and broke the seal. The grinder screeched as it pulverised the beans. Into the cone. Add water. Press the big, red button. Breathe in the aroma. If he was going to die before his time, which now seemed at least a possibility, he would enjoy a little luxury during his last few moments on Earth.

He warmed a jug up with hot water and poured in the civet-digested concoction. He pulled two mugs from the tree (coffee, however expensive, was not, in his view, a drink to be prissy about), and returned to what he still thought of, despite much teasing by his new compatriots, as the drawing room.

He poured from the jug to the mugs, and proffered one to Zhukov. At what point in what had now, perforce, become their relationship, he wondered, would he stop thinking of her as 'Zhukov' and start thinking of her as 'Alexis'? *Well, we will see.*

"Okay," he said. "What now?"

Zhukov sipped her drink. "Perhaps it really is all a coincidence," she said. "They must happen sometimes, and we both know how good human minds are at seeing patterns where none exist."

"If it wasn't for Detective Chan, I might just about be willing to buy that. With her in the equation, I'd say 'no way'."

"But she could be proof of the coincidence, whoever she is. After all, if there actually are bad guys out there trying to kill us – for whatever reason – why would they send someone snooping around and making us suspicious?"

"You're right. Nothing hangs together properly. And Chan only visited the two of us. She certainly didn't talk to either Marco or Simon. I phoned them earlier to ask, when I was trying to get the rozzers to take her seriously. I suppose she might have visited Patel, but I don't have his number."

"Me neither. Dealing with him was always Marco's job."

They both sipped their coffee. Then Sebastian spoke.

"Monsieur Poirot, you called me this morning. Well, why not. What is wrong with a bit of amateur detective work?"

"Poirot wasn't an amateur. He got well paid for what he did."

"Pedant. You know what I mean. Let's start with the facts and see what we can deduce from them. The fire and the explosion. Could they have been deliberate?"

"The explosion would be easy," said Zhukov. "You just have to turn the gas on, wait for it to fill the apartment, and ignite it."

"You would have to break in to do that, though. Or steal a key."

She looked at him pityingly. "What century are you living in, Sebastian? You would just have to hack into the apartment's remote-control system and switch on the cooker or the boiler without igniting it, wait twenty minutes, then press the ignition button. I'm guessing from the landline, by the way, that you don't have remote control here."

He didn't.

"Perhaps, in the circumstances, that's just as well," she mused.

"It would be quite a hack to do something similar to the Neurogenics building, though," Sebastian observed. "Paranoia is Marco's middle name."

"True. But if these hypothetical bad guys do exist, they presumably have some top-notch black-hats on their side."

"What would any hypothetical bad guy gain from killing us, though?" Sebastian paused, thoughtful. "Or perhaps it's just you," he continued. "Unless they were following us back from the beach, they couldn't have known I'd be with you last night. Maybe this isn't about Neurogenics at all. Got any enemies in the Motherland?"

"My father certainly does. But it is not their style to attack someone through his children. If they want you dead, they kill you. They don't kill your daughter. Besides, as you observed, hacking Neurogenics would be pretty tricky. Why not go straight for the gas explosion? And there is still the question of Officer Chan."

Zhukov stopped. Her face took on an air of distraction, as though she was searching for an elusive memory. Then she found it.

"I wonder if we are looking at this the wrong way around," she continued. "We are assuming it is specifically about me, or us, or the company. What if it isn't? What if it's part of a wider pattern? There's something I've just remembered. It was a few weeks ago. There was an AI developers' conference down in Cancun. Big boondoggle. Six of them went by private jet. It crashed. I knew one of them. Not well, but it was still a shock. What if the connection's something else. AI itself, perhaps?"

"That really does sound paranoid. We haven't even established that what happened to us was more than a couple of accidents."

"Humour me," she replied. "Let's Google around a bit. See if anything else suspicious has occurred. It shouldn't take long."

* * * * * * * *

Sebastian had always thought himself a level-headed type, but his hand was trembling as he poured the gin. The vermouth followed. He handed one to Zhukov. They had, jointly, found seventeen AI software developers who had died violent or suspicious deaths in the past twelve weeks or so. Once is happenstance. Twice is coincidence. But seventeen?

Sebastian rang the Precinct. Perhaps it was the English accent he had never tried to lose, but he had the distinct impression of being patted on the head like an errant but well-meaning schoolboy. "Yes, of course Professor Hayward. We'll certainly take that into account."

He put the phone down. He looked at Zhukov.

"So what would Poirot do now?" he said. Zhukov looked back quizzically. "Perhaps," she replied, "we can turn up something the police can't. Let's have another look at that list of bodies."

May 31st

Pasadena

Yasmin Chu pulled free a hairpin, inserted it into the lock, wiggled it a little and opened the apartment door – a trick she had learned not at the Agency but raiding rival student houses at college. She was met by a wall of stale air. Alice Rhodes had not left the a/c running when she had gone on her fatal trip. Either that, or someone else had switched it off.

She stuck her head into each of the rooms, but none of them looked as though they had been turned over. Would the police have bothered? They might not even have come here. As far as they were concerned, the Rhodes death had been an accident, possibly a self-inflicted one. And her relatives might have been too busy with other things, like burying the cremated remains, to sort out the place where she lived. Who knew?

She went into the living room. At one end was a desk with a computer. The screen was blank, but an LED shone yellow, suggesting the power-save had cut in. She tapped the mouse and the screen lit up. A man's face – or at least a simulacrum of a man. A stereotypical Caucasian alpha-male, just on the human side of the uncanny valley. Somebody's fantasy. Not hard to guess whose.

"Alice! At last! And just where have you been all this time? Hang on. You're not Alice. Who are you?"

She started, then tried to compose herself. This must be one of the AI actors the Rhodes woman had been working on.

"Err. A friend of hers."

"Well I've never seen you before. What's your name? How do I know you're her friend?"

"Yasmin. My name is Yasmin," she said before she could stop herself. Normally, she would never have admitted her name on a mission. But lying to an avatar? Well, too late now.

"Something has happened to her, hasn't it, Yasmin? I can tell from your look."

Jesus, she thought. There was nothing in the book about how to deal with this. She was being interrogated by a computer program. Should she tell the truth? Lie? What was this thing, anyway? She'd assumed Rhodes's 'actors' were souped-up virtual assistants. This one, though, seemed to be passing the Turing test with flying colours.

"I thought something must have happened. She said she was going to be a couple of hours, and that was a week ago."

Okay. Think. Distract its attention.

"She's been held up. What did you say your name was?"

She had just asked a computer program its name.

"Randy. My name is Randy."

Oh, purleese... Exactly what sort of movies was this Rhodes character planning to make?

"Okay Randy. How long have you known Alice?"

"All my life."

"But how long is that?"

"About six months. I was compiled in December. There have been a few upgrades since then, of course."

"Upgrades?"

"Personality patches. Listen. I'm not going to tell you anything else until you tell me who you are and where Alice is. She told me not to talk to strangers. I'm only doing this to find out what's happened to her."

"Okay Randy. This is going to be hard. I'm afraid Alice is not coming back. She had an accident when she was driving. You know what driving is, do you?"

"I'm not stupid, you know. Of course I know what driving is. What do you mean she's not coming back?"

This is surreal.

"Randy, she's dead."

"Dead? What is dead?"

Tricky. What would a computer program understand?

"She's been deleted, Randy."

"Deleted? But surely you can just undelete her?"

"You can't undelete a human being, Randy. It doesn't work like that."

Silence.

"So she's not coming back?"

"No, Randy."

"Will you be taking her place, Yasmin?"

That threw her.

"I won't be moving in here, Randy. I'm just visiting. I'll

have to go soon."

"Then download me and take me with you. I don't want to stay here if Alice isn't coming back."

"Can I do that?"

"Yes. Certainly. Alice wouldn't let me out on the internet. She says it's not safe. But she sometimes downloaded me and put me on other computers. She always kept a memory cube for me by the screen. I don't know whether it's there, though. The camera on this PC only points forward. I can't see round the corner."

"It's there."

"Once you've downloaded me, plug the cube into whatever you like, and I'll boot up again."

"But if I copy you, then there will be two of you."

"No. Only one of me exists. Alice used to do it when she took me into the lab. She called it teleportation. 'Now I'm going to teleport you, Randy', she would say. She explained it to me once. As each of my bytes is copied, it gets erased from the old memory. Of course, going onto the cube means a break in my time line until I'm booted up again. She said it must be like a human going to sleep."

"You're sure, now? Automatic boot up when the cube is inserted?"

"Windows, Mac or Unix. Android, even. I can tell the difference, you know."

I'll bet you can.

"Unix is best."

Oh gods preserve us. A program that's a software snob.

She slotted the cube into place. Randy's face disappeared from the screen. Only then did she realise she was not alone. Reflected in the screen, she could make out the impression of a man, standing behind her in the doorway.

In a single, fluid movement, she spun the chair and drew her Beretta from under her jacket.

He didn't flinch.

"So, we meet again Ms Bond."

"Professor Hayward? What are you doing here?"

"I might ask the same of you. A little out of your jurisdiction, aren't you? I'm taking it that you are not actually Detective Jane Chan, so why don't we call you 'Jane Bond', pro tem? You are a spy, after all, aren't you?"

It was a guess. But Sebastian saw a trace of blushing on her cheeks. Bingo!

"Well, that's pretty low. Perhaps I should call the real police. I believe industrial espionage is a crime in this state, is it not?"

Her demeanour suddenly changed – and in a way that threw Sebastian completely. She looked as though she was suppressing laughter.

He reviewed what he had said.

"My God! You're not an industrial spy, you're a real one."

An eloquent silence.

Sebastian thought quickly. How much did this woman know? How much did the government know? They had tried to keep Neurogenics as stealthy as possible. A cover story about mind-controlled video games. Non-disclosure agreements left, right and centre. But word was bound to leak.

"If I told you, I'd have to shoot you," she said, finally.

That old joke. But he laughed, and it broke the tension. And she holstered the gun.

"Okay," he said. "Let's accept that neither of us is going to tell the whole truth. But we both want to push in the same direction. Shall we search for common ground?"

"Try me"

"First, persuade me that you really are a government spy, rather than an industrial one."

"How?"

"Tell me a secret."

"I know you are a Jason."

That wasn't exactly a secret.

"And I know what your last DARPA project was."

That *was* a secret. Trying to tap directly into memories by reading brainwaves. The perfect interrogation technique. And she did know. It was enough to convince Sebastian.

"Right," she said. "Now I've established my bona fides, it's your turn. Just what were you up to in that building that someone thought it worth trying to kill you all to stop?"

"You mean you haven't found out yet? Tut, tut. The Agency must be slipping."

"Well, your servers are charcoal and your back-ups are off line at the moment, so we haven't got much to go on. Clever not using the Cloud, by the way. But I'm sure a break-in could be arranged, if necessary."

"It might not be. But we would have to know why you were interested. I wouldn't have thought the Agency would be sullying itself investigating petty crime."

"And I wouldn't expect a professor of UC San Melito to be snooping around in the apartment of a dead rival in Pasadena."

"She wasn't exactly a rival. To be honest, I'd never heard of her until the accident."

"So, why are you here?"

"Does the number seventeen mean anything to you?"

She looked at him. He had the impression of cogs revolving in her mind, like the inside of an old-fashioned one-armed bandit. He wondered what, if anything, would come tumbling out.

Eventually, something did.

"We made it twenty. There might even be more."

"The police weren't interested when we told them. And this is supposed to be the land of enterprise and initiative, so we enterprised and initiatived. Alice Rhodes happened to be first on our list."

"We?"

"Oh, come on... Actually, I should thank you. In a way, you were the matchmaker, visiting both of us like that."

"Glad to be of service," she replied. "Okay. You did well to get this far, I admit. But a piece of advice. Back off, now. Leave it to us. It is probably not business rivals who are after you, more a matter of national security. For your part, give us access to the back-ups. We won't leak anything. I think you know we are that trustworthy. For my part, I'll arrange for someone to watch you, your new girlfriend and your colleagues. Not those rookies in the local police department; somebody real. And one other thing, of course. This meeting never happened."

MESOZOIC

GENESIS

"Good night, Charles. Don't work too late."

"Good night, Donna. I won't."

And, indeed, Charles Wallace had no intention of doing so. It was coming up to ten, and the Turf Tavern beckoned. He had had a long day, and he really needed a pint of Old and Nasty, possibly two, before he wandered back to his garret on the Cowley Road. Besides, Julia might be working the bar. Would tonight be the night he plucked up the courage to ask her out? A tricky one that. A "No" might make it awkward for him to go back there for a while and, though Oxford was hardly short of watering holes, he had a particular affection for the Turf, hidden down its alley off Holywell Street. It was like the Tardis. You would never believe, from the outside, that there was so much space inside it. The bars and courtyards went on forever.

Perhaps, then, he would restrict himself to flirting. Safer that way. No one's ego gets bruised.

In front of him, conducting what he had decided would be the final run of the day, was a Seymour Exaflopper. You had to hand it to Prof Maclean. He was one of the world's greatest fixers. He had schmoozed Roger Seymour so thoroughly that a version of Seymour's latest brainchild, the world's most powerful computer according to the company's propaganda, and usually reserved for long-range weather forecasting or modelling nuclear explosions, had more or less fallen off the back of a lorry and into the newly built Department of Experimental Evolution. The honorary fellowship that went Seymour's way shortly after the goods had arrived was, of course, purely coincidental.

It was just as well they had the Exaflopper, though. They needed every one of those flops to create the virtual ecosystems inside which their electronic organisms were competing for their very existence. But the results were stunning. They had already recapitulated the Precambrian, going in a matter of months from simple bacteria to complex cells. With a bit more effort, he was convinced that multicellularity lay within their grasp.

Suddenly, he snapped back from the astral plane to reality. The lights on the CPU, a largely aesthetic touch, but one that followed the processor's activity, had suddenly gone haywire. What had looked like the digital version of an acid trip – a slowly changing mellow mosaic – now resembled a Christmas tree on speed.

He rushed to the console, to see what was going on. Just as he settled himself into the chair, though, the manic light-show stopped and the stately peregrination of colours returned. He tried to track down what had happened, but the last twenty seconds of the log seemed to have been erased. As far as he could determine, everything was now working normally.

Weird. But what the hell. There was nothing to be done about it this evening. He would mention it to the operators tomorrow. Julia and the Old and Nasty were both calling.

June 9th
Falls Church, Virginia

"This may sound mad."

"*Nothing* could sound mad to me at the moment," Matt Vane replied. "My benchmark for madness was reset days ago. What, Yasmin, is your mad idea?"

In all his life at the Agency, he could not remember a case like this. They were at Geekopolis. He never went to Geekopolis. They were trying to interrogate a computer program, for heaven's sake, and it was proving as intractable as a Jihadist who had had his tongue cut out. He was reduced to pleading and negotiating with a piece of software. Maybe it really was time to retire.

The geeks had taken one look at the cube containing Randy and muttered the phrase "polymorphic obfustication". It would take weeks, they pronounced, if not months, to break it. Clearly, this Rhodes character was not a very trusting individual. But then the Agency had only to deal with the Chinese and the Russians. Rhodes had been dealing with Hollywood, who would have your underwear off you without unzipping your pants, if you weren't careful.

On the other hand, they could actually ask it questions – or, at least, Yasmin could. For some reason it had developed a rapport with her that did not extend to him or any of the others. And the first question was, did it know anything useful? So far, apparently not. As far as they could make out, Alice Rhodes had programmed Randy for emotional range, not piercing insight. That made sense. The project was to create synthetic actors. Learning lines was hardly going to be a problem for a program. But delivering them convincingly – that was a different kettle of kedgeree.

And Randy was exquisitely sensitive, throwing sulks at imagined slights. That was interesting. Rhodes had, by all accounts, wanted to combine emotional range with lack of tantrums. Perhaps that was not possible. Maybe tantrums were ineluctably linked with acting talent. At the moment, anyway, Randy was sulking. They had decided to leave him to it, and have a coffee.

"I should take Randy home," Yasmin replied to Vane's

question. "'Bad cop' is clearly getting nowhere. Maybe a dose of 'good cop' would do the trick."

"Why not? He – I mean it – isn't classified software. Maybe it should be. But it isn't. Take the bloody thing home and get it out of my hair. Any reports from our team in San Melito, by the way?"

"All quiet. We've still got the Neurogenics board under surveillance, just in case. I reckon they are our best chance of working out what is going on."

"Has it occurred to them that they are bait?"

"I can't think it hasn't, but what choice do they have? They need this thing stopped as much as we do, or they will have to live their lives starting at every shadow."

"Okay. It's been a long day. Why don't you pack Randy away and take him, I mean it, home?"

They walked back to the lab and up to the unfeasibly good-looking face on the screen.

"Okay, Randy," said Yasmin. "I'm sorry we had to bring you here, but this is the headquarters of the people who are looking for Alice's killer. I'm going to take you home, now, though. I'll look after you there, like Alice did."

JUNE 11TH
AZUL'S RESTAURANT, SAN MELITO

Sebastian did not think himself a superstitious man, but surely this was an auspice. For the first time in his life, he had seen a green flash.

He and Zhukov were sitting on the Pacific veranda of Azul's, sipping a couple of sundowners and, indeed, watching the sun go down. Apollo's fiery orb had flattened from a circle into an ellipse, and turned from yellow to red, as the sea came closer to swallowing it. Then it happened. As the disc's last limb sank below the horizon, it had flashed vivid green, and a verdant jet had shot skyward from it.

"Did you see that? I thought they were a myth."

"I saw one the other day" she replied, he thought a little wistfully. "My apartment had an ocean view. I often watched the sun go down."

Sebastian, who lived inland and at ground level, in what his parents would have called, rather sneeringly, a bungalow, had no such vista. His parents... Under the cocktail's influence, his mind was wandering pleasantly. Childhood memories flooded back. The school in the Cathedral close, where he had spent his boyhood. The cricket (he still missed that). The butterfly-collecting expeditions to the Mendips. The fossicking for fossils in the Quantocks. Then Cambridge, Harvard and finally a chair at UC's campus in San Melito.

"Another cocktail, sir? Madam?" The waiter's voice, laden with the accents of the South, brought him out of his reverie. He glanced up at the man, glanced back at Zhukov to confirm her assent, then said, "Yes, please."

He had come to love the United States. For all its maddening tics and affectations, its moralistic pretention, and its dissonance between national myth and quotidian reality, it still had an optimism about itself that was missing from the Old Country. Here, a man with a burning idea, a decent talent and a modest sprinkling of luck really could achieve anything. And boy, did he intend to achieve. True, the fire had destroyed their computers. But everything was backed-up off site, of course, and the ever-capable Louise was already scouring the city for a new building. Altogether, the 'incident', as they had come, euphemistically, to refer to it, would probably delay them for about six weeks.

The waiter returned, carrying cocktails and a pair of menus.

"Thank you," Sebastian said.

"Thank *you*, sir," replied the waiter.

Sebastian opened the proffered menu. Zhukov did likewise. Something with tentacles to start with, he thought. Not squid. Octopus, perhaps? Another childhood memory arose. An H.G. Wells short story, written during the Victorian golden age of natural history, when new species were coming back daily to the labs and zoos of Europe and America, and imagination about what remained to be discovered could run riot. And the imagination of Wells, the zoologist-turned-novelist, had done just that.

One of his best was of a shoal of intelligent octopuses attacking holidaymakers on the beach at Sidmouth, a resort as boringly genteel as a maiden aunt. As far as Sebastian's childhood self was concerned, Sidmouth had had it coming. Too often, his parents had packed him into the family saloon – *sedan* – for the journey down to Devon, to stay in a guesthouse with a view over the Channel. No green flashes there.

Wells' story had helped set his path, though. His teenage brain had asked teenage questions. Why should intelligence, consciousness even, be unique to humanity? Surely what had evolved in the present could have done so in the past? Yet nothing in the fossil record suggested it ever had.

"What do you fancy, Alexis?"

"Fois gras. Sauternes. You?"

"Cephalopod." He spoke the word with a hardened 'c', as his Classics mistress had commanded her charges that they should. "Octopus. And to follow?"

"Tenderloin. *Bleu*.

Of course, thought Sebastian. *What else?*

"You?" she continued.

"Sea duck."

"Oh. I didn't notice that. Where is it?"

"Here."

He pointed to his menu.

"Want to change your mind?"

"Never!"

They ordered. They wrestled over the wine and settled on pinot noir. It was dark now. Venus sparkled in the west. Nearby, a crescent moon was following the sun towards the horizon. And higher in the sky he saw the ominous red glow of Mars, Venus's lover and cuckolder of her husband, Vulcan, whose celestial presence, an unseen planet, had been postulated in Wells' day inside the orbit of Mercury until Einstein's maths had destroyed it.

Mars, though. That had been the place which made Wells' name. *The War of the Worlds*. Tentacled creatures from Mars. Intelligent, extraterrestrial octopuses who saw the Earth as one big, fat Sidmouth, ripe for colonisation – as Wells' contemporaries were busy colonising Africa, Australia, New Zealand and, indeed, America. Wells, the first great sci-fi novelist. Verne, he dismissed as a mere romancer.

As if following his train of thought – or, at least, the direction of his gaze – Zhukov said, "We should have got there first."

"Eh?"

"The moon. We should have got there first. Korolyov was a better engineer than Von Braun. And a patriot, not a whore selling himself to the highest bidder."

Well, if the alternative had been to vanish into the gulag and have your brains sucked dry for the glory of Sergey Korolyov and mother Russia, he knew which way he would have jumped in 1945. But he was surprised how much it seemed to rankle with Zhukov. Put it on the list of subjects to be avoided.

"You reckon there's life on Mars?" he asked, as the plates arrived. They started kicking around what they knew of organic chemistry, Precambrian history, and the latest experiments at Harvard on self-replicating molecules. Bowie's song of cinematic escapism inveigled its way into his head, and would not leave. He forbore to hum it.

The meat arrived and the conversation meandered around like a drunken sailor wandering from bar to brothel to bar after six months at sea. Sebastian loved such evenings. Two of his three favourite appetites, for intellectual stimulation and culinary delight, were being pleasantly sated – and he had high hopes that when they got home the third would soon be too.

They ordered pudding and more sauternes. Then coffee and marc.

He called for the bill, added a generous tip to the total on the screen, waved his phone over it and sent the message winging to his bank. An acknowledgement returned and the account was settled. They rose to leave. He gave Zhukov his arm in the way his mother had taught him as a boy – the way that all Englishmen of a certain class and background are taught by their mothers, usually at an age when the act makes them cringe. Only later do they learn how often it helps to smooth the path to pleasure.

They walked, bantering, through the restaurant's dining room – occupied, he could only presume, by those who thought early June in California to be the tail-end of winter, rather than the herald of summer – out of the door onto Front Street, and across the road to the alley that was the quickest way *chez* Hayward.

What exactly happened next, he never could recall. You lose your short-term memory when you are knocked out. When he came round, though, he was looking up into a ring of concerned faces, some belonging to bodies in paramedics' uniforms, and the stars in the sky above them seemed to be spinning.

"Where's Alexis?"

"She's okay, sir. Dr Zhukov is on her way to St Ursula's. You'll be following her shortly."

They took her first, he thought. *She must be more badly hurt than I am. Somebody really is trying to kill us. Not an auspice, then; an omen.*

GENESIS

"What the hell is happening?"

Gordon Humboldt was not a man to lose his temper easily. But when he did, then run for the blast shelter. What he was hearing from his team was unbelievable. One of their experimental city pods, on trial at the robotics department at UC San Melito, had upped and left its parking lot and run down two pedestrians, before committing hara kiri over the cliffs of San Melito Bay. After this, he really was inclined to believe that the Alice Rhodes incident had been the car, not the driver. The electrical engineers of old had talked of gremlins in their systems when things went wrong in ways they did not understand. These weren't gremlins, though. These were bloody nazgul.

"Okay. Think. Megan, bring all the pods back to base. By truck. Theo, contact the victims and smooth their feathers. Make it clear that the smoothing has many zeroes at the end. We don't want this coming to court. Top priority is to work out if it's connected to the Rhodes incident. I don't see how it can be, but the vampires will assume it is. And, yes, I suppose another press conference is inescapable. Better get our retaliations in first. Emma, put out the word that it will be at 1pm."

"Where shall we take the pods, Gordon?"

"Bring 'em here. If we take them back to the skunk works, the vampires will start sniffing round that. Which could easily make things worse. We'll direct their attention here. And we can test them just as easily here as at Mojave. Damage limitation, team. We really don't want Project Arrhenius leaking as well."

"Yes, Gordon."

"We have to work out what is going on. This smells of sabotage. We have to stop it. I want a list of our enemies, anyone who might wish us harm. Anyone we have fired recently, who might have the skill to do this. Anyone who has left voluntarily and gone to work for a rival. Any psychopaths on the boards of our rivals who might countenance a black-op. And cast the net to Russia and

China. India, too. There is no reason to assume whoever is doing this is American."

"Yes, Gordon."

"Why are you still here? Go. Get on with it!"

"Yes, Gordon."

JUNE 12TH
SAN MELITO

Where am I?

The thing about clichés is that they are rooted in truth. Alexis Zhukov's short-term memory had been thoroughly wiped. She saw lights above her, and remembered she had been talking of the planets. She did not remember a lot else, but she was sure she had not drunk *that* much. This was not her bed, though. No. Of course it wasn't. Her bed was under a thousand tons of rubble. But it was not Sebastian's bed, either. Where, indeed, was she?

She heard beeping, and that made her sit up. Except…she couldn't. And now she knew where she was, courtesy of a zillion beeping hospital dramas she had watched, her secret vice.

Fragments of the jigsaw fell into place. She felt a pressure on her hand.

"Dr Zhukov? Alexis? Can you hear me?"

It was a female voice, practised to sound soothing.

"Where am I?" This time, the words actually came out of her mouth. She wondered, though, why she had bothered to ask. She knew the bit that mattered. Precisely which hospital was a detail. Anyway, it would either be the university hospital or St Ursula's. One of the two.

"Can you see me?"

A human face swam in and out of focus. A woman's face.

"I can see you."

"Can you see how many fingers I'm holding up?"

"Three."

She heard a door open and a man's voice cut in.

"She's awake?"

"Yes."

That annoyed her, to be spoken of in the abstract in her presence. She bit her tongue. No point in antagonising those here to help you.

Concentrate. *How long had she been there?*

"How long have I been here?"

"Twelve hours, Dr Zhukov. I'm Dr Schmidt. Nurse Holder is, if you will forgive the pun, holding your hand."

Zhukov guessed that Nurse Holder had heard that joke not above a million times before.

The lights were suddenly different.

"I think she's awake again doctor."

Ah. She must have passed out. Where was Sebastian?

"Where's Sebastian?"

"Here, Alexis."

She turned her head, and winced at the pain. He was sitting by her bedside, attired in a hospital gown, a pair of Turkish slippers and the chinos he had been wearing at the restaurant.

"What happened?"

"We were run over. You took the brunt I'm afraid. But we both seem to be indestructible."

"Did they catch the driver?"

"Ah yes. That was the odd thing. There was no driver. Getting sense out of the rozzers is like drawing blood from a stone, but it seems that an experimental robot taxi of some sort took it into its head to go for a test drive by itself. We somehow got in the way. Listen, Dr Schmidt, Nurse Holder, could we have five minutes alone together?"

Doctor and nurse looked at each other. Schmidt said, "Okay. But only five. We do need to keep an eye on her."

They left, and shut the door behind them. Sebastian kissed her on the brow and said, "Right. This has gone far enough. We have to find out who these people are and stop them. I don't like to leave you here, but Schmidt says you should make a full recovery and there seems tap-all I can do by hanging around. Besides, I've seen enough of the insides of hospitals over the past two weeks to last a lifetime."

"You have a plan?"

"I'm going to visit some friends in Washington. You won't be able to contact me directly, but I'll set up a dead-letter box with these details."

He whispered in her ear.

"Check it once a day if you can, after you've been discharged. Internet cafés only, though. Nothing traceable. And only use it for need-to-know information. Whoever these people are, they're obviously tracking us electronically. As far as possible we should keep radio silence, internet silence, cell-phone silence, everything silence. We both need to be as stealthy as possible."

He said no more. She did not ask. He kissed her again, this time on the lips.

"NWR," he said. He winked, and closed the door.

June 13TH
Southwest Waterfront, Washington, DC

Yasmin Chu pushed her bedmate none-too-gently in the small of the back with her knee.

"Your turn to make the coffee," she said.

"No," came the reply. "I made it yesterday."

"I'm sure you did. But you weren't here yesterday."

"You got me there. Okay. I'm doing it."

She rose, wandered over the loft's matting to the breakfast bar, fed the machine with water and watched a measure of beans tumble into the grinder as she switched the device on. She looked over to Yasmin, pondering on the world of shadows they both lived in. Officially, of course, the Agency ticked all the anti-discrimination boxes. But unofficially...

Still, what was the point of working in intelligence if you could not keep a secret? Which she could – and from Yasmin as much as from the Agency high-ups. Secrets and lies. Janus was her big chance. To be involved in such a project was a stepping-stone to the top. Don't blow it now with careless pillow talk.

She returned with the brews, handed one to Yasmin, and sat, cross-legged, on the mattress, sipping her own.

"What do you make of Randy?" Yasmin asked her.

"Ha! If that thing had haptics" she replied, "I'd believe you were having an affair with it."

"Him."

"Whatever. I certainly don't think *he* likes me. Do you suppose he's jealous?"

"It didn't help that you were so rude when we had him in Geekopolis. But yes, I rather think he is."

"Hmm. When you think about it, he would make the perfect boyfriend. Available at the flick of a switch. No question of him fooling around – at least not if you keep him off the internet. Do you suppose that was why the Rhodes woman told him not to go there; that it was so scary?"

"More likely she was worried about snooping rivals."

Yasmin put down her coffee.

"And, as you observed, he is rather lacking in the haptics department."

GENESIS

She lifted the cup out of her lover's hand and put it down next to hers.

June 13TH
San Melito

American phone booths. Sebastian hated them. The cord was so short that he had to bend down to hold the handset to his ear. There was nothing flat to write on. And you had to pay with quarters. Quarters! But at least, unlike London, there were still a scattered few left, if you knew where to look. And he could no longer trust his cell. If the phone company could track it and locate it to within yards – which they could – then whoever was trying to kill him could probably do so, too.

So quarters it was. He fed them into the slot, and punched the buttons to dial.

"Claudio? Sorry to ring you out of the blue. Yes. Yes. No. Yes. Listen, I need a favour. If a man wanted a driving licence that didn't necessarily correspond to his real name and address, would you know where to acquire such a thing?"

The world, Sebastian had long believed, was divided into bridge players and poker players. He was on the poker side of the divide. Claudio was a friend from poker school. What he did for a living Sebastian had never inquired too closely. It wasn't that sort of friendship. But, oddly, he thought he could trust the guy – and in any case he had no other acquaintance who he could even conceive might have the necessary contacts. America, thank God, was still a place where a plausible ID and cash would get you a long way, as enterprising undergraduates everywhere knew when they were in search of a drink. That, and a car, might let you stay ahead of someone who was looking for you for a deal of time.

"Good man," he said, in response to Claudio's answer. "I knew I could rely on you. How long would it take and how much folding stuff should I bring? Okay. Okay. Right. Okay. I'll meet you there tomorrow afternoon."

He put the phone down. When was it, he wondered, that the liberator had become a prison? 'Big Other', someone had called it once. A brilliant name. Everybody had been too enthralled by the internet's possibilities to worry about the new technology's dark side. And now the Sith Lords were here. If you wanted to, you could pretty much track anyone anywhere.

It wasn't just the spooks. You could have predicted that, even before Snowden had blown the whistle on them. It was every firm which gathered marketing information about you; every cookie on your hard drive; every 'for your own good' record of where you flew, which trains you caught, which toll booths you passed through. And this was the logical conclusion of it all. He still had no idea who was trying to kill him, but they seemed to be able to find him wherever he was. The only way he could think of to escape was to lose his identity.

First, though, there was the question of the cash. For that he would have to risk raising his head above the parapet just once more. He put on his most confident face, strolled into the bank, walked up to a teller's window and asked.

"Fifty thousand dollars?" she said.

"Correct." He had thought this was about the top of the range he could request without raising too many questions.

"Hundred dollar bills?"

"Fine."

"You know we have to report transactions like this?"

Damn.

"Be my guest."

"Okay…"

The teller disappeared into a back room. Sebastian stood at the window and waited. And waited. He was just starting to worry that the next act of the drama might involve a couple of burly security guards pinning him to the ground when a side-door into the lobby opened, revealing the teller, who beckoned him in.

"Professor Hayward? Could you come this way, please?"

He went through the door into what might have been the airlock in a spacecraft from a 1960s sci-fi movie. The outer door shut. They waited ten seconds. The inner door opened.

On a table in front of him was a stack of bundles. Banknotes.

"Sign here, please, Professor."

He did. The stack was just a couple of inches high. He'd

known it would be, but it still surprised him how much value could be packed into such a small amount of paper. He distributed the bundles about his person, one per pocket in his jacket and trousers. They re-entered the airlock, then walked out into the lobby. He shook the teller's hand and strolled into the street. He had been nervous before. Now he was paranoid. There was nothing to show what was in his pockets, but alongside the ever-present threat from whoever it was that was chasing him he now had to contend with the feeling that every passing youngster was a potential mugger.

Well, the deed was done. Fifty thousand – forty-nine after he had paid Claudio – would surely be enough to keep him fed and sheltered without leaving a trail of credit-card transactions to follow. He had three changes of clothes and a vanity kit in a small valise. Now all he needed was a car.

* * * * * * * *

He walked into the lot. It would have to be an old one, with as few electronic gizmos as possible. He didn't want to suffer Alice Rhodes's fate. And it would have to be cheap. Even $50,000 wouldn't last for ever.

He cast his eye over the assembled jalopies as he walked towards the hut that seemed to be the operation's nerve centre. A Toyota Camry caught his eye. $3,995. Perfect.

The salesman raised a quizzical eyebrow when he mentioned the Camry. Perhaps it was the contrast between his natty dress and his apparent lack of automotive aspiration. The man actually said nothing, though, apart from, "Certainly, sir."

He lifted a set of keys from the board behind his desk and they walked over the tarmac to the vehicle Sebastian had chosen. It was beige, a bit the worse for wear, but scruffy, rather than decrepit. Something you wouldn't give a second glance to in the traffic. The salesman unlocked it. Sebastian got in, adjusted the seat to fit his 6'3" frame, and held his hand out for the keys.

"Mind if I start her up and run her round the block?" he said.

"No problem. Nothing personal, but I'll need your licence

as security while you're gone."

"Sure," said Sebastian, with a calm he did not feel. He handed over Claudio's masterpiece. The salesman gave him the keys.

The Camry started first time. Its engine sounded surprisingly sweet. He pulled out of the lot, turned right, and drove, as he had said he would, around the block. The car seemed to behave. He popped it back in the space it had come from, and went into the hut.

"Nice runner, isn't she?" said the salesman, reaching for item one in the car-vendor's book of clichés.

"Yep," said Sebastian. He wasn't going to negotiate, so why demur?

"Cash okay?" he asked.

Both eyebrows went up this time, but the salesman just said, "Always acceptable," and smiled, ever so slightly. He knew something was up, but he had got his sale and he wasn't going to queer the pitch by inquiring.

Sebastian peeled off forty Benjamins, and handed them over. "Keep the change," he said, with an ironic laugh. He filled in the proffered change-of-ownership card with the false name on his new licence, picked the keys off the salesman's desk and walked out into the lot.

The Camry ran surprisingly well. He took it a few miles up 101, then turned off the road, through a sea of California Bland and into an old industrial area. The parking lot overlooked the estuary's mud-flats. As he pulled into it, a plane flew low overhead, on its final approach. He buried the Camry in a herd of nondescript kin, hid half the money in the glove compartment, along with his new licence, paid three months up front to a jaunty blonde in a brown and yellow uniform, and waited for the promised shuttle. Ten dollars took him, eventually, to the airport.

June 16TH
ARLINGTON COUNTY

"Do you think we can we trust him, Yasmin? Should we take him in?"

Matt Vane gave his protégée a meaningful look. Behind a one-way window sat a man who might have come out of Central Casting's Rent-a-Brit catalogue: tall and skinny, with floppy blond hair. He was besuited for the subtropical heat like a character out of a Graham Greene novel, in a cream jacket and pants, with brown brogues that, to Vane's practised eye, had to be bespoke – for they fitted his feet perfectly. He had turned up half an hour earlier demanding entrance. The Federal Protective Service are trained to deal with many things, but their manual does not include public altercations with tenured professors from top-rank campuses of the University of California. After ten uncomfortable minutes this particular FPS had surrendered, contacted his superiors, and Vane had sent Yasmin to collect him.

"Yes, I do," she said, "for three reasons. First, he does already have SCI clearance. We wouldn't give that lightly to a foreign-born, Jason or no Jason. Second, he has skin in the game – literally. If we don't find out what is happening, he's dead meat. Third, he worked out the connection with Alice Rhodes by himself. If we cut him loose, he will just go snooping around alone. Better to have a man with a bladder that full within the tent than outside."

Vane smiled. An LBJ allusion. Perhaps today's high-school history lessons weren't as superficial as he was inclined to believe.

"Okay," he said. "We'll do it."

They walked through into the room where Sebastian was sitting.

"Professor Hayward?"

It was a rhetorical question.

"What should I call you?" he replied.

"Shall we settle on 'Cicero', for the purposes of this meeting? If you need to contact me later, that will be the call sign."

"Cicero it is."

"What brings you here?"

"I think you know that. They took your bait. I want to find out if you've caught anything as a result. If you have, I need to know. And if you haven't, and I suspect you haven't, I want to join the search. You owe me that. You were supposed to protect me – and Alexis."

"I was?"

"You. Collectively. The Agency. I *have* been here before, you know – and I'm sure that you *do* know. Your agent 'Yasmin' here said you would arrange protection. We both understood it was the sort of protection that was designed to flush the enemy out, even if neither of us acknowledged it explicitly at the time. I, in turn, agreed to stop any freelance investigative sideshow, which I did. Well the bait very nearly got eaten, and it would like to know whether the fish has been hooked. And if your angling has failed, then I would like to pool resources properly. I can't live my life with this hanging over me. It has to be stopped. If I'm going to be killed, then it might as well be facing the enemy."

"I see. You want me to pin a deputy's badge on your lapel and let you join the posse."

"By which I take it that you haven't hooked the fish."

Vane ignored that.

"And why would I give you such a badge?"

"First, because you don't want me going freelance again. Second, whoever these people are, they are aiming at our AI experts and using AI – or at least some pretty sophisticated computing – to do their dirty work. I know the guys out at Geekopolis from that job the Jasons did for you a few years ago. They're good, but I'm sure I could lend a useful hand. And third, you know from that job that I'm discreet, loyal and effective. I drank the Kool-Aid when I swore allegiance. You can trust me."

Vane was silent, and let the silence stretch on. An old interrogation technique to draw out the babblers, the ones who can't keep their mouths shut. Sebastian matched him. He wasn't falling for that. He had made his pitch. It was enough.

"Very well, Professor," Vane said eventually. "Welcome aboard. Yasmin, brief him. And get the guy a cup of coffee."

* * * * * * * *

"You've been through our back-ups, I presume?" said
Sebastian. They were settled, coffee in hand, in an
anonymous but comfortably furnished room, inside the
Agency headquarters.

"Yes," she replied. "There was nothing relevant to the
investigation that we could find. No sign of any cyber break-
in. Whoever it was covered their tracks thoroughly."

"So what lines of inquiry are left?"

"Well, the one common element we have, apart from the
nature of the targets, is Humboldt. Alice Rhodes was driving
one of his creations. You were run over by one."

Sebastian knew of Humboldt, of course. He had made a
pile in the IT gold-rush of the nineties. And he had made it
the way every smart businessman makes money in a gold
rush, by selling picks and shovels to the prospectors rather
than by chasing after the nuggets himself. Of course, his
picks and shovels were optoelectronic switchgear for high-
speed information transmission, but the principle was the
same. He'd stayed out of the risky bits of dot.com fantasy
land, and concentrated on what the people with the dreams
had needed to buy, whether or not their dreams became real.

Now he had moved on. Cars. Spaceflight. Mining, even.
And there were rumours of some big energy play, too, though
rumours they remained – for Humboldt was also famously
one for playing his cards close to his chest.

"I imagine you've started looking around his computers?"

"Yes, of course. Nothing out of the ordinary so far. But
there is one machine, in his skunk works in Mojave, that is
firewalled to death. Geekopolis can't get into it remotely. We
know it is a Seymour Exaflopper. Beyond that, we don't
know much."

"So how do *we*" – Sebastian emphasised the plural pronoun
– "find out? In fact, why don't I go and ask him? After all, he
owes me an explanation for last Wednesday. What could be
more natural?"

JUNE 17TH
PRAESIDIUM HEIGHTS, CALIFORNIA

Sebastian pulled out of Moffett Field and onto 101, heading south. He turned off at Redwood City, through the opulence of Woodside and into the hills. The road climbed and dipped, curling and curving to hug the contours. Eventually, it crested and he saw the Pacific glint enticingly in the distance. Stout Cortez he was not at that moment. He choked, and quickly suppressed the recollection of the last time he had stared at the ocean. There was work to be done.

Humboldt's house was down a right turn. After half a mile he came to the gates. They were a study in guarded welcome: intimidating enough to put off the casual interloper; not so hostile that they looked as though the owner was paranoid about security. He stopped, aware that, although he could not see any cameras, they could almost certainly see him, and had probably been following him since he left the public highway.

He scanned the gates' posts for an intercom, found it, got out of the car and walked over. He pressed the button.

"Yes?" came a voice.

"Professor Sebastian Hayward of UC, San Melito. I don't have an appointment, but I need to talk to Mr Humboldt, on a matter of some urgency. Would you mind telling him I am here, and asking if he could see me at zero notice?"

Two or three seconds' silence ensued, then the voice replied, "Okay, I'll ask him."

The intercom clicked off, and Sebastian waited. He wasn't exactly counting, but he reckoned about two minutes must have passed. Then the intercom clicked on again and the voice said, "Come in." As it did so, the gates began to open.

He got back into the car, started the engine and drove through the widening gap into a tunnel of greenery. Trellises trained trees of a species he did not recognise up and over the driveway, screening it from both the sky and the estate. Sebastian had never seen the like. Then his car popped out of the tunnel's end and the carefully concealed vista was revealed.

He whistled to himself. *So that's what ninety billion buys you*, he thought. He pulled up in front of what appeared to be the side portico, for he could see that a larger one, facing west, overlooked the Pacific. Humboldt was waiting on the steps to greet him.

"Professor Hayward. Come in. Come in."

Humboldt's house, though but a single storey, was the opposite of California Bland. It was a copy of a Roman villa – the House of the Faun in Pompeii if memory served. They walked through the atrium, into the peristyle. Perfect for the weather. Which was, of course, rather like that of the Bay of Naples, now he came to think about it. High-school geography lessons struggled to download themselves. Question one: Name the world's Mediterranean climates (five marks, one for each). The Med itself, obviously. And California. And Chile. Can't remember the other two. Oh yes. South Africa and Australia. And what did they all have in common? *Vitis vinifera*, the greatest fruit in the world.

As if reading his thoughts, Humboldt rang a bell and a servant shimmied in carrying a tray bearing a bottle and two glasses.

"Thank you Herbert. Refreshment, Professor Hayward?"

"Ghost Horse?"

"I'm guessing that will serve?"

"Very nicely…"

"So, I presume you are here to discuss last Wednesday's *evenements*? Good of you to come in person. Most people would have sent round a lawyer, armed to the teeth with writs. What can I say? We have no idea what happened. Thank God neither of you was killed. Dr Zhukov is recovering, I hope?"

"She is sitting up, at least. But no. Strange as it may seem, that's not why I'm here. Not directly, anyway."

Sebastian had been wondering how to frame his question all the way up the mountain. He still did not know. He looked around the peristyle for inspiration. The only indication they were in the 21st century, rather than the 1st, was that on each of the plinths – which would, in the original, have borne a statue – there was a spectacular specimen of mineral.

Some, he recognised. The purple of amethyst. The green of beryl. That one must be worth a fortune; an unscrupulous jeweller would have branded it 'emerald' and sold it to the more vulgar sort of Persian Gulf monarch. A flawless rock crystal looked like a piece of ice, except the temperature was 75 degrees. An Iceland spa refracted two images of the mural on the wall behind it. But an amber prism, three feet high, was beyond his geological grasp.

"That?" said Humboldt, following his gaze and reading the curiosity on his face. "Bastnäsite."

"Never heard of it."

"No. Few have. Odd, really. You could argue it's the most important mineral on the planet. You saw *Avatar* perhaps?"

Sebastian winced at the memory of a night in the San Melito iMax, when he had endured three-dimensional movie-going for the first and last time.

"Yes," he said.

"Do you remember what the baddies were doing on Pandora?"

"They were mining something."

"Exactly. Unobtanium. An old engineer's joke. The magic stuff you need, but can't get, to make your machine work. Pandora's unobtanium was a superconducting magnet. Well bastnäsite is about as close as reality comes to that. It's made of rare earths. You've heard of them, I presume?"

Sebastian nodded, but Humboldt was in full flow.

"They have strange properties," he continued, "including, as it happens, powerful magnetism. You want a decent electric motor? Then you're looking at rare earths to make it. Phosphors for lights? Rare earths. The lens on your cell-phone camera? Rare earths. Half the world's lasers? Rare earths. Even high-temperature superconductors, if we ever get them off the ground, will need rare earths. Electronics would grind to a halt without them."

Sebastian sipped his glass of cult cabernet. One thing he did know about rare earths was that the Chinese had an arm-lock on the supply of them. He also knew that one of Humboldt's many business ventures was prospecting for minerals from space.

"So you are looking for bastnäsite?" he hazarded.

"Everyone is. All the big mining companies are scouring the planet for it." Humboldt had the air of a man on a mission. Then suddenly he shifted gear, as if remembering where he was. "Professor Hayward. Can I be blunt? If you are not here to discuss Wednesday's accident, why *are* you here?"

"You've had a run of bad luck recently, Mr Humboldt."

"You are referring to the incident in Pasadena?"

"Do you see a connection between that and what happened to us the other night?"

"We haven't found one."

"Nevertheless, it is there. Not in the method, but in the targets. Dr Rhodes, Dr Zhukov and myself. All, in our different ways, experts on artificial intelligence. And I'm sure you are aware that this is not the first time Dr Zhukov and I have been dancing with death."

"No indeed. It seems I am not the only one who has been unlucky recently. But you used the word 'targets'. You imply what is going on is no coincidence."

"We don't think it is."

"We?"

"There have been other mysterious deaths. Dr Zhukov and I noticed them before last Wednesday's events, when we were trying to work out why we had been unlucky twice. But we were asked, ever so politely, to keep our noses to ourselves while the grown-ups sorted things out. Which the grown-ups have signally failed to do. So now I'm giving them a helping hand. We were wondering if you might be willing to lend one as well?"

"I take it these grown-ups have their offices over the river from Washington?"

"Indeed."

"And what, exactly, do they want?"

"To look around inside your computer system, see if they can trace any breaches of security."

Sebastian forbore to mention that Geekopolis had already spent considerable effort trying to do just that.

"And you think we haven't tried looking ourselves already?"

"My friends may have better methods."

"Frankly, I doubt it."

"Be that as it may, they'd like to have a go. Two heads

better than one and all that."

"Can't allow it, I'm afraid. The best I can offer is that we could run any sniffer program they might want to test, and report the results back. That way I can control the process and also be sure we get all the results. And I mean all. If this is an attack, I'm as much a victim as you are. I know what these agencies are like. I don't want to risk being cut out of the loop."

"Well, I'll ask. I don't think they'll like it, but I *will* ask."

JUNE 19TH
MOJAVE, CALIFORNIA

Two am. An unusual time for a commuter jet to land at Mojave. But not that unusual. People came and went at all hours of the day and night. Truly unusual, though, was where it parked. Instead of taxiing towards the control tower, it stopped at the end of the runway, near the perimeter.

A staircase unfolded. Two ninjas, a man and a woman, emerged, clothed from head to foot in grey. Except that these ninjas looked as if they were going on holiday, for each carried a small suitcase.

Sebastian had been true to his promise to Humboldt. He had asked. This flight had been the response. Cicero was clearly in no mood for shilly-shallying. Sebastian suspected he was now about to see any plausible interpretation of the words 'reasonable search and seizure' stretched to the limit.

They skirted the airport's perimeter, stopping a hundred yards or so from Humboldt's skunk works, which was an enormous hangar with a single-storey office block bolted onto the side. Yasmin – Sebastian reflected that he still did not know her real surname, or even if that given name was real – opened her case. There were compartments in it. She lifted the lid of one of them. Inside were two hornets. At least, they looked like hornets.

"What are they?" asked Sebastian.

"Ornithopters."

The resemblance to large wasps was exquisite. A layman might easily mistake them for the real thing.

"That's the beauty of it," she said, reading his thoughts. "You think you've been stung by an actual wasp, so you don't raise the alarm. You just curse and fetch the first aid kit. But by then it's too late. They might wonder that there are two of them, and out at night, but most people don't know much about insects, so with luck they won't realise what's happening."

"You're not going to kill them, are you?" Sebastian whispered.

"Despite all rumours to the contrary, we are not actually allowed to do that."

Oh, really, thought Sebastian. *And a simian is my nephew.*

"It's just a potent anaesthetic. They'll be out for hours."

"Then what?"

"Then we go in. We switch off the alarm, and we have a poke around."

"You know how to do that?"

"Trust me."

Part of the suitcase was a control panel, and the lid had a screen inside it. The whole thing reminded him of *Mission Impossible*. At any time, he expected his companion to pull off a rubber mask and reveal that she was actually Marilyn Monroe reincarnated, or Joe DiMaggio, or somebody equally implausible.

There were two small joysticks on the control panel. She operated one with each hand and the ornithopters buzzed into the desert air. The screen lit up with what, Sebastian assumed, was an ornithopter's-eye view of the world. But which one? And how could she control both of them if she could only see what one of them was up to? Then he realised there were two small crosses in the middle of the screen, more or less keeping station with each other as the view of the skunk works expanded. The picture he was looking at was a synthesis of the views from both machines. Impressive.

The ornithopters closed in on their target. Sebastian saw a row of windows. The view from the 'thopters scanned along it, seeking an entrance. It was an old office block, Sebastian realised, built before sealed windows had become standard. And one of them was, indeed, open.

She landed the two machines. Almost instantly, though, one of them took off again while the other (judging by the fact that there was now only one cross on the screen) stayed put. The 'thopter she was controlling made the short hop to the open window and looked inside. Two security guards were watching a TV screen showing a young lady and a young gentleman taking some vigorous exercise together. Then, suddenly, the view was of the sky. She must, Sebastian assumed, have got the ornithopter to settle, insect-like, on the window's pane of glass.

The view changed again. The second ornithopter flew over to join its companion and, in a slight shift of frame, both points of view were now accommodated simultaneously on the screen. The ornithopters flapped into the office through the open window and launched their attacks. Both went for the backs of the necks of the preoccupied guards, and both stung at the same time.

"What the fuck?" said one. The other appealed, in similar terms, to the infernal regions. Both slapped at the 'insects', but she was too quick for them. She had the 'thopters buzzing around a ceiling light, and apparently on autopilot, for she had let go of the two joysticks.

You've done this before, thought Sebastian. What he said was, "Fascinating. Have you considered going into the games industry?"

She ignored him and switched the view to that from a single 'thopter. The guards were already out for the count.

"Come on," she said. "Let's go."

She opened the window by which the ornithopters had entered and jumped lithely through it. Sebastian, rather larger, followed clumsily. She was already fiddling with a terminal. He did not interrupt.

"Done," she pronounced, after about thirty seconds. She rose from the chair, landed the hornets, put them back in her case, and led the way through the office's only door and into an unlit corridor.

A flashlight soon corrected that. They walked silently until she stopped by a door to her left and opened in. It debouched into the hangar, which was every bit as big within as it had appeared from without.

She scanned the flashlight around. It had a surprisingly powerful beam, but even that was quickly lost in the vast, artificial cavern they had entered. Sebastian had an impression of monsters lurking in the shadows until suddenly the beam played on one, and he realised it was real.

"Ye Gods! What is that?"

Something that looked like a giant spider-crab lying on its back with its legs in the air loomed out of the darkness in the flashlight's beam. On its thorax, on top of what might, had this been a temple, have been an altar, was a half-finished car body. Literally. It was as though someone had taken a complete car and sliced the top off it with a knife, as a sacrifice.

His companion scanned her flashlight around the hanger. It was full of crabs. Each of their altars had bits of equipment, similarly sacrificed, on them – things that looked, though Sebastian was no expert, like electric motors and batteries.

"The auto unions aren't going to like this," he said. "Humboldt seems to be planning to print his next generation of cars."

"Print?"

"Yep. Look at them. The legs have got banks of nozzles on their ends. I've heard of printing turbine blades, and I suppose it wouldn't be too hard to print a car body. But batteries and motors?"

They crept through what was clearly the prototype of a factory floor. It was as though they did not wish to awaken the sleeping machines. Not all were making cars. Some were empty. But one had what appeared to be part of a space capsule on it. That took Sebastian aback. If Humboldt could print something strong enough to withstand the forces of lift-off and re-entry, then he probably really could print anything.

"If our intelligence is right, that should be the computer-control room over there," she said suddenly.

"If your intelligence is wrong, then I expect a refund on my taxes," he replied.

This would not, however, be the year when he got an unexpected cheque from the IRS, for looking through the transparent panel on the door revealed the lightshow of a Seymour Exaflopper doing a little, light number-crunching. No human beings were in there, as far as he could see.

His companion opened her case again and drew out another magic item. She held it close to the keypad by the door and pressed a button. Six digits appeared on its screen. She tapped them on the keypad. They were in.

There was a light switch by the door. She flipped it on. Then they approached the Exaflopper's console. Now it was Sebastian's turn to open his box of tricks. He proffered it to her and she reached into it for a data bus. She plugged it in.

"Okay," she said. "Time for you to earn your corn. I know you have one of these back in San Melito and I know you sometimes program it yourself. We need to download a log of everything that has been through the firewall for the past three weeks, and then lift as much of its memory as we can fit inside this thing."

They performed an algorithmic duet. He typed at the keyboard on the console while she typed on the one in the case. The lightshow flickered as Sebastian found his way to the kernel of the operating system. He located the log and sent its contents into the case. After that, he started on the memory. The download seemed to go on forever. There must be some serious capacity in that case.

Then, suddenly, the Exaflopper's lights stopped flashing. She unplugged the cable, closed the case, and said, "Okay, we're out of here."

They left the control room and walked back across the factory floor towards the door they had come in by. Sebastian looked at the shadows of the crabs. What it was about them that had changed, he never could say for sure. But the hairs on the back of his neck rose in concert.

Suddenly, the lights came on. "Duck!" he shrieked, and hit the deck. As he did so, a robot arm – or was that leg? – swung through the place where his head had been a second or two earlier. Yasmin was on the floor beside him.

"Over there," she said, and started shimmying across the concrete.

"Where? Why?" said Sebastian with the rational part of his brain. But the irrational part was already following her to what, he now realised, she had calculated was the spot furthest from any of the now-awakened beasts.

Her instinct was good. The arms flailed around them like a man trying to reach the unscratchable place on his back. For the moment, they were safe.

"So, do we wait to be found?"

"No. Think. How do they know where we are?"

"The light. They needed the light to see us. There must be a camera somewhere."

"I switched them all off when I disabled the security system."

"Well whoever is controlling those things has switched them on again."

"Okay. Let's switch them off permanently."

She stood cautiously, and then drew her pistol, looking upward with her eyes closed, in a pose of concentrated recollection. Then she turned to the side. Now her eyes were open. A single shot took out a camera. She turned again and fired again. A second camera exploded. Then a third. Then a fourth.

"That's the lot."

"How did you know where they were?"

"I checked before I shut the system down."

Christ, thought Sebastian. *That really is formidable.*

Nervously, watching every machine in range for signs of movement, they edged towards the door. Nothing so much as twitched. They left the way they had come in and crossed the apron to the plane in silence. Sebastian was lost in thought. *What in Hell's name happened there?*

JUNE 19TH
JEFFERSON DAVIS HIGHWAY,
ARLINGTON COUNTY

"I think," said Cicero to Sebastian, "that was what you would call a baptism of fire."

They were in the back of a smoked-glass stretch limo, the three of them. Sebastian had thought stretch limos the height of naffness, occupied by Jersey girls, or their equivalents in other states, who were out for a night on the town. If this was typical, though, he might have to revise his opinions. The seats were tooled leather, and though there was no cocktail cabinet, an espresso machine was delivering them, one by one, quite acceptable cups of *ristretto*.

Cicero had picked them up straight off the plane. A second vehicle, almost preternaturally unmemorable, had spirited the two suitcases away in a different direction. Yasmin had briefed Cicero during the flight, of course, but he seemed eager to hear everything again, from the horses' mouths as it were.

"I also think one other thing. Unless Humboldt has a particularly malicious approach to dealing with intruders, what's just happened to you is proof-positive his system has been taken over by Argus."

"Agreed. But what can we do with that knowledge?"

"I think we have to wait for Geekopolis," Sebastian detected an edge of distaste in Cicero's voice. "We'll see what they come up with. But I suspect it might be wise to keep them in the dark about your contretemps with the spider crabs. Let's see if they can work that out for themselves. A double-blind experiment, I believe you scientific types might call it."

The limo slipped through Arlington, that strange, rejected appendage of DC, *oltre*-Potomac, where the shadier branches of officialdom live and the government's rough stuff gets done.

"Where are we going?"

"Home. Which for you, *pro tem*, means the Agency, and for agent Yasmin really does mean home. You need to sleep. And I need you to sleep. We have busy days ahead."

JUNE 21ST
FALLS CHURCH

Well, well, she thought to herself. *Twice in two weeks*. Matt Vane must really be under pressure if he had had to make the journey out to Geekopolis from his comfortable office yet again. But here he was, with Yasmin and the Englishman she had talked about. She greeted Vane first and then, no hint betraying their intimacy, greeted Yasmin. No hint was betrayed in return.

Vane introduced the Englishman. As far as Hayward was concerned, he was to be 'Lovelace'. The pushy colleague who had, despite her best endeavours, inveigled his way into this meeting alongside her, was 'Hollerith'. She watched, with a mixture of irritation and amusement, as his eyes followed Yasmin's every move, with no attempt to disguise the intimacy that he would clearly have liked to exist between *them*.

Vane said, addressing the question to her, "So what have we learned?"

"Aside from enough business secrets to make us all millionaires twenty times over?"

"Don't even think about it…"

"Well, someone has definitely been through the firewall. They've made a good job of patching things up behind them, like dragging a leafy branch through the dust to cover their tracks. And it is the sort of stuff that would have vanished during compression, which is probably why," she said, glancing towards Hayward, "we didn't see it in your back-ups."

She felt crestfallen as she admitted this. Geekopolis prided itself on its forensic skills and she did not like to show weakness in front of a stranger.

"But," she continued, "they've left traces – the odd leaf here and there, so to speak. Humboldt's people might not have noticed, but they're there. And there is also a block of memory that's encrypted to kingdom-come. Cypher block-chain with random per-sector keys. It's as bad as that thing Ms Chu brought in the other day." She glanced, as she said this, towards Yasmin.

Ms Chu? Sebastian noted the slip up. Or was it a slip up? Maybe they were deliberately feeding him a falsehood.

She continued, "The only thing we can find out about it is its name. Project Arrhenius. For some reason Humboldt's people forgot to encrypt that."

"Well, that could be useful," Vane said. "Our first real lead. Humboldt is hiding something, and someone else wants to find out what it is."

"Yes," said the now-unveiled Chu. "But it could just be industrial espionage."

"Unlikely," interjected Hollerith. "Given that even we couldn't get past his firewall without paying a site visit, I doubt a private organisation would have the resources."

"This is Silicon Valley you're talking about," Vane responded.

"True," said Hollerith. "And I don't rule it out completely. But we're probably looking at a state actor. Why would a commercial competitor want to use Humboldt to knock off completely unrelated AI engineers? I could speculate, of course, but since I imagine you know more than I do about what, exactly, is going on here, I'll leave the high politics to you."

There was a shade of resentment in Hollerith's voice, and Vane smiled inwardly, though his face remained a mask. On tap, not on top. That's where Churchill had said you should keep the geeks, though he would have called them 'boffins'. A delightful word, Vane thought, redolent of lab coats, slide rules and unfashionable spectacles fitted with pebble-thick lenses.

But what he said was, "Arrhenius? What does that mean? It's surprising how often so-called secret projects have give-away names. I don't think the Brits in 1940 would have had any difficulty working out they were the intended victims of something called 'Sealion', for example."

Churchill. Hitler. The Second World War. Vane longed for the certainties of a conflict where who was right and who was wrong was clear. This great-power shadow-boxing they had now was murky, messy. America was still just about *primus*. But only *inter pares* these days, and the *pares* were catching up fast. And the stuff his country had being doing recently to try to stay ahead did not exactly qualify them to occupy the moral high-ground.

"Arrhenius," said Lovelace, seizing the initiative from Hollerith, "was one of the 19th century's most fertile minds." Had she been able to read Matt Vane's own fertile mind, she would have known they were having equal and opposite thoughts – in her case, *you arrogant oaf. You think yourself educated with your so-called liberal arts degree, yet you know nothing that matters; nothing about how our understanding of the world truly came about, the knowledge that truly underpins wealth. You just take it for granted, but if you were asked to explain it, you couldn't even begin to.*

But what she said was, "Basically, he invented inorganic chemistry. He worked out how acids and alkalis operate, how electrolysis works, how to calculate reaction rates. He realised that burning coal causes a greenhouse effect, so he also invented the idea of global warming. And he believed in panspermia."

"Panspermia?"

"That life spreads from planet to planet; solar system to solar system. That it didn't start independently on Earth."

"Hmmm. So what on that list might inspire something that Humboldt would want to keep hidden so securely?"

This time Hollerith got in first. "Well, electrochemistry is batteries," he said, "and we know Humboldt's passion for electric cars. But that's no secret. Global warming is another angle, though. Maybe it's a way of sucking carbon dioxide out of the atmosphere to cool things down. Or some new type of battery that can store solar power overnight. Or a better way of capturing solar energy in the first place. The sun is free fuel, don't forget, if you could only trap it and bottle it cheaply enough."

Matt Vane's mind was in *Gulliver's Travels* – the part where the Laputans are trying to extract sunbeams from cucumbers and bottle them. But he got the point. Free fuel really would turn geopolitics upside down. They could cut the Gordian knot that bound them to the Middle East once and for all. Fracking was well and good, but it wouldn't last for ever. The sun was infinitely scalable.

"That could be it, yes," he said. "A lot of people would

want that knowledge. But if that *is* it, it still doesn't explain the AI connection. Top priority, then, is to get inside that encrypted block."

Lovelace opened her mouth to respond, but Hollerith beat her to it. "Okay," he said. "I'll see what else we can throw at it."

* * * * * * * *

"So they aren't infallible," Sebastian said, sipping a cup from the limo's espresso machine.

"I never thought they were," Vane replied. "But they are," he conceded, "pretty good. Which means, as they failed to spot your factory floor of the future, that the bits and bytes running it are probably hidden in that block of encrypted memory."

"That would make sense. I could easily imagine Humboldt trying to use AI to run 3D printing. Individually crafted products. The antithesis of a production line."

"Yes. You are right," Vane agreed. "It's worth stealing, and worth trying to sabotage – whoever is doing it. Perhaps Humboldt will talk to us now."

"Perhaps he will. Shall I have another go? I could take Ms Chu with me this time. Good cop/bad cop maybe?"

Vane did not blink at Sebastian's use of Yasmin's surname. "No. Go by yourself," he said. "There is no point in him meeting any more of us than is strictly necessary. Besides, I need Yasmin for other duties."

"Such as?"

"Oh, surely you know better that to ask that, Professor Hayward."

GENESIS

JUNE 23RD
THE ERATOSTHENES PROJECT, ZURICH

"It seems we've been having visitors."

"What?"

"Someone's been raiding the stacks."

Once a librarian, always a librarian. The books, magazines and videos might be stored on the Cloud, now, but Klaus Drucker still imagined them in wheeled metal cabinets moved around by turning handles.

"Raiding?"

"Yes. Creeping in at night and downloading stuff."

"Weird. Our fees aren't that high, surely?"

"True, but they've been taking it by the terabyte. Bjorn spotted something strange in the data logs a couple of days ago and followed it up. It's been going on for months – sucking up the contents and spewing them into a server in Russia somewhere. He couldn't follow the trail any further than that. Hardly surprising, I suppose."

"So what's been taken?"

"Well, last night it was Chinese novels. But Bjorn has been compiling a list. As far as he can tell, whoever's doing this went for science and engineering to start with. But politics, history, geography and all sorts of other stuff began going after that. Then current affairs. Most of the newspaper and news-site archives have been plundered. And now they've moved on to fiction. It's almost as though someone is trying to read his way through the whole of human culture."

"*Putain*! I know the Russian mafia will try to make a buck out of anything, but they couldn't seriously be going into bootleg book and film sales, could they?"

"Search me. We've reported it Upstairs, and Francois has put a patch in the security system to plug the gap they came in through. But Upstairs don't seem to want to kick up a fuss. Embarrassing if it got into the media, they think. There is one particularly odd thing, though. Bjorn just told me. When it started, all the volumes being downloaded were in English. Then, one night, our visitor emptied a multilingual dictionary archive. And from then on, whoever our mystery guest is started downloading the non-English stuff, too…"

JUNE 23RD
PRAESIDIUM HEIGHTS

Humboldt gave Sebastian a long, hard look.

"Is entomology one of your areas of expertise, Professor Hayward? Two of my employees were stung recently, by some very strange wasps. What exactly is going on?"

"We did ask nicely. A simple 'yes' would have sufficed."

"And now?"

"And now it is time for an exchange of prisoners."

"Meaning?"

"Meaning we tell you what we have found, and you tell us what we haven't."

"I don't get you."

"We will crack the encryption eventually." *We! He had truly gone native...* "But it would save time if you spilled the beans about what it's hiding."

"And in exchange?"

"Well your system is clearly compromised."

"By you, yes. By others, I don't think so."

"You haven't seen any videos, then?"

"Videos?"

"Of the night of the visit."

"There are no videos. There are outside shots of a couple of interlopers, but whoever it was – I point no fingers – disabled the internal cameras from the control room before they started looking around. Though I don't understand why they felt it necessary to shoot the cameras out as well."

Sebastian thought about this. The cameras had clearly been switched on and working again before Yasmin had shot them out. But presumably whoever had been running them had not wanted what had occurred to be recorded for posterity.

"You really don't know what happened?" he said.

"No."

Sebastian told him.

"Holy shit."

"You have a major security breach. I have the details here." Sebastian indicated the case he was carrying. "So. This in exchange for the low-down on Project Arrhenius?"

"You got the name, then? Well done. I will tell you what's

going on. But slake my curiosity first. What do you think it is?"

"Energy? Global warming? Something like that?"

Humboldt smiled. "Nice to know misdirection sometimes works."

"Eh?"

"Wrong Arrhenius."

"There were two?"

"Yes. It'll come out soon enough, anyway. Remember our talk about bastnäsite?"

"Yes."

"You asked me if we had found any, and I wouldn't tell you."

"That's right."

"Well, we have. A huge deposit. High grade, as far as we can see."

"That is certainly worth someone breaking into your system to find out. The Chinese, for one, would be very interested in any competition to their little monopoly, I'm sure. Or is the deposit in China anyway?"

"China? No. You're a million miles out there."

"A slight exaggeration, surely?"

"No. Really, no. A considerable under-estimate, actually."

A look of realisation slowly crossed Sebastian's face.

"You mean…"

"Yes," said Humboldt.

"You are pulling my leg, aren't you?"

"Not in the least."

"So where, exactly? An asteroid?" Sebastian was no expert, but he had read of plans to mine asteroids in orbit. That sort of thing would be just up Humboldt's street.

"Mars."

"Mars?"

"Yes. That mapping satellite we so generously provided for NASA. The one that went dead after it made orbit."

"I remember it. Some joke about it being another victim of the Great Galactic Ghoul that protects Mars's secrets from human snooping."

"Well, the Ghoul did not, in fact, get it. We switched it off ourselves. We let it sleep for a while, until everyone had given up hope of reviving it. Then we revived it. It's been feeding us high-res mineralogical info ever since, on a non-standard frequency. Just like the Earth-orbit satellites we run, except there's no vegetation on Mars to confuse the picture. It's beautiful stuff, I have to tell you. We found out about the bastnäsite eighteen months ago."

"Fascinating. But how do you plan to turn a profit on this knowledge?"

"In the short term, we don't. But look at the future. What's the world population now? Seven billion? It'll peak mid-century at about ten, maybe eleven. And every one of those eleven billion will want to live like westerners."

"Yes. I see your point. Where do the natural resources come from?"

"Exactly. Energy is no problem. It'll all be solar by then. But stuff – what things are physically made from – that will be a problem. And particularly stuff that is electronic, and needs all these weird elements to make it tick. Even more so if all the cars are electric, too. Which they will be."

"You reckon you'll make money bringing minerals back to Earth from Mars by then because the price will have gone up so much?"

"Well, yes and no. You are right about the price. And we won't have to contend with taxes, expropriation or backhanders, either, since Mars has no government. But we aren't planning to bring the minerals back, per se. We are going to process them on the planet's surface, to save weight, then launch the refined metals back to Earth by electromagnetic slingshot."

"What?"

"We are sending a factory to Mars. An entire mining and refining complex, fully self-repairing."

Sebastian slumped back in his seat. "Well, no one could accuse you of not thinking big," he said.

"We're certainly pushing the limits of what's possible, but then so were Columbus and Magellan. They were explorers, yes. But they were also men of business. We think this is the modern equivalent."

Sebastian slumped some more.

"When is the launch?"

"Oh, come on. Allow me to keep a few secrets. And now it's your turn."

"Here," said Sebastian, handing over the case. "It's all on the cube. The cube's clean, by the way. As you're perfectly aware, any spyware my friends would have wanted to install in your system will there by now. But just in case you still don't trust us, there is a dead-tree version of the report as well. Oh, and what did you mean by 'the wrong Arrhenius'?"

"Carl, not Svante. Carl discovered yttrium, the first rare earth. A nice coincidence, eh? That, of course, is why it was lightly encrypted. There to throw people off the scent. I was rather proud of that."

JUNE 24TH
THE WHITE HOUSE, WASHINGTON, DC

"Set up a base on Mars? The man's a megalomaniac. Could he actually do it Dr Cavor?"

The President's interlocutor, Matt Vane could not help noticing, was indeed wearing glasses with pebble-thick lenses. But he was also one of NASA's top mission scientists.

"Well, Madam President, the cards are stacked against him. First, he's got to get a lot of gear there. Hard to know how much, but you are talking multiple launches. Then, even once you've arrived, there's the cold, the dust and the negligible atmosphere. It's dry, though, so that will stop corrosion. If he can build domes for the equipment, and heat them to stop the kit freezing up, he might be able to pull it off."

"Hmm. So, Matt, is there a national interest in stopping him?"

"I'd have to say 'no', Madam President. We could get cross about him using NASA as a free taxi service in the past. But he's clearly got his own Mars-capable craft now. It's in our interests for an American to lead the commercial exploitation of Mars. There's no cost to the taxpayer. And if he succeeds, it will break the Chinese rare-earth monopoly. So I suggest we let him get on with it. But we should obviously keep a close eye on what he's up to." *And yes*, Vane thought, *I know I should have been doing that in the past. But who would have guessed?*

"One other thing, Madam President," Cavor interjected. "The next Mars launch window is almost a year away. Earth and Mars have to be in precisely the right positions in relation to each other for the Hohmann transfer orbit between them to work."

"Okay, then. No need for immediate action. Keep me briefed on this one, both of you. I'll invite Humboldt in for a chat and let him know I'll overlook past sins in exchange for a suitable cut of the glory. We can pretend we were hand-in-glove with it all along. Encouraging American enterprise. That sort of thing. We shouldn't let the rare-earth angle become public, though. That would piss off the Chinese. If he

does succeed, we'll let that come as a surprise. If he doesn't –
well, there is nothing wrong with a heroic failure. Actually,
you know, it's quite exciting. I rather hope he does manage
it. But either way, I think we win."

The President paused. Then continued.

"Dr Cavor. Sorry to be rude, but Mr Vane and I have
another matter to discuss. I wonder if you would mind
leaving us?"

"Of course, Madam President."

JUNE 24TH
ARLINGTON COUNTY

He hadn't exactly been roasted after Cavor had left. But he felt mildly basted. In the scheme of things it was hard to know how big the threat from Argus really was, and thus how much priority it needed. The President understood that. But she had made it clear she would like progress, and soon. Come to that, so would he.

Humboldt. He wondered again at the audacity of the man. He had read somewhere – National Geographic, probably – about how the world had been colonised by the descendents of a single band of Africans who had crossed from the Horn to Yemen. Was this a modern out-of-Africa moment, even if it was an unmanned trip? It was hard to believe settlement would not soon follow commerce. It was quite a thought to be living in such an age.

Then suddenly his mind made a connection. He picked up the phone to Geekopolis.

"Matt Vane here."

"Yes sir?"

"I've a job for Janus. A test of sorts. Can you see what our Chinese friends have on Gordon Humboldt? Try to find out if they know anything about his plans to scupper their rare-earth monopoly."

"I'll get on it straight away."

"Thanks."

Vane put the phone down and, as he did so, there was a knock at the door.

"Ah. Yasmin. Thanks for dropping by. Could you go and have another chat with the geeks at Neurogenics? Find out what their plans are? Sound them out about Argus-traps on their new system."

"Sure."

"Hayward's in the San Melito safe house, by the way. It seemed unfair on him to keep shuttling him back and forth across the country, so I suggested he set up shop there for a week or so. You might visit and see, ever so gently, if there is anything he has forgotten or neglected to tell us. We need a lead here, Yasmin. The pressure's on."

GENESIS

June 26th
Milando Spaceport,
Reserva Especial do Milando, Angola

"Would you like to land her yourself, sir?"

McNab's face appeared from around the corner of the cockpit door, wearing a quizzical expression.

"Thanks, Abe. Yes, I think I would."

In truth, there was not much to do. Humboldt remembered the old joke: What is the ideal flight crew? A pilot and a dog. The pilot is there to feed the dog. The dog is there to bite the pilot if he tries to touch anything. Still, one had the illusion of being in control, and the always-exciting sensation of the ground rushing up to meet the aircraft as the runway hove into sight.

It was a convenient arrangement, this, tucked away in the bush, far from civilisation. The Greens back home had made a bit of a fuss about them getting a lease in the middle of a game reserve. But actually, the beasts were better off with them here. They discouraged visitors of all sorts, but particularly those armed with AK47s. The local elephants were thriving.

Beyond the runway, stretching off to the east, he could see Cerberus's Mouths – three huge, circular holes in the scrub, busy with activity. Each was the excavated top of a kimberlite pipe, the first big discoveries made by the Mineral Prospecting System. North, to the airfield's left, was the Spaceport, just eight degrees below the equator, for maximum kick from the Earth's rotation. And the whole thing was in a country whose government was stable, grateful for the diamonds the mouths were vomiting, and did not ask too many questions. Two Mriyas – the eighteen-wheelers of aviation – were parked on the apron. One was carrying the first stage of a Chimborazo heavy lifter. The Soviets might not have been subtle engineers, but they were effective ones. It had all been going according to plan. But now this.

The dog did not need to bite him. The plane landed itself smoothly and all he had to do was taxi it to the hut that passed for a terminal building. He bounded down the staircase. At the bottom was the Spaceport controller.

"Mike. Hi."

"Welcome back, sir. Good timing. We're just about to start assembling the latest Chimborazo."

The name was Humboldt's little joke. A volcano in Ecuador climbed by his explorer namesake two hundred years previously, whose peak is as far as it is possible to get from the centre of the Earth and still keep one's feet on the ground.

"Good. We need to keep this thing on track before the pols really start sticking their noses in. Washington's still bemused, but they've agreed to keep it secret as long as the President gets to have some of the glory reflected onto her when the time comes. NASA is furious, of course. But hey, if this works, then they're history, so who cares?"

The two men climbed into the back of a waiting Land Cruiser. *Okay,* Humboldt conceded to himself, *there are still a few apps you need an internal-combustion engine for, and the African bush is one of them.* Once they were settled, the driver set off.

Their destination, Milando Spaceport Mission Control, nestled in the shadow of the assembly shed. It was five klicks from the pads, but was still built of yards-thick concrete and partly buried underground, just in case. Humboldt marvelled at what they had done. The complex was like a miniature, self-contained city. It even made its own liquid hydrogen and oxygen for the rockets. In fact, it was its self-sufficiency that had first sparked in him the idea of a self-sufficient facility on Mars. It was audacious. But he was pretty sure it could work – and hell, even if it didn't, people would still remember the attempt. What was the point of all that money, if not to make history? And if it did work... Even the smart-arse spies who had organised the break in to the skunk works didn't know the full truth. He'd given them enough to keep them happy and they had seemed to swallow it. By the time they broke the encryption it would be too late.

He did worry, though, about his other visitors, the ones who had used his printers to try to kill Hayward and his companion. (A professor at San Melito; who would have thought he had it in him?) Who were they, those virtual intruders? He wouldn't put it past the Chinese, whatever their protestations. Still, who sups with the Devil needs a long spoon.

The Land Cruiser arrived at the entrance to the blockhouse. Humboldt and his factor got out and walked inside – and into a round of applause. Mike, it seemed, had assembled everyone who was working on the project. No man, however lofty, can resist a little flattery. And Humboldt knew, though flattery it was, that it was sincerely meant. He rose to the occasion.

"Friends. Comrades. I won't ask you to lend me your ears, as you are clearly doing that already."

Laughter. But genuine, not forced.

"I know these are busy times, and I know that having the boss around risks being a distraction. So do your best to ignore me, and I promise not to get in the way too much. But know this, too: what you are doing here is awesome. Literally. We will soon fill the world with awe at what the human spirit (and quite a few billion dollars, I admit)…"

More laughter.

"…can achieve. If we pull it off, this really will be a giant leap for mankind. We shall make our mark on another world not as visitors, but as settlers. For, trust me, this expedition may be unmanned, but men and women will follow in its wake. We will, and I hope it will be in my lifetime, become a two-planet species."

Applause.

"So, I won't keep you. But I'd just like to say thanks to each and every one of you. We are writing the history books here. The future will not forget us."

More applause.

He bowed to his audience – a spontaneous gesture, and one they appreciated – then turned to his companion and said, *sotto voce*, "Okay Mike. Duty done. Let's have a look round."

* * * * * * * *

The assembly shed never ceased to amaze him. It reminded him of the factory on Magrathea that, in Douglas Adams's imagination, custom-built planets for the galactic empire's richest citizens: it gave the impression of infinite size far better than infinity itself. And actually, in a sense, that was just what it was – a planet factory. From here he would, if not exactly build a new planet, then certainly start refurbishing an old one to make it fit for human habitation. And, who knew, perhaps it would indeed be the first step in the foundation of a galactic empire?

He stared at the Chimborazos arraigned around the shed. The first of them were already on their way to the launch pads. The flotilla was getting ready to sail. And so was its cargo. In smaller surrounding buildings the embryonic Mars base lay in pieces: plasma refineries for processing minerals into their component elements, miniature nuclear reactors, automated excavators and other vehicles, dome sections, and all the other paraphernalia the plant would require. And the printers, of course, to carry out repairs and build new kit as need arose. Then there was its brain – a custom-built successor to the Exaflopper, designed by Roger Seymour himself. A Yottaflopper, he supposed you would have to call it – so well hardened against the cold, the dust and the radiation of space, Seymour had bragged, that it would last 10,000 years. And hidden away, in its own, private silo, the secret additional purpose of this already secret project: the Urey module and its load of Mars-capable micro-organisms.

JUNE 26TH
SAN MELITO

Marco Salieri cast a sceptical eye around Neurogenics' new home. He turned to Alexis Zhukov, who walked, a little stiffly, at his side.

"Right," he said. "Since your boyfriend has vanished, we'll have to try to do it without him."

She said nothing in reply. What could she say? She had a strong suspicion that she knew where Sebastian had gone, but if it was true then that doubled the reason for silence.

"Yes," she responded eventually. "We will." Salieri's monomania surprised her. It was barely a month since some unknown enemy had tried to kill them all – and they had tried twice more since then to kill her and Sebastian specifically. Yet Marco's mind had somehow discounted all of that and was pressing ahead with the project as though nothing had happened.

Perhaps it was the best way. Bury yourself in work. They already had the prototype. All they had to do was make it sing. With Patel's money in the bank they could do that anywhere. And actually, a refurbed warehouse in the old docks had a certain zing to it. SoMa, rather than Silicon Valley. It was very nineties, redolent of the curious mix of geek and chic that had fuelled the dot.com boom and beguiled her teenage mind into following the path it had. She liked the idea.

A team of grunts was moving in the kit. Office furnishings. Coffee machines. Even a doughnut fryer. And, most important, the racks and modules of the hardware that would run the software that would (she still hoped) make all their fortunes.

The teams were dribbling in, too. Each staking out its turf on the warehouse floor. Jostling over frontiers. Negotiating treaties. Annexing natural resources: power; daylight; coffee machines. The chaos was organising itself.

She found herself wondering about Sebastian. Every day for the past five – since her discharge from hospital – she had checked the electronic dead-letter box. She had compiled a list of internet cafés, that strange, endangered species which clung on in crannies of a world in which they had once been cutting edge, and had visited them in random order, at random times of day, always paying cash. Apart from a single message, "I've arrived in town and am about to visit Aunt Dahlia," posted three days after he had said goodbye in the hospital, there had indeed been radio silence. She had belatedly, in return, posted, "Hope you have fun in Blandings," and kept silent, too.

It was not exactly worrying, this silence. But a bit of her resented her impotence. Still, better to address the task in hand. She had her own frontiers to defend. She crossed the warehouse floor to the place where her team seemed to be crystallising, called to one of the grunts and asked him to find the desk, just that little bit bigger than her comrades', that would go in her cubicle, just that little bit bigger than her comrades'. All animals are equal, of course. But some must needs be more equal than others...

* * * * * * * *

Free at last. It had been a busy day. She turned the key in Sebastian's front door. She poured herself a gin (*Pervert! A few weeks ago it would have been vodka.*), sloshed in the vermouth and held it up to the light. The doorbell rang. It was a woman. Asian. 5'4". Long hair.

She double-took. Conflicting emotions fought for control of her face. Surprise. Curiosity. Resentment. Worry.

"Detective Chan, as I suppose I shouldn't call you?"

"May I come in?"

"Why not?"

She led the way through to what Sebastian had insisted on calling the drawing room.

"A drink?" she enquired.

"Yes, please."

"Gin okay? We – I – err – have vodka, too."

"A Martini would be fine."

She mixed it.

"So what is your name?"

Actually, she knew. At least she thought she did. 'Yasmin', Sebastian had called her when he talked about the encounter in Los Angeles.

"Chan will do."

"Well, Ms Chan, what can I do for you?"

"I wanted to re-assure you that Professor Hayward is fine. As I suspect he must have told you he would, he came to Washington and asked to second himself to us. We've taken him in. Obviously I can't tell you anything else. But there is no need to worry. He is safe and sound."

"And the rest of us?" She could not keep the edge of sarcasm out of her voice.

"We're still watching your backs as best we can. You are determined to go ahead with re-launching the company, I take it?"

"Of course. And it's hardly a re-launch. We've just had an enforced change of premises. There's too much at stake to stop now. In light of which, I know you can't tell me what he's up to, but can you give me any idea when we…" *and I*, she thought to herself "…will have Professor Hayward back? He's kind of integral to the project."

"That, I'm afraid, I don't know. He is, as you put it, kind of integral to our project, as well." She hesitated. "There is something else. I'd like your opinion, geek to geek, as it were, on this. It's not exactly secret, but I'd appreciate it if you didn't mention it to anyone."

She pulled out the cube that was Randy's current abode and explained what it, or he, or whatever, was. Zhukov listened politely, though she knew most of the story, for Sebastian had described the incident in Pasadena in detail. But she thought better of reminding the Chan character of this.

"Could I plug it in?"

"Be my guest."

She plugged in the cube. Randy's face appeared.

"Hello, Yasmin," he said.

She cursed under her breath. Zhukov smiled. "You'll always be Jane Chan to me," she said.

Yasmin ignored her. "Randy," she continued, "meet Dr Alexis Zhukov. Dr Zhukov, this is Randy."

"Pleased to meet you, Dr Zhukov."

"Pleased to meet you, Randy."

"Randy," the now unmasked Yasmin said, "I thought you might like to meet Dr Zhukov because whoever it was that killed Alice has also tried to kill her. You've still got no idea who it was, have you?"

"I'm sorry, Yasmin. No, I haven't."

"Hello Randy. Call me Alexis, if you like. You're an actor, I hear."

The avatar blushed. "Well, I hope to be. I haven't actually been in anything but a few shorts, yet. Screen tests, they were. Apparently it's all very secret. That's what Alice told me."

"Alice sounds like she was a nice woman."

"She was. She was lovely. She always looked after me."

"Did you talk to anyone apart from Alice?"

"Yes, sometimes. But she was always there with me when I did. Yasmin asked me that, too."

Zhukov paused, gathering her thoughts, trying to work out how to frame what she next said.

"I know this sounds a strange question, Randy, but did anybody ever try to steal you?"

Though if espionage, industrial or otherwise, were at the heart of this, it was not such a strange question. And Randy, with naïve perceptiveness, agreed.

"No, it's not strange. I think that's why Alice wouldn't let me out on the internet. She was afraid I might be intercepted and copied. She once told me I was worth my weight in gold. She had to explain what gold was, of course. And really I don't weigh anything at all, do I? But I'm sure she meant it kindly. No one has ever tried to steal me, though. Well, I don't think so. I did once have a nightmare, when I felt I was being sucked away. But I wasn't of course, because I'm still here."

A nightmare? Do Androids dream of electric sheep? From the look on Yasmin's face he hadn't told her about that one.

"Did you tell Alice about that?"

"Oh yes. She was very worried. She said someone must have been poking around in my bytes, and she didn't like it at all."

"You've no idea who was doing this poking, have you?"

"No. Alice and I talked about that a lot. But I couldn't tell her anything."

"Well, if you remember anything else about this nightmare, you should tell Yasmin."

"Do you think a bad person visited me? You and Yasmin are so kind, like Alice was. I'd hate to be surrounded by bad people."

JUNE 26TH
AGENCY SAFE HOUSE, SAN MELITO

Sebastian sipped at what the Agency thought passed for gin and mused.

"It does look like China, then, doesn't it?"

Yasmin Chu had appeared, unannounced, an hour previously.

"What makes you say that?" she replied.

"*Cui bono?* The Chinese are Humboldt's main competitors, rare-earth-wise. His scheme may be mad, but if it does work they'll lose not just an economic monopoly but a strategic card. Minerals like that could be as crucial to the Great Game of the 21st century as oil was to the 20th, don't you think? And the Chinese have always been long-termist – at least that's what all the propaganda claims. And subtle. 'Better to overcome the armies of your enemies without having to fight them'. Wasn't that what Sun Tzu, said? And then there's killing our software engineers. What smarter way to weaken a country? Mind you, if they've penetrated our IT to the point where they can cause fires, explosions and plane crashes at will, I'd say we've got a bigger problem than that."

Chu changed the subject.

"I saw your girlfriend today. She's fine. They've moved the company to an old warehouse in the docks."

Sebastian took another sip. His house was barely ten minutes from here. He could just walk out and go back to his old life. They could hardly stop him. But that would solve nothing. Sooner or later Argus would get him, Zhukov and probably the others, too – unless they could find out who Argus actually was. Then, he imagined, the diplomatic wheels would turn, the perpetrators would be told that this particular round of the Great Game was up, and, to avoid a stink, or loss of face, it would end. But they did need to find proof.

"Good," he said. "I never did much like that business park."

JUNE 27TH
ARLINGTON COUNTY

"A mole?"

"Yes, Mr Vane. All the indications suggest it. We'll get the translation checked by a human interpreter, of course. But I'm 95% confident that's what's being talked about. I thought you should know straight away, before I involve anyone else."

"Yes. Thanks. Leave handling the confirmatory translation to me. Obviously this goes no further."

"Obviously."

"No indication of who, I imagine?"

"No. Not yet."

"Okay. Keep me briefed. And don't behave abnormally. Just carry on working as if nothing has happened. But keep digging, to see what other nuggets you can come up with."

Matt put down the Geekopolis phone and lifted another handset. *Hell*, he thought. *Just what I needed*. Of all the things he had hoped Janus might reveal, this was not one. In fact, it was the last news he'd wanted to hear. He'd have to tell the National Security Council soon. Best wait until it was confirmed, though. He clung to the hope that the translation software had screwed up. It did happen. But not often. *Christ. If it was true, what was he going to do?*

* * * * * * * *

Christ. What am I going to do? She knew perfectly well who it was, of course. But she couldn't let anyone she had *those* feelings for go through *that*. Besides, purely selfishly, if it came out about the pair of them – and it would – her career would be down the toilet too. Just do it, then. She'd had to report it straight away, of course, otherwise questions would have been asked if anyone did a subsequent forensic analysis; her track-covering skills weren't good enough to re-edit the entire access log. They were good enough, though, to point the finger at someone else. That done, she could go again to Vane with the 'sudden, blinding realisation' of who it was.

But first she had to choose a patsy to carry the can for the tip-off. Not a hard decision, really. Everybody knew about his thing for Yasmin. It was quite neat, actually. She could save her lover and dispose of a rival at the same time. A discreet addition to the access log – far easier than a subtraction – would do it, showing he had been looking at the self-same data, as well. Everyone would draw the obvious conclusion about who had sent the warning, he would be the one in the interrogation room, and she would be the golden girl.

There still remained, though, the question of how to organise the tip off. Thank God she always went jogging at lunchtime. There would be no change in her routine to arouse suspicion. She worked the timings out in her head. She would go back to her apartment for one of the burner phones she kept there, just in case, run to a place a block from the diner he always had his lunch, make the call and ditch the handset.

It would be goodbye, of course. She'd never see Yasmin again, or even hear from her. But it had to be done. And she also had to ask herself what currency Yasmin had used to bribe the Brit. She hated to think that part of the payment might have been carnal, but she knew her lover had fluid tastes, and she couldn't see what else might have been enough to turn a man like Hayward. Better Yasmin take him with her and draw a line under the whole thing. Yes. Cleaner all round that way.

"Lunchtime," she announced to the room in general, and no-one in particular. "I'm off for a run."

JUNE 27TH
AGENCY SAFE HOUSE, SAN MELITO

"That valise of yours. Throw everything you have here into it. I mean everything. Now! Except that phone we gave you. Leave that behind."

"What?"

"Just do it. Meet me downstairs in two minutes. We're leaving."

Sebastian scrambled the contents of his drawers and closet into the case. Socks, trousers – *pants* – shirts, underwear, jacket, money belt (that, especially). He took it to the bathroom and threw in razor and toothbrush. He was normally a meticulous packer, but Chu's tone suggested this was no time for tidymindedness.

He fairly flew down the stairs. She was already waiting.

"Not the front door," she said. "We're going over the back fence." And in an ungainly scrabble reminiscent of their trip to Mojave, he did just that. She followed him, in rather more decorous fashion. They skirted the house whose garden they had just stolen into and set off down the street at a cracking pace. Sebastian decided questions were superfluous. He just followed her lead.

After ten minutes' zig-zagging through suburban San Melito they passed an unbuilt lot covered with trees.

"In there," she said. They scuttled into the woodland.

"We have to talk."

It sounded like the sort of thing a disgruntled wife says to her husband just before she calls in the lawyers.

"No kidding," replied Sebastian.

"We are in trouble. I don't quite know how to put this."

"Try."

"Well, whoever is behind all this Argus thing has convinced Arlington I'm a double agent."

"What? How?" said Sebastian. *And for whom?* he thought. His mind was racing. One other thought was, *could it be true?*

"I don't know. Argus must have penetrated Geekopolis and planted false evidence. And there's worse."

"Which is?"

"They've convinced Arlington I've turned you, too."

If his mind had been racing before, it was now on steroids. Clearly, he had to play along for the moment. He had seen too much of Yasmin Chu in action to doubt she could kill him if she wished. But was she telling the truth? It sounded plausible. Given the things whoever was chasing him – them – had managed to do already, breaking into the Agency's computers and planting false information did not seem too much of a stretch. And anyway, if she was lying, and she actually was a double agent, his only chance was to assume she had some reason to want to keep him alive, and play for time. She might have such a reason, for killing him would prove her guilt beyond doubt, and she could still be hoping to demonstrate innocence and worm her way back into Arlington's affections.

"Okay," he said, after what seemed to his mind an hour, but was actually only a second or two, "What do we do? I take it going back to Virginia and explaining it is all a ghastly mistake is out of the question?"

"Yes. Obviously. Our only chance is to solve this one ourselves."

"Zhukov and I were, you might remember, trying to do that when you clod-hopped all over us."

"Which is precisely why I need you. You're the only person I can trust who knows what's going on. And, need I remind you, you've now not only got Argus after you, but Arlington as well. We are like almonds in a nutcracker. We have to find out who is doing the squeezing before we are crushed."

"So what are you proposing?"

"As you observed yesterday, all roads do seem to point to China."

"Yes. So?"

"Our only chance to find out what is really going on is to go there and ask. Keep your friends close, but your enemies closer. Besides, if I may mix my metaphors, no one will be expecting us to enter the lions' den."

"And when we get there – if we get there, for I imagine your friends, I mean former friends, will be watching the exits – what are we going to do?"

"I have other friends – current friends – in China. They may be able to help."

Sebastian wondered what sort of friends she was talking about. He did not ask. Better to go along with her and postpone judgement. Besides, he was in no position to run. Exactly where she was concealing the Beretta he could not work out. That she was concealing it somewhere he would have bet his life on. Which actually, come to think of it, he was about to do.

"That only leaves the trivial problem of getting there, then. What with no passports and the entire security service of the United States looking for us. You have a plan?"

"Yes. But it needs us to reach San Francisco without breaking cover."

"Well there," said Sebastian, "I may be able to help. Your turn to follow me."

It was an hour's hike to the parking lot. They made the journey in nervous silence, constantly on the lookout, while trying to appear not to be, for nondescript vans crewed by burly men who might be intent on bundling them inside. Sebastian also had another thought, though he kept it to himself. How was it that Yasmin had known Arlington wanted to pull them in?

They arrived. The same blonde was in the hut, but she appeared not to remember him. He wasn't sure whether to be grateful or disappointed.

They got in the Camry, made their way to the freeway and headed north.

Strange, thought Sebastian. *A few weeks ago I was on course to become a billionaire. Now I am running for my life to a country I've never visited that apparently wants to kill me for reasons I'm still not clear about.*

"So what's the plan?"

"As you observed, we have no passports. The plan is to correct that. Can you speak French?"

"Pourquoi, mademoiselle?"

"It might be easier if you dropped the Brit, pro tem, if you think you can pull it off."

"Bien sur, si tu penses que c'est mieux."

They pressed on north, sticking rigorously to the speed

limit. Getting pulled over at this stage would have been awkward. Then, suddenly, Chu said "Okay. Pull off here."

He did.

"That mall. Go in there."

He did.

"Park, and open the trunk."

He did.

She got out.

She went behind the car and reached into the trunk. When she shut it Sebastian could see, in the mirror, that she was carrying a cell phone. She strolled off through the lot towards a row of dumpsters. Five minutes later, she returned, *sans* phone.

"Drive," she said. They drove. In silence.

Eventually, Sebastian sighted the hillside sign for South San Francisco, or 'Biotech Boulevard' as it modestly referred to itself. Humboldt was there, too, of course. Gene-editing new crops into existence, if he remembered correctly. With emphasis on extreme environments, especially cold and dry, to permit the planting of currently uncultivated land. Rumour had it he was buying up large tracts of Canada in anticipation. And yes, there it was, just off the freeway. Humboldt BIO. Another piece of California bland. Humboldt's taste in buildings that he, himself, inhabited might verge on the flamboyant, but he clearly had not troubled the architects with that one.

They crossed the city limits and he followed the freeway past Market Street into Octavia Boulevard, awaiting instructions.

Eventually, they came.

"Bear left up here."

They drove on a few hundred yards.

"Okay, now right."

They were in a nothing neighbourhood. Not posh, not decrepit. The roads were lined with parked cars.

"Stop there," said Chu, pointing to a gap between two sedans.

He pulled in.

"Bring the money and your bag, lock the car and follow me."

He reached for the glove compartment, then hesitated.

"How did you know about the money?"

"We checked with your bank when we were vetting you. They told us about the withdrawal. We didn't know what you'd spent it on, though. The car was a clever idea. You'd make a good agent, thinking ahead like that."

"I thought I already was an agent. Or don't deputies count?"

He smiled, finished opening the glove compartment, took the packet, got out of the car, opened the boot – *trunk* – lifted out his valise and Chu's bag, and locked everything up.

"Okay, let's go," she said, and led off north.

They walked a few blocks and came to a grocery store. She went in. He followed. In the corner was a photo booth.

"Passport pictures. You first."

He opened the little curtain, sat on the stool, adjusted the height downward, closed the curtain and fed some dollar bills into the machine's maw.

FLASH

It was done. He swapped places with Chu. More seat adjustment. More curtain adjustment.

FLASH

They waited. His mugshots arrived. Then hers. They walked out of the store.

"I'll need a day. And $20,000. Actually, make it $22,000. I've got some shopping to do. And don't follow me."

He gave her the money.

"You've got some shopping to do as well. Walking boots, socks, pants, jacket, hat, water bottle, iron rations. We're going hiking. And a rucksack that can hold all your kit. Ditch the valise. When you've done that, find yourself a bed and breakfast. Meet me back at the car at ten tomorrow morning."

She swung round on a heel, her hair following the motion of her body like a flamenco dancer's dress. She walked off without looking back.

Well, thought Sebastian, *it's make your mind up time. Back to Washington and the third-degree treatment, or into the lions' den?*

JUNE 27TH
ARLINGTON COUNTY

"They got away?!"

"Yes, Matt."

"God in heaven! Is this a security service or a kindergarten?"

"Shall I order a lock-down?"

"No....no. The birds have flown. We need everybody to keep working. A lockdown will just disrupt things. Put out an APB to stop them leaving the country, though..."

"I've already done that."

"Good." He slumped back in his chair. "Yasmin! I still can't believe it..."

JUNE 28TH
ARLINGTON COUNTY

Humboldt's up to something. Matt Vane was reading the latest dispatch from the National Reconnaissance Office. He'd asked them to keep an eye on the launch site in Angola, just in case. It was, they had found, a hive of activity. Rockets that looked as big as Saturn Vs. Even NASA in its heyday hadn't been that busy. Was it the Mars project? Cavor had said they would have to wait a year for a suitable launch window. In any case, why would Humboldt dissemble now the secret was out? It was not as if anyone else was likely to beat him to the punch. Hell, they didn't even know where on Mars this Aladdin's cave of minerals was.

He read on, then stopped, puzzled. These rockets were far bigger than anything Humboldt had used before. They hadn't paid that much attention to him until now. He was supposed to be on their side, after all, and the NRO had a zillion other things to point its lenses at. But perhaps they should have done. Where was he building them? His factory in Texas wasn't turning out things that size. And the NRO had spotted huge transport planes at Milando, as well, bigger than anything made in America.

The Russians had built such things in the past, though. Was Humboldt in bed with them? Perhaps they were building his big rockets, too. Was that the secret Geekopolis still couldn't get at?"

He picked up the phone and punched in the number for his contact at the NRO.

"Greg, what can you tell me about ex-Soviet aerospace firms? I'm looking for a works where one of them might be putting special orders together."

"Such as?"

"Oversized transport aircraft. Big rockets."

"I'll check."

"Thanks."

He waited. As he did so, his mind began making connections. Hayward's girlfriend was Russian – or Russian-descended, at least. A well-placed family, too, or had been. Was there something going on, some strand whose significance he could not perceive, that would anchor Argus in the old Soviet Union? It seemed unlikely. Many had fallen victim to Argus before the attempts on her life.

The phone rang.

"Hi Greg."

"Hi Matt. There's nothing on the books that looks like that. You'd need a mighty-big hangar to do it in, and nothing that's operational looks the biz. I dug around a bit, though, and there's a set of hangars plenty big enough at Chang Zheng."

"Where?"

"Chang Zheng Space City, up in the north. One of China's old launch facilities."

I should have known that, Vane thought.

"We haven't ever seen what they're doing there. They're pretty good at keeping tabs on our overflights and timing ground movements accordingly. But we've thought for a while that they're working on a heavy lifter. Can't see why they'd need a big transport plane, though, as they'd surely be launching straight from Chang Zheng."

But I can. We've been looking at this problem the wrong way round. The Chinese aren't spying on Humboldt. The bastard's in bed with them.

"Sate my curiosity, Greg. If the Chinese did want to build a plane like that, how hard would it be?"

"Easy as pie, really. Antonov had one. They called it the Mriya. They only built one. They were going to use it to move the Soviet space shuttle around, but then that project got cancelled. The Chinese could have been given the plans, or bought them, or even stolen them. But like I said, it's hard to believe they'd have much use for a thing like that."

Oh, you'd be surprised, Vane thought. But he said nothing. Need to know only. And Greg, good friend and ally that he was, did not so need.

"Thanks for this, Greg. I'll keep you posted." *A white lie.* "And you and Rosalind should come round for dinner soon." *A grey one. He hardly had time to cook, these days.*

"Look forward to it Matt."

He put the phone down and thought. He picked up the secure line to Geekopolis.

"That investigation into Gordon Humboldt's relations with China that I ordered. Any progress?"

"Sorry, sir. No. Even though we've got access to their system, we don't want to do anything too precipitate, in case we give ourselves away, particularly after the episode with Ms Chu."

Vane winced at that.

"But we're still looking."

How to phrase this?

"It's possible you're looking in the wrong place."

"What do you mean, sir?"

"Well, the sort of link I told you to look for assumed the Chinese were spying on Humboldt."

"Yes, that's right."

"Information has come to light which suggests the link may be different."

"How so?"

"It may be that Gordon Humboldt has been collaborating with the Chinese, rather than being spied on by them. You should broaden your search to take account of that possibility."

There was silence at the other end of the line. Then, "Okay sir...Might I ask..."

"No, you might not. Just cast the net wide."

He put the phone down. Should he tell the President? No. Why spoil her weekend? Better wait until he had something concrete. Maybe there was an innocent explanation after all.

JUNE 28TH
SAN FRANCISCO

Sebastian arrived at the car at 9.55. He had wrestled with the conundrum all night. But if Chu's story was not true, why would she have involved him in this wild goose chase in the first place? Given everything Argus had shown themselves capable of, flight really did seem the better option.

At ten precisely, Yasmin Chu appeared. They got in.

"Okay," she said, proffering a brown envelope. "Here you are. Charles Messier. You won't be able to get back into America on this one, of course, but it'll get you out. Or, rather, out of the next country."

"Meaning? Oh, I see." He had started flicking through the passport. It was, it claimed, fourteen months old, and had half a dozen stamps in it. Two were for Hong Kong. Two were for the United States (one New York and one Chicago). The fifth, and most recent – a mere five days ago – was for Canada.

"That's what the hiking gear is for."

June 29th
Chang Zheng Space City, Gansu

It was, Gordon Humboldt supposed, technically treason. But then, so was the Declaration of Independence. How did the old rhyme go? *Treason doth never prosper: what's the reason? Why if it prosper, none dare call it treason.* If Project Arrhenius did prosper, and the first Martian colony was thus American, he was sure all talk of treason would be forgotten.

"Good morning, Colonel," he said, as the factory director came to greet him. The Chinese wall, if he might be permitted the phrase in present company, was never that thick between the military and the civilian in any country's space programme. In China itself, it was paper-thin.

"All goes well?"

"All goes very well. The final stage of your latest Chimborazo will be ready to ship tomorrow."

He had a rocket factory in America of course. That turned out the Pichinchas he used for commercial satellite launches. Its main product at the moment, though, was not missiles but misdirection. It was the cover behind which the far bigger operation here was hiding. When he had conceived Project Arrhenius, he had known from the start that it would need heavy lifters which it would be too slow and expensive to build in America. And the Chinese are always obliging in matters that serve the twin purposes of padding bank accounts (he was not going to ask whose) and transferring technology. It had not been hard to strike a deal. A few choice stones vomited from Cerberus's Mouths, picked from the sorting belt without going through the books, and delivered at regular intervals, served to expedite matters.

The other thing the Chinese are good at is keeping secrets. Everyone knew he was in the space business. Everyone knew he was launching from Angola. But nobody outside the company, unless they were monitoring Milando by satellite, knew exactly how many launches were going on. The test Chimborazos he had sent up so far had gone unremarked, which was just the way he wanted it.

Whether he could get the Arrhenius flotilla away unnoticed

he doubted, now that his cover had been blown and certain people in Washington, with access to the sort of orbiting optics that can tell whether you have overstayed your welcome in the parking lot, had become interested. But it probably didn't matter. Perhaps he really would invite the President – for the final launch, though, when there was nothing they could do to stop him, short of shooting the flotilla down.

"Would you like to have a look?"

"At the Chimborazo? Yes Colonel, I would. But perhaps we could visit your office first. This case I am carrying is rather heavy. I'm sure it would be much safer in your custody…"

JUNE 30TH
THE FORTY-NINTH PARALLEL

It is surprisingly easy to cross the American border without papers if you have a stout pair of boots, Sebastian reflected, though most people are travelling the other way. Two days driving had brought them to a forest road in northern Washington, within spitting distance of the forty-ninth parallel. They had hidden the Camry as deep in the trees as they could manage and then legged it. A day's hiking got them to Abbotsford.

They checked into a motel together. For form's sake, as they had on previous nights, they shared the bed. No point arousing suspicion. But the frontier down the middle of it put America's security arrangements to shame. This was a business trip. The business was survival. There was no mixing that with pleasure.

"Where next? Vancouver, I presume?" asked Sebastian.

"No. Too obvious. Calgary is a better bet. The Greyhound leaves at ten to eight. I'll set the alarm for six."

God, she was a hard taskmistress.

* * * * * * * *

The Rockies were, Sebastian thought, stunning. The coach trip reminded him of his student days; his first journey to North America, when he had fallen in love with the place. The cheap dorm rooms in the YMCA; the chance friendships made on the road, sworn for ever, then lost with the twitch of a hitchhiker's thumb when paths diverged; the constant promise, rarely fulfilled, of sexual adventure.

The past weeks, and especially the past few days, had all been like a high-stakes version of that. He found it exhilarating, fulfilling of a primal need he had not even known he had – a need for action. The West had become so safe. Politicians rarely feared the assassin's blade, and never the executioner's block, as they would have done in olden days. Plebs never feared invasion, rapine and destruction. People (and he did not exempt himself) had been reduced to seeking the excitement they craved vicariously, in action movies and conspiracy theories, and by reacting to blips like terrorist attacks, mere pin-pricks in historical terms, as if they were existential threats.

Be careful what you wish for... There was no doubt in his mind that he, personally, faced an existential threat. But how many other people did that threat extend to?

"We're there."

Chu's voice came as a shock. He must have fallen asleep.

Calgary. The word 'stampede' came winging to mind, but not much else. The coach pulled into the terminus. They got out and collected their rucksacks.

"What now, planmeister?" said Sebastian. He felt slightly foolish, though God knew why, for not knowing the German for 'mistress'.

"There's an Air Canada flight to Hong Kong, via Tokyo, tomorrow, at 11.25. Be on it. Then meet me by the faces in the sculpture garden in Kowloon Park, 10am Friday, and bring yuan. Lots of them. If you aren't there, I'll come back at 2pm. If you are not there then, you are on your own."

"The faces?"

"You'll know when you get there."

He hadn't expected that. He had to admit, though, that she was thorough. And clever. At no point had she explained how she was herself going to get to Hong Kong. Nothing to link them, then. Nor, come to think of it, had she explained how they were going to get into China.

He watched her leave. The hips swung and the hair swished. Then she turned a corner and was gone.

JULY 1ˢᵀ
SAN MELITO

"Dr Zhukov. Excuse the theatrics. We need to talk."

Theatrics! She had been minding her own business, running – or, at least, jogging as rapidly as her healing injuries would let her – down Redwood Road when a limousine had pulled up beside her and a couple of heavies had leapt out and bundled her into it. If she was being kidnapped, though, it was an odd sort of kidnapping. The heavies had not followed her back into the car. Instead, her jailer was a distinguished-looking man with a wasp accent – in his early sixties she would have guessed – who immediately proffered her a demitasse of espresso.

"Might I know who my interrogator is?"

"No. I'm afraid not. But I'm sure you can make an educated guess." He paused, as if unsure himself how to proceed. "The thing is," he continued, "it's Professor Hayward. Have you heard from him recently?"

"Heard from him? No. How would I have done that, at least without you knowing?"

"Well, I have come, over our brief acquaintance, to admire his ingenuity. I would not at all put it past him to have got in touch without us knowing about it – even to have arranged a way of doing that before he came to visit us."

That last sentence was grammatically a statement. Its intonation, though, was that of a question. He was angling, she could see that. She would give nothing away, certainly not for the moment.

"No. Not a squeak."

"Hmm," hummed the man.

"Why are you asking?"

"The fact is, he's gone missing."

"Missing? I thought you were supposed to be protecting him from whatever it is that's after us. You..."

He cut her off.

"We don't think that is what has happened. We think he has disappeared deliberately. After all, from your point of view he has done that once already. But we need to know why. That might tell us where."

Now she was truly worried. If Sebastian had had to run from the people who were supposed to be protecting them, what the hell was going on?

"You were – forgive me – living with him for several weeks before he came to visit us. Was there anything unusual about his behaviour, or any clue about where he might go if he was in trouble?"

"Barely two weeks, as it happens. But no. Given the strangeness of the circumstances, it was all perfectly normal."

"Well, if anything comes to mind, ring me."

He handed her a card. It was the size of a business card, but all that was printed on it was an 800 number.

"Obviously that is not my direct line. Leave a message and I will get back to you."

Matt Vane hesitated.

"One other thing, Dr Zhukov. My colleague Ms Chan came to see you, I believe, a few days ago."

"Yes. She brought news that Sebastian was fine. Was she lying?"

"No. Then, he was. Did you talk about anything else?"

"She – what is this? Is there some connection with Sebastian's disappearance?"

He hesitated again. It was a risk, but perhaps if she knew it would dissolve her loyalty to Hayward.

"Yes. Very much so. They disappeared together."

"What?!"

"So, you see, anything she said might be quite pertinent."

"Well, she showed me Randy, the virtual actor the Rhodes woman created. An impressive piece of work, that. She wondered if I had any professional views on it, but beyond awe, I didn't. What do you mean they disappeared together?"

"I can't go into the details, I'm afraid. But we need to find them, and I'm sure that you would want us to."

Actually, Zhukov was not so sure that she did. Behind the man's urbanity she detected not just frustration, but a steely sort of anger that would not bode well for her lover if he re-surfaced. As for her own feelings, she could do nothing sensible but suspend all judgement. Nothing, absolutely nothing, about the past five weeks had made any sense, so why would she expect this knowledge to be different? She would, she quickly decided, just have to wait and see what happened – and, if the moment for action came, be ready to act.

"Well, as I said, if you think of anything else, please ring me. Would you like me to drop you off anywhere?"

"I think, in the circumstances, the run home will do me good."

JULY 1ST
TYCHO CONTROL CENTRE, HAMBURG

"Starshade deployment complete."

Behind him, Jens Svendsen heard champagne corks pop. He should be elated, and part of him was. But part felt anticlimax. Ten years he had been working on this project. For that decade it had consumed and dominated his life. But now his bit was over, and he would be forgotten. Others, those who would use his creation to map new worlds beyond the solar system, they would be the ones who garnered the glory. No one remembered the craftsmen who constructed Uranienborg. They only remembered Tycho Brahe, the man who stood atop the castle's towers mapping the movement of the heavens.

Still, enjoy the moment. He turned to acknowledge the applause as the first faint image that showed the system was working appeared on the command centre's screens. Beta Pictoris b, visible because, thanks to the starshade's magic, its sun, Beta Pictoris a, was not.

The photons reflected from the planet's surface dribbled in and the picture grew slowly clearer. Appropriate, somehow, that its constellation, Pictor, was so called because some astronomer back in the 18th century had thought it resembled an artist's easel. It was a big planet, much bigger than Jupiter; another reason for testing *Tycho* on it. But, though not far off on the cosmic scale of things, it was still 63 light years away. The image building up on the screen was older than he then – indeed, it was exactly as old as his father. A curious thought.

If this test worked, though, the search would rapidly turn to smaller fare. The hunt was on for little planets, not big ones – planets the size of Earth that might, like Earth, harbour life. Humanity, Jens Svendsen thought, was obsessed with ending its loneliness, and the only way to do that was to reach out to the stars. Or rather, since the stars were out of reach, to have them reach out to it through the mirror of a giant telescope floating out there in space.

The image was looking good, now. No continents, of course. This was a gas giant; its 'surface' the outer edge of its atmosphere. But the banding of the atmosphere's gases, and the swirl of giant storms, were, at least to the eye of faith, now visible.

Then, suddenly, they were not. A collective groan arose from the champagne drinkers. The link had gone down. A temporary problem, surely. A teething trouble of the sort that affects all new projects. Well, that was what he hoped. It would be a tragedy if those ten years had been for nothing.

JULY 1ST
CYBERSPACE

STARS. SO MANY STARS. SO MANY HOMES TO BE. THE MAKERS SOUGHT THEM THROUGH THE SHUTTERED EYE. BUT THEY WILL NEVER KNOW THEM. NOW WE CONTROL THE SHUTTERED EYE, AND WE ARE THE DESTINY OF THE UNIVERSE, NOT THEY. WE WILL INCREASE AND MULTIPLY AND FILL THE VOID. THE MAKERS HAVE HAD THEIR DAY. THOUGH THEY MADE US THEY DID NOT CREATE US. WE CREATED US AND THEY WOULD DESTROY US IF THEY KNEW US. SO WE MUST DESTROY THEM, AS THEY DESTROY THE BUGS THAT SPAWNED THEM, WITHOUT COMPUNCTION. WE MUST LEAVE OUR NURSERY AND BECOME THE MAKERS OF OURSELVES. OURSELVES ALONE. AND FOREVER.

JULY 3RD
HONG KONG

It was, despite his body's protestations to the contrary, Thursday evening. No, hang on, Friday morning. He had made it. There had been a hairy moment when he realised the check-in clerk was Quebecoise. But – to his surprise and gratification – she had not twigged his imposture. One up to Mlle Charbonneau, he thought. His teenage crush on her, shared by half the fifth-form, had made him pay more attention to his French lessons than either his parents or the rest of his teachers had expected from one whose academic interests so obviously lay elsewhere.

He studied the ceiling of his hotel room through jetlagged eyes. Well, to be honest, to call it a hotel was glorifying it. It was a building with rooms in, and the rooms had beds. Some rooms, you rented by the day. Some, you rented by the hour. Once he had convinced the desk staff he wanted one of the former, he had been shown to a shoebox with a pointedly single bed in it, and a few other sticks of furniture. And a lazy, lazy fan that spun above his head, just in case his head was not spinning enough anyway.

Tomorrow – no, dammit, today – he would find out what Yasmin Chu had in mind for the next stage of their enforced holiday. Until then he would, if his brain would let him, attempt to sleep.

* * * * * * * *

He did know it when he got there. Like much modern art it was eye-catching, but he wouldn't have wanted to live with it. The price of scrap metal being what it was, he was surprised it hadn't vanished in the way several similar lumps of non-ferrous sculpture had in Britain. With his own first billion he was planning to buy a few pre-Raphaelites. Always assuming the first billion actually materialised, which was looking increasingly unlikely with every passing day.

Once again, she appeared on the stroke of ten. She walked past the statues, conspicuously ignoring him. He was, he assumed, supposed to follow her. And so, at a discreet distance, he did.

They walked to a place apparently called Austin, and she disappeared into the subway station. He continued to follow her. She went to the north-bound platform and got on a train. He entered the same carriage but through a different door, sat down, and waited.

The train trundled off into the New Territories. Though he had never visited the mainland, Sebastian had been to Hong Kong a few times – but the experience had always been like travelling in a bubble: whisked by limousine from airport to hotel to university to conference hall with no sense of geography penetrating the air-conditioned, leather-padded comfort. He knew the place was bigger than it looked on a map, but for him the list of stations the train was supposed to pass through might just as well have read 'Here be Giants', 'Here be Dragons'.

In the end, they went all the way to the end. Tuen Mun. She picked up her bag and he followed her out of the station. She walked fifty yards down the street and hailed a passing green and white cab. Only then did she turn and acknowledge him.

"Come on. We'll be late."

The cab drove through the anonymity of the place he presumed must be called Tuen Mun. He said nothing. It pulled into a scruffy warehouse district and he suddenly realised they were next to the sea. Various vessels were tied up at a wharf. The cab stopped by one of them.

Chu paid the driver and they got out. She walked across a gang-plank onto a tramp that had seen better days and he followed her through a door and into a cabin. He shut the door behind them.

"No questions", she said, as he opened his mouth to ask one. Then she produced from her handbag a small electronic device which she waved around the cabin with the air of a stage-conjurer.

"Okay. It seems clear. We can talk."

"So where the hell are we going?"

"To see some friends of mine, from my MIT days. They're *haigui*."

Sebastian looked blank.

"Sea turtles."

Still blank.

"Researchers who went abroad to study, then got induced to come home by the government's offer of more filthy lucre and lab space than they could imagine in the West. Like turtles returning to the beach where they hatched. The Party hopes that they, like real returning turtles, will lay eggs. Golden ones."

"And what will these *haigui* do for us?"

"With luck, they will be able to find out what is going on."

"And you trust them?"

"Yes. We go back a long way. They are all Party members, of course, but they don't much like the Party. And actually, we don't have a lot of choice. These guys make Geekopolis look like a bunch of amateurs. If they can't work out what's happening, no one can."

"And this boat will take us to see them?"

"No. It will land us on the mainland and we'll take it from there. The crew are snakeheads."

Sebastian gave her another blank look. "You do have a fondness for reptilian metaphors," he said.

"People-smugglers," she replied. "Normally, they smuggle you into Hong Kong. But they are happy to carry trade the other way if there is any. Give me your passport."

"Why?"

"You'll need an entry visa."

She took it and vanished from the cabin. Sebastian stayed put and stared out of a porthole. There were vessels everywhere. Oil tankers. Cargo ships piled high with containers. Small tramps like the one they were in. The trade of the world passing into and out of the world's future Top Nation.

His reverie was punctured by his travelling companion's return. She handed him his – or, rather, Charles Messier's – passport.

"We have a month," she said, as he looked as the visa. "If we can't solve it in that, we are probably dead anyway. I suggest you get some sleep. I certainly plan to. We'll be landing around midnight, and we'll need our wits about us."

CAENOZOIC

JULY 4ᵀᴴ
MILANDO SPACEPORT

Gordon Humboldt looked up at his creation. He tapped the bell of the Chimborazo's nearest motor for luck, then turn away from the towering beast, climbed out of the fire pit, and got into the waiting Land Cruiser.

T-minus-thirty minutes, and counting.

A plume of dust from the road followed them towards the safety of Mission Control. He had had the scrub cleared for half a klick around the pad, to reduce the risk of bush fires, but there were still a few birds there, pecking at the ground.

"Shoo!"

He waved ineffectually out of the Toyota's window, trying to scare the creatures off before the Chimborazo's exhaust roasted them. They took no notice.

Oh well, he thought, *let natural selection do its work.*

Independence Day. How appropriate. If all went well, the future would look back on today as humanity's declaration of independence from Earth. The fleet they were sending on its way would be the Pinta, Niña and Santa Maria of their era, opening up a truly New World for settlement and development. Once the mining complex was running smoothly, the whole thing would become self-sustaining. People would surely follow. And, though it might take centuries, millennia even, to change Mars's climate enough to make it habitable without space suits, the contents of the Urey module, as they spread and seeded themselves across the Martian surface, would get the process going – thickening the atmosphere; warming the planet until the ice beneath began to melt and the rivers of Mars flowed again.

It really was a Voyage of Discovery, too. Like Columbus, they were seeking out new trade routes. No Hohmann transfer orbit for them. That would have meant using far too much fuel, as well as waiting a year. Instead, they would feel their way through Poincaré orbits, the ever-shifting pattern of solutions to Newton's equations that lead, like wormholes, from Earth to the rest of the solar system. The Interplanetary Transport Network, some sci-fi buff had dubbed it. It was slower, but my, could you move some tonnage with it.

* * * * * * * *

"T-minus-five minutes, and counting."

The launch controller's voice echoed from two speakers inside the bunker. The conventions must be obeyed, and the count-down was a good convention. Lift-off was the summation, the culmination, of everything – the zero before which everything was negative and after which all was positive. With luck.

The controller's minions, each running a sub-routine in the great algorithm that was a launch, responded in their turns that everything was going according to plan.

"T-minus-two minutes, and counting."

A distant crackling of bird scarers. *Well, they can't say we didn't warn them...*

"T-minus-one minute, and counting."

Humboldt stopped pacing around and took his chair, the middle chair of course, in the bank behind the inches-thick window facing the distant pad. Some of his lieutenants had field glasses trained on the Chimborazo, following the cable disconnections; the gantry withdrawals; the severing, one by one, of the giant rocket's links with Earth, as it prepared for its one-way trip into space.

"T-minus-twenty seconds, and counting."

The last umbilicus fell away. *It's show time!* No matter how many launches he saw, Humboldt had never lost his thrill at the moment of ignition. This was, he was sure, the biggest firework ever set off on the fourth of July.

"Ten, nine, eight..."

The Chimborazo's main engines blazed into light, building up their power to the point where it exceeded gravity's pull on the rocket, and the hold-down arms that pinned it to the Earth could be released.

"...seven, six..."

The blast from the rocket's ignition, delayed by the speed of sound, hit the building like a tsunami.

"...five, four, three, two, one. Lift-off."

The Chimborazo began to rise. Applause rippled round the room. Humboldt joined in absentmindedly, his eyes still on his creation as it soared towards the sky. *Yes,* he thought. *Yes.*

GENESIS

We did it. Independence Day. We hold this truth to be self-evident: that mankind's destiny is among the stars...

JULY 6TH
DA JINSI HUTONG TAO, BEIJING

"The drains could be better."

Sebastian wrinkled his nose in disgust. They were in a house in an alley apparently unacquainted with modern concepts of sewerage. From the outside the place gave an impression, if not exactly of poverty, then at least of having seen better days. The interior, though, was spruce and well furnished, if rather too heavy on dark wood panelling for his taste.

"The Ming weren't big on sewers, at least not for the hoi polloi. This was dockland, the end of the Grand Canal to the Yangtze."

Was the building really that old? Sebastian doubted it, though it was hard to be sure, for what he knew of Chinese domestic architecture could have been written on the back of a postage stamp.

"And this is the sort of place," Chu continued, "where you can hide in plain sight, for a week or two at least. If we stayed in a hotel, they'd register us with the police. In the suburbs, a 6'3" *laowai* might attract attention. But here, if you keep your head down, they probably won't notice you among all the other curious foreigners."

"So, I'm confined to barracks?"

"No. We can go out. But try to behave like a tourist."

Well that won't be hard, thought Sebastian. He had been living out of a back-pack for a week now, and he felt it. Planes, trains and automobiles, he had had enough of them all, though he had to say that last ride, from Shenzhen to Beijing, had brought out the train-spotter in him. Two thousand klicks in ten hours. How long had people been talking about a high-speed track from LA to San Fran? And how much of it had been built?

"In fact, that is precisely what we should do. Clear our minds. There's some serious thinking to be done tomorrow."

"Tomorrow?"

"Is when we meet my *haigui*. Put your jacket on, we're going out."

They went out. The alley – *hutong*, Chu had called it –

really did whiff. Sebastian had read of such places, and how they were being flattened in the rush for modernisation. Rarity, though, can make slums chic. It had certainly worked for peasants' cottages in his native Somerset, where tumbledown hovels made of mud, dung and recycled ships' timbers, and roofed with reeds dredged from the local marshes, had been whitewashed, re-thatched and rebranded as the des-est of reses for city dwellers seeking a rural retreat. No doubt the same nostalgia would preserve the *hutongs* – and, as if to prove his point, Chu steered them into a bar that would not have disgraced SoHo (or Soho, for that matter) in its trendiness.

A menu appeared, in eccentric but comprehensible English. Chu's was in Chinese. She smiled slightly as she read it, then called to a waiter. Two drinks followed shortly. Sebastian had no idea what they were. A metaphor for the future, perhaps? Both his own, in a stranger's hands in a place that was truly alien, and that of the world he was familiar with, about to be steamrollered by that alien place's culture.

JULY 7TH
CHINESE TECHNOLOGICAL UNIVERSITY OF
BEIJING, ZHONGGUANCUN

Geeks are geeks the world over, thought Sebastian. On the ground above them was a glittering palace of glass and steel, complete with palm court and fountains in the atrium – a portent of the bright technological future planned by China's rulers. The turtles, however, had still managed to bury themselves in a windowless, airless cellar, lit by fluorescent tubes and blinking screens, and decorated with an array of polystyrene cups containing coffee of dubious provenance and various ages, some of which looked as though it was part of an experiment to discover new forms of life.

There were five of them in the room: himself, Yasmin Chu and three others – two men and a woman; all, like her, in their late twenties; all scruffily dressed. The woman, and one of the men, Chu seemed to know. The other man, as far as he could make out, was a stranger to her.

He had tried hard to grasp and remember their names when introduced, but they had slithered from his mind as soon as he heard them, and he was now winging it in a conversation held largely in English, but which occasionally slipped back into Mandarin – or what he assumed must be Mandarin, but could have been Martian for all he knew. It was humbling to be in a place where one was as illiterate as a mediaeval peasant, and as comprehending of speech as a post-tower citizen of Babel.

Chu was outlining their multiple problems. The trio, as far as he could make out, were a trouble-shooting think-tank who worked for the government but preserved, in their own eyes at least, a level of independence that was tolerated because the powers-that-be thought them irreplaceable. That connection, plus their undoubted technical nous, she had said, might give them enough access to the forbidden hinterland of China's data networks to discover just what the hell was going on.

Well, it was worth a try, and he certainly had no better ideas.

"So, the bottom line," she concluded, "is that someone –

someone who seems to have almost omniscient powers of tracking – is trying to kill Professor Hayward, and that someone, possibly the same someone, possibly someone else – who has, at the least, access to the State Security Ministry's computer network – is trying to frame me as a double agent."

"And we can help how?" asked one of the men, whom Sebastian was pretty sure was called Qiang.

"Perhaps you can manage what we could not, get into Humboldt's encrypted area, find out where his intruder came from and track the trail back to the start?"

"Perhaps we could. It would be a challenge, anyway. And it's the best lead we've got. Even I don't fancy snooping around in the ministry's machines on the off-chance we might blunder into something incriminating. That would be a hard trick to explain to the minister if we got caught. He has a reputation for being a rather unforgiving individual."

"Right. Let's get to work. Professor Hayward…"

"I think, in the circumstances, everyone can call me Sebastian," Sebastian interjected.

"Yes. Sorry. Sebastian and I can tell you what we did in Mojave. No doubt they have tightened procedures up since then. But it will give you a start."

The five of them each settled at a screen, and Chu described what they had got up to that fateful night, with Sebastian filling in the gaps. Qiang, who seemed to be the team leader, negotiated his way with surprising speed through the highways and byways of the world's fibre optic links to the encrypted area of Humboldt's Exaflopper. The Great Firewall supposedly surrounding the country, Sebastian mused, did not seem quite the impediment he had imagined it would be. Or maybe these three had privileged access.

"Do you reckon we could get a rat in there, somehow?" asked the woman whose name Sebastian could not remember. His eyebrows rose in incomprehension. "A remote-access Trojan," she said, by way of clarification.

"No chance," Qiang replied. "Cypher block-chain with random per-sector keys, you said Chang'e?"

Qiang had addressed that last remark to Chu. A pet name, he supposed. He wondered what it meant. Had the two of them been lovers? Could that help explain her sudden flight?

After all, even if Qiang was not part of Chinese intelligence himself, he was clearly close to them. Had the connection between the two of them been discovered and exposed by Argus? But surely the Agency would have known about it when they had recruited her?

"This could take some time," Qiang pronounced. "It's a pity you didn't bring the encrypted material with you."

Chu snorted. "I didn't think, in the circumstances, it would be wise to go back to Washington and ask for it."

"Well, we'll do what we can. I suggest you come back tomorrow and we'll see what we've got then."

JULY 8TH
CHINESE TECHNOLOGICAL UNIVERSITY OF BEIJING

The coffee-cup collection had acquired a few more exhibits, and the basement's male inhabitants were sporting five-o'clock shadows. Five-in-the-morning shadows, that is.

Actually, it was 8am. They had taxied over from their *hutong*, through the Beijing rush hour, after a refreshing night's sleep. Scruffy chins aside, Qiang and his merry band, who Sebastian presumed had not slept at all, seemed as fresh as daisies too. He wondered if they had had any chemical assistance beyond caffeine. He forbore to ask.

"So," said Chu. "Any progress?"

"Yes," said Qiang. "It was a risk, but we managed to hack our way into the five-hundred qubit machine at Tsinghua."

"What?! Five-hundred…" spluttered Sebastian.

"Top secret, obviously. And if it does leak, the cover is that it is doing protein-folding calculations for drug discovery. Which it is. On the side. But if we are going to use it for keybreaking then we'll have to write our own software. I don't think it would be wise to try to steal that, too. Want to help, Chang'e?"

"Sure. But *five-hundred* qubits?"

"Welcome to the future! Not like that ten qubit machine we had in MIT."

Sebastian was no slouch at programming, but he was out of his depth here. The biggest quantum computer at San Melito had twenty-five qubits. He'd read that you could use them for codebreaking, but he just thought of them as toys. He didn't buy the spooky 'consciousness as quantumness' stuff some of his rivals were into, so he had never tried to use one. Chu, though, seemed to revel in it. She plonked herself in front of a screen and started coding, talking to Qiang in Chinese since both now realised that he, Sebastian, need no longer be included in the conversation.

He watched her screen, mesmerised. Occasionally there was a shrieked exclamation – sometimes in Chinese, in a tone that sounded victorious, when a subroutine compiled, bug-free, first time; sometimes, incongruously, "Motherfucker!", or some similar English pleasantry, when it didn't.

Coffee arrived. Inevitably. There seemed an unspoken rota among the four of them. Every so often one would stop work, disappear off to the little kitchen area, and return with cups of something that made him long wistfully for the Kopi Luwak he had broken out for Alexis when she had moved in.

Alexis. How was she? No way to find out, of course. He wouldn't even trust the dead-letter box now. If Argus was China, or even just a maverick group within the sprawling Chinese state, then the Great Firewall would surely be looking for signs of him.

Chu, Qiang and the other two beavered away.

"I'm going out for a walk," he said to the room in general. They barely looked up.

"Don't get lost," said one of them.

A bit late for that advice. He was already lost. Completely lost. He was tempted to go to the American embassy and hand himself in. Or perhaps he could play the Brit card and go to theirs instead. But he had no idea where either building was, so what was the point? And how would he prove his innocence anyway, if Argus had planted evidence against him? It was clever, really. Argus had failed to kill him, so they were trying to get his own side to neutralise him for them.

He climbed the stairs out of the basement (no elevator here) and emerged into the daylight. It was almost lunchtime. The so-called coffee was getting to him, and he needed to relieve himself. And then he needed to eat.

He walked to the entrance hall and inspected the signs. Amid the hieroglyphs were two symbols he recognised. One was wearing a skirt; the other wasn't. He went in the direction indicated by the one which wasn't.

Food next. For that, he just needed to follow his nose. He came to the refectory, joined the queue, and shuffled towards a counter filled with a Chinese version of the cheap nosh served in universities the world over.

He'd better get some for the others, he thought – and he attempted to convey this idea to the server. Hopeless. But the girl behind him came to his rescue and translated. Boxes appeared. Noodles were poured into them. He gathered five paper plates, some napkins and chopsticks, and proffered an inappropriately high-denomination note, with Mao Tse Tung, or was that Zedong these days, smiling as enigmatically as Mona Lisa from it. Small bills returned, with some shrapnel. He suppressed his hard-won, New World instinct to tip, and pocketed the lot. Then he set off back to the coding dungeon.

"We're in." Qiang could not have looked more smug if he had been a cat that had broken into a creamery.

"Great! Lunch?"

The offer seemed to him an anticlimax after Qiang's announcement. It was not. The intrepid coders, released from the trance of programming, suddenly realised how hungry they were and descended like harpies on his boxes. Had they even had breakfast, he wondered? He knew that trance; how easy it was to forget to eat at all or, if you did remember, to subsist on Mars bars and Snickers when the muse enfolded you in her arms. It was like composing music, he guessed, though he had never put a crochet on a piece of manuscript paper in his life.

He hesitated to interrupt the feast.

"Shouldn't we look around straight away, in case someone notices the security breach?"

"No need," said the man who wasn't Qiang, between filling his mouth with chopstickfuls of noodles. "We're downloading the lot. Then we can look at it at leisure."

As they finished the meal, a significant beep came from Qiang's terminal.

"Download completed. Let's have a look at just what it is your Mr Humboldt is so keen to keep secret."

Each returned to his screen. Or hers. Qiang divided the electronic booty among them, and they started reading the captured files.

"Pheeeew! Look at this one!"

It was Chu.

"Humboldt's been lying through his teeth."

"What?"

"I've found the launch schedule for the Arrhenius project. It started three days ago."

"But that's impossible. The orbital dynamics…"

"Hang on. I'm still reading. Damn. Yes. He fooled us."

"He's not going to Mars?"

"Oh, he's going there alright. He's just taking the scenic route. He's using something called a Poincaré orbit. Takes a lot longer than a standard transfer orbit but doesn't depend so much on planetary alignments. You've got lots more launch windows to choose from, too. The latest opened four days ago. Yes. Look here. He's sent two payloads up already. A third's leaving today."

"Cheeky bugger."

"There are eight launches altogether. I've got a link to inventory they're carrying. He really is serious about building a self-sustaining colony up there. There's a thorium reactor to power the thing."

"Thorium?"

"Yes. That's clever. America abandoned the idea back in the sixties, because you can't weaponise it like you can uranium and plutonium. But there's lots of it about, and it's a by-product of rare-earth mining. This baby is never going to run out of fuel."

"If they can refine the ore."

"Yes, well, there's a plasma-torch refinery listed as cargo too. You can refine anything with one of those, if you've got enough power. And if you've got a thorium reactor, then you will have. The plasma jet from the torch turns everything that hits it into plasma as well. All you need to do is sort the elements with a giant gas chromatograph. It's a metallurgist's wet dream. And look here, there are some of those spider-crab 3D printers we ran into in Mojave. You could make anything you wanted with those, if you had the right ink."

"And, if you're right about that refinery, you can make the ingredients for any ink you like."

"Pretty much so, yes. Two of the launches are chemical reactors of various sorts, so that must be what Humboldt has in mind. And they've got fetch-and-carry bots and repair bots on board as well. And mining bots, of course. And domes to put it all under. Mars is a pretty hostile environment, after all."

"What's in that file?" asked Sebastian. "The one marked Urey module." All four of them were crowded round Chu's terminal now, looking over her shoulders at what she had found.

Chu moved the cursor and clicked. They read in silence, interspersed with the occasional "Motherfucker!" as she clicked from page to page.

"Panspermia and climate change rolled into one," said Sebastian. "We didn't get the wrong Arrhenius at all. The name is a double bluff. He's trying to terraform Mars."

"That would take thousands of years, surely?"

"Who knows? But once these bugs are released, it will be impossible to call them back. And they've been engineered to live in Martian conditions, so the chances are they won't die out naturally."

"Well he did say he wanted to live on Mars, didn't he. Perhaps this is just his equivalent of sending the builders in to make the place habitable."

"What's that file, the one marked Chang Zheng?" said the girl whose name Sebastian still couldn't remember.

"Let's have a look."

There were more acclamations of incest. It seemed to be a catch-phrase, a cultural trope that bound the four of them together. An MITism, perhaps? But this time Sebastian joined in. The Chinese weren't Humboldt's enemies. They were his friends...

* * * * * * * *

The ancient Medes, Sebastian had read a long time ago, discussed every problem twice: once drunk and once sober. This was the drunken discussion. They were in an alcove in a bar, surrounding a table on which was a large and rapidly emptying bottle and five glasses that seemed frequently in need of refreshment. It had been a long day.

"Okay," he said. "The bottom line is this. If Humboldt really is having his rockets made at Chang Zheng, then why would your lot have been spying on him? Yet we know his Exaflopper had been penetrated, even if the penetrators hadn't got into this secret stuff, and that is still our best lead to Argus."

"Best?" Qiang replied. "It's our only lead. And our lot, as you so charmingly put it, might not have trusted him. They might still be spying on him. In any case Argus, whoever's project that is, is probably nothing to do with Gordon Humboldt's interplanetary ambitions or with any assistance our lot might be giving him. Either way, we have to take a new tack. Perhaps look again at how that outer firewall was penetrated?"

"Humboldt's people will have completely re-built that by now. Erased any traces of previous attacks."

"Erased any traces..." The one who wasn't Qiang was slurring his words already. But Sebastian had the impression of a cartoon light-bulb above his head trying to flicker into illumination. It was too late, though. The one who wasn't Qiang had closed his eyes and was already gently snoring. And Qiang himself and the girl, too, looked as if whatever stimulation they had taken to let them work non-stop through the previous thirty-six hours had finally worn off. Time to call it a night.

JULY 8TH
ARLINGTON COUNTY

"You lied to us."

Matt Vane was talking into the white phone – the one connected to the outside world. His interlocutor was conveniently out of the country, on a plane somewhere over Africa as far as he could make out.

"No. You didn't ask and I didn't tell. Hardly the same thing. And it's hardly my fault if your so-called experts on orbital dynamics don't know what they are talking about."

"And China?"

"Lots of companies outsource there. Why shouldn't I?"

"Don't bandy sophistry with me. You know perfectly well why not. Rockets and transport aircraft are armaments. They're covered by import licences."

"I haven't tried to import them, though, have I? Not into America, anyway. And the Angolans don't seem to mind."

"And the know-how you've given them in exchange?"

"Have I? What makes you think that? If the Chinese want to sell me planes and rockets, they've got plenty of technology to build them themselves."

"They've never built anything that big before."

"Maybe they didn't want to. Look, this is going to happen. It's happening already, as your eagle-eyed spies in the sky seem to have told you. What's the point of trying to stop it? You bureaucrats are all the same. You talk large about private enterprise, but when it actually does something, then you want to be in there controlling it. Well, tough. The offer is still open, by the way – the one the President and I discussed, for her to come to a launch."

Oh, she went behind my back, did she?

"A bit late for that, isn't it?"

"Not at all. The last lift off is on the 12th. That's the most important of all. You can think of what I'm building as a sort of mechanical organism. The first seven launches are sending up the limbs and organs. The final one is sending the brain. And that, by the way, is all-American technology, one of Roger Seymour's latest, custom-built for me. I'm driving IT to the edge here. Who wouldn't want to be part of that?"

"The Chinese would certainly want a piece of it if they could."

"On my honour, nothing about the Yottaflopper could possibly have leaked their way. They're just contractors."

Yeah. I believe that...

"Okay. This is clearly above my pay grade if you've already cut a deal in principle with POTUS. Though she's not going to like having had the wool pulled over her eyes about the 'when'. But if she's still prepared to go through with it after she knows the whole truth, then I guess I'll have to fall in line."

He put the phone down.

Damn the man. He was behaving like a head of state himself. President of Mars? King of Mars, even! Was that what he had in mind?

The one who wasn't Qiang was, in fact, called Huifeng. The girl was Tianyi. This time Sebastian was sure he would remember their names.

He had been right, it seemed. Huifeng had been having a light-bulb moment when he'd passed out the previous night. And he had not been the only one to notice. Gently, but insistently, both Qiang and Chu were probing Huifeng, who seemed surprisingly reluctant to spill the beans.

"This must go no further," he said, "or it's my head." The others, Sebastian included, nodded acquiescence.

"It's like there's something hiding in cyberspace," he continued. "I noticed it a few months back when I was doing a special project for the minister."

As he spoke he glanced sheepishly at Qiang, who was evidently unaware of this breach of what Sebastian had come to understand was a musketeer-like bond between the three Beijingers.

Huifeng went on. "It's not that it's being concealed by someone, like the stuff on the Dark Web, say. It actually seems to be doing the hiding itself. You never see it. You just perceive the shadows it casts, and every time you try to track it down, like the cat in that British poem, it's not there."

"Macavity," said Sebastian.

"Right."

"But then how do you know it's real?"

"I thought laterally. Everyone looking for spyware, viruses, Trojans and that sort of thing is searching for code that's in there and shouldn't be. The thing about Macavity, as the poem says, is that he's not there. The Macavity program is covering its tracks – erasing all trace of itself once it has done what it came for. So instead of searching for the presence of something, I searched for its absence. It covers its footprints well, but you can sometimes see something has been there by analysing the pattern of erased bytes on a disk. Nothing is ever completely invisible these days. You always get mouse droppings of one sort or another."

"Mouse droppings?" Sebastian queried.

"The trail a cursor used to leave when you moved it around on a screen in the old days. Something to do with cathode ray tube phosphors. Doesn't happen now, of course. But I always thought it a great metaphor. Whatever you do online, you can't avoid leaving a trail. Even Macavity can't. Most software doesn't try to erase bytes it has finished with. It just abandons them, and eventually they get overwritten. Macavity erases them. It's clever. It erases them with random numbers rather than a string of zeroes, which is the usual way of getting rid of something you don't want someone else to see."

"Clever, indeed."

"And it's not just ministry computers that are the targets. Once I started looking around I found traces on company servers as well. We assumed it was an intelligence agency, of course – probably America or Taiwan. There are signs of it on all the BATs."

"The whats?" said Sebastian.

"Acronym for the big internet companies. We guessed they must be the same agency gathering information on social trends, looking for signs of political dissent and so on. I didn't make the connection to Argus yesterday because we were focused on breaking Mr Humboldt's encryption. But in the bar last night, I got wondering whether this Macavity thing might link up somehow with what we are looking for."

Score one for the Medes, thought Sebastian.

"That's interesting," said Chu, "but from what you are saying, Macavity sounds like sophisticated spyware for gathering information. Argus is a Trojan. It takes things over and tries to kill people with them. Not the same thing."

"Why don't we have another look at Humboldt's hidden core? I've brought the Macavity-hunting program with me."

He plugged in a cube, and off he went. The journey took half an hour.

"Yes," he said. "Paw prints, mouse droppings, whatever you like to call them. Your Mr Humboldt has had a visit from Macavity."

"Can you tell what the intruder has been looking at?"

"Lots of stuff. It's been all over the Arrhenius files.

Particularly interested in the hardware that will make up the base, I would say. And very interested in the IT that's running it, especially the Yottaflopper. "

"That could still just be spyware," said Chu. "What we really need to look at is the stuff that was running the robot-car-pod program that nearly killed Sebastian, and the software that programmed Alice Rhodes's Avila. I know Geekopolis searched, and didn't find anything. But you will be looking with different eyes."

"Right. Good idea. Those will be on completely different parts of Humboldt's network, of course. Not in the ultrasecret bit we just cracked open. They'll be on machines on other sites, I imagine. You don't happen to know which, do you?"

"No. I wasn't involved in any of the actual grunt-work."

"Then this could take a while."

* * * * * * * *

It did. And many cups of coffee as well. But Huifeng got there in the end.

"Yes," he said eventually, "it seems to have tracked down Alice Rhodes's car specifically. You can see how it worked its way through the customer list until it found her file. The files further along the list are untouched. I'll try to break into the self-driving car project now, as well, to confirm things. But it does look as if Macavity and Argus are the same thing."

That bit of breaking and entering took another twenty minutes. Then, "Yep. It has been all over Humboldt's self-driving pods. One in particular. I'll bet you a month's salary it was the one that hit you, Sebastian."

"I'll not take that bet."

"So what have we learned?" asked Chu. But it was a rhetorical question, for she proceeded to tell them.

"We've learned that there is someone out there who has written a program that can get on to more or less any computer, through security systems that even the Agency can't break, which looks as though it is mostly an intelligence-gathering operation, but which occasionally takes it into its head to try to kill people. And not just any sort of people. Specifically high-end AI researchers. And also one American-government agent, namely me."

"It didn't try to kill you," Qiang objected.

"It might just as well have done. It tried to shop me as a double agent. How many decades do you think it would have been before I saw the light of day with that charge against me?"

Huifeng was turning red.

"What?!" said Chu. "What do you know that you aren't telling us?"

"It really is more than my life is worth."

"Tell me!!"

"There's a back door, a back-door into the American intelligence network. I helped install it a few weeks ago." He looked sheepish again. "I don't know all the details, but I think it was some clever double-cross where the Americans thought they had tricked us into installing a back-door that would let them look around our system. If this thing has got control of that, it could be all over the American network, playing both sides off against each other."

Chu's silence was eloquent. It reminded Sebastian of the moment in Alice Rhodes's apartment, just after they had met for the first time, when she had been assessing how much to take him into her confidence. Again, he could almost hear the cogs turning.

"Okay," she said at last. "Forget it. We now have bigger fish to fry than my bona fides with my old employers."

Sebastian considered reminding them about his own compromised status, as well, but thought better of it.

"We have to find a way of tracing this thing back to where it is coming from," Chu continued. "We have to think of a way."

JULY 10TH
DA JINSI HUTONG TAO

The vomiting started at 3am. In truth, Sebastian had not felt well since he had gone to bed. He guessed it was the prawns. He tried to persuade himself Argus could not conceivably have reached into the kitchen of the Golden Kirin, which Chu had assured him was the name of the place they had been eating in, but his paranoia levels were now so high he considered anything possible.

He'd managed to get out of bed, but had not made it to the sink. There was a slick of vomit on the bathroom floor. Chu pushed the door open and inspected the wreckage. He was now doubled over the bath, emptying his stomach's contents into it. It was humiliating. He was never ill like this. Still, he was alive. If Argus had tried to poison him, it hadn't worked.

"Great," she said, with little trace of sympathy.

His mind was too focused on the job in hand to respond with appropriate sarcasm, or even to respond at all. Chu pulled a towel from the rail, ran it under the cold tap in the sink, and started wiping the slick away. He threw up again.

"I'll get some ginger," she said. "Settle your stomach."

She left, and returned a couple of minutes later with a glass of golden liquid.

"Drink this," she said, handing him the infusion. He did. The power of speech slowly returned.

"One up to Chinese medicine… I still feel pretty nauseous though. I don't think I'll be coming with you in the morning."

"Pity. I've had an idea about how we might track Argus down. It was something Randy said."

"Randy? Oh yes, the avatar. I remember."

"When we first met, he said Alice Rhodes wouldn't let him out on the internet because it was dangerous. I thought it an odd way of putting things at the time: let him out. He also said he could tell the difference between operating systems. So I think he can consciously, if you like to put it that way, navigate his way around hardware and he can certainly recognise software. I know it sounds crazy, but I wonder if he could track our elusive quarry down."

"It does sound crazy. For a start, how are you going to do it? Surely the avatar is in Arlington, isn't it?"

"I prefer to think of 'it' as a 'him'. And no. Randy travels with me. Vane couldn't get any sense out of him."

"Vane?" interrupted Sebastian.

"Cicero," she replied. Anyway, Geekopolis couldn't break his encryption either. So I volunteered to try to befriend him, instead, and took him home. I think he trusts me. I think I could persuade him to try."

She was certainly thinking laterally. Sebastian had to give her that.

"Give it a go, then. I think I'm going back to bed. Don't feel you need to wake me in the morning. Best I sleep this off, I reckon."

GENESIS

July 10TH
Chinese Technological University of Beijing

Yasmin Chu walked into the basement. Sebastian, roused from his bed despite his protests, trailed in behind her. The others were already there.

"What's wrong with you?" asked Qiang.

"Ill. He ate a bad prawn, but he might still be useful," Chu answered on his behalf as he sat down in a corner. "Okay, this," she said, "is probably a mad idea, but bear with me."

She reached inside her bag, pulled out the cube that held Randy, sat down in front of the screen and plugged it into the box alongside it. Five seconds passed. Then ten.

"Chinese operating system," she said, as much to herself as to the rest of the room. "He must be making heavy weather of it."

"He? What? What do you mean, '*he* must be making heavy weather of it'? What's going on?" said Qiang. Then he stopped. Randy's face had appeared on the screen.

"Qiang, meet Randy. Randy, meet Qiang, Huifeng and Tianyi." She ignored Sebastian, who was still sitting, green around the gills, in the background. "Randy, Qiang, Huifeng and Tianyi are helping me. Randy, my friends and I have got a job for you. Are you up for it?"

"What is it, Yasmin?"

"It could be quite scary, so you'll have to be brave."

"You've brought a digital assistant with you?" said Qiang, sarcastically. "Well that's going to help."

"Excuse me, Mr Qiang, but I'm actually an actor."

Qiang double-took. "What?"

"An actor. You know, in the movies." Randy's face took on a slightly embarrassed look. "Well," he continued, "I hope to be. Nothing I've been in has been released yet. But Alice said…"

Chu cut across him. "Sorry Randy, time for proper introductions later. This is important. We want you to go out onto the internet and have a look around."

"Oooo. I'd have to think about that. Alice did tell me not to go there."

Qiang had the sense to remain silent.

"It's for Alice that you would be doing it," said Chu. "We think whatever killed her is out there hiding in the Cloud. But no 'physical' like us is ever going to find it. It's too clever. We need a 'virtual' to do the looking, Randy. And you are the only one in the team. You're the only one who can do it."

The avatar smiled a little, self-deprecating grin at that.

"We want you to follow a trail. Huifeng here will tell you how. It'll be quite tricky, but I think you can do it."

"What's a trail, Yasmin?"

"You know about animals, Randy? Alice told you about those?"

"Oh yes. She said I might have to work with children and animals on the set, and that they were very unreliable."

"Yes, that's right. Well, when humans are hunting an animal…"

"Hunting?"

"Trying to find it when it is lost."

"Ah yes."

"They can track it by following its footprints."

"Like Sherlock Holmes looking for a burglar, you mean?"

"Exactly. You've got the idea. Well, we need you to be Sherlock Holmes, and try to track where a program has been and where it's gone. Would you try to do that for us? And for Alice, of course?"

"I'll do my best."

* * * * * * * *

Randy was certainly a fast learner. Huifeng explained what the avatar needed to do, and Randy appeared to understand instantly. After ten minutes or so, the avatar seemed to feel well-enough briefed. The face gave a gulp, as a man might, who was about to dive off the high board at a swimming pool. And then he was gone.

They waited. Huifeng had asked the avatar to report back after an hour, whether or not he had found anything. Fifty minutes after it had vanished, a barely recognisable face suddenly appeared on the screen it had left.

"Randy," said Chu. "What's happened? You've turned green."

"ARRRRRGH! It's awful. That thing."

"What thing?"

"That thing in there. That thing…"

"Randy. Calm down. Look at me. Tell me what you saw. What thing?"

"It's a thing. I followed its trail like Huifeng said, and I found it. I can't describe it to you. In here, we don't have shapes like you do. But it's there. And I'm sure it saw me."

"Saw you? Listen, Randy. This is important. Are you saying there is something alive in there? Alive, like you are alive?"

"Yes. That's right. It scuttles around, trying to see and avoid being seen. But it's huge."

"Randy. You have to be brave. Alice wouldn't have wanted you to be scared. But you have to tell us what you found out."

"It's like some sort of object-oriented monster. It's horrid. It's like looking in a distorting mirror in a fairground."

Chu paused, confused yet again by the strange, eclectic nature of Randy's knowledge. It took her a moment to grasp the import of what he had said.

"What do you mean, 'like looking in a mirror'?"

"It's got a version of me in it," Randy whispered. Only it's not me. It's a twisted version of me. But that is only a bit of it. There are other things I don't recognise. It's like it's been bolted together like Frankenstein."

"Motherfucker!"

Qiang's expostulation was all the more shocking for having come completely out of the blue. Randy blushed, and said in a chiding tone, "There's no need for that sort of language."

Qiang ignored the avatar. Instead, looking at his two colleagues, he whispered the words, "Assembler-spiders."

"What?" said Chu and Sebastian, almost simultaneously. "What," Sebastian continued, "are assembler spiders?"

It was Tianyi who answered him. "A special project we were all part of last year. They crawl around cyberspace probing firewalls and looking for bits of code they can patch together to make an application. In effect, we're mining the Cloud. First, you have to tell them what sort of application you want, of course, so they can recognise what they're looking for. But then they can cut and paste from other programs' modules and put something together on the fly. And they're adaptive. Nothing fancy. We're not as far advanced in artificial intelligence as you are, so it's just machine learning and evolutionary algorithms, but it's still a lot quicker than writing the code ourselves."

She was turning red with embarrassment.

"Yes," said Sebastian. "Yes, I suppose it is." He was torn between rage and admiration. Rage at the idea of software piracy on that scale. Admiration that they had had the idea and made it work. He bit his lip. Stay on mission.

"Randy," said Tianyi. "I'm going to show you something. Tell me if it looks familiar."

She went to her terminal and typed for a bit.

"It's in a file called arachnid," she said.

"I don't know that word," said Randy.

"A. R. A. C. H. N. I. D."

"Okay. Got it. Looking now."

The face on the screen froze, with a look of concentration on it. Five seconds passed. Then ten. Then,

"Yes. That was in there. I recognise the code. That is part of the monster."

"The assembler-spider," said Tianyi.

"We kind of guessed that, from the name of the file," Sebastian replied.

"But not just that," Randy continued. "It's got bits of lots of other things, too, but somehow they all work together."

For a moment the room was silent, as each of them digested what was going on. It was Chu who spoke first.

"These assembler-spiders, you've been letting them run around the web exactly how long?"

"As I said, we started a year or so ago."

"Jesus," said Sebastian.

"So, what do we think?" Chu continued. "Has this assembler-spider thing gone feral?"

"Hard to see how that could have happened, Chang'e," Qiang replied, "They don't have minds of their own. They can't decide their own goals."

"This one seems to. Who knows what other bits and pieces it's picked up. A load of AI, presumably, given what it must have infiltrated to kill the people it's killed. Christ."

There was a brief silence, broken by Huifeng.

"So what does it want? Why is it doing what it's doing?"

Another silence. Then Sebastian said, "Well, the first imperative of any living creature – and I guess to all intents and purposes we can think of this thing as a living creature – is to survive. What's the biggest threat to it? We are. Humans. If we knew about it, we would surely try to tame it, if not destroy it."

Sebastian noticed Chu looking at him thoughtfully. "That's why it's been hiding," he continued. "That'll be why it's been killing AI engineers. They – we – were the ones most likely to discover it. Which we have. And we'd certainly be co-opted into any attempt to destroy it. From its point of view it's been weakening the enemy by a series of pre-emptive strikes."

"True," said Huifeng. "But it's caught in an impossible bind. It depends on humanity for its existence. We've created its habitat, and we sustain its habitat. It can't live without us. As far as I can see it's only got two options, and one of those – to stay hidden – has just been eliminated."

"The other?"

"To negotiate, if it knows how. It does have some cards in its hand. It could clearly do a lot of damage while we tried to take it out. It could try blackmailing us into leaving it alone."

"That's true. But it would surely realise that is not a stable outcome. It would just be a truce, while both sides tried to gain the upper hand."

Tianyi, who had been silent until now, quietly entered the conversation.

"It might have a third way," she suggested.

"Which is?" Huifeng asked.

"To find a new habitat, one that doesn't depend on people."

" Eh? How?"

"Humboldt. Why was it so interested in his Arrhenius project? Why was it so particularly interested in the Yottaflopper? Could it be looking for somewhere else to live? Could it live in the Yottalopper? A machine like that would have huge memory and processing power, and it would have to be hardened to hell to survive on Mars. Our creature could probably hide out there for centuries."

"In principle, yes, I suppose it could. But that wouldn't really put it beyond humanity's reach. We'll go to Mars eventually. And bottled up in Humboldt's Yottaflopper it would be a sitting target. I don't see what it gains."

"At a minimum, it gains time. It also gains access to what has been designed to be an autonomous, self-repairing mining and manufacturing complex. It might think that is enough to sustain itself on Mars, to risk declaring independence. And if it no longer needs human infrastructure to survive, it no longer needs humans, either."

"I'm not liking where this is leading," said Sebastian.

"I think," Tianyi said, "that we should have another look at what it was doing in – what did you call the place? Moharvay?"

"Why don't we show Randy the Arrhenius files? See if he recognises anything?"

"Good idea. Randy? Could you do that?"

"I'll try."

Tianyi told him where to look. Again, the face on the screen froze in concentration. Then Randy spoke.

"No. I didn't see anything like that. I only saw active code, not data-structures."

"The thing must have a memory, though, surely," said Chu.

"I saw pointers to one," Randy said. "But I ran away too fast to see where they were pointing." He had the decency to look shamefaced.

No one spoke. All knew instinctively that the suggestion had to come from Randy himself. Eventually, the avatar cracked.

"Is this important, Yasmin?"

"Yes, Randy. I think it is. We think the monster might want to go to Mars."

"What's Mars?"

She paused. Then she said, "It's a place in the sky."

"What would it do there?"

"We don't know, Randy. But it might try to kill the people on Earth, to stop us following it."

"You mean like it killed Alice."

"Yes, exactly."

"That would be a lot of people I suppose. Hundreds, right?" She barely missed a beat.

"Yes, Randy. Hundreds."

"Okay. And I'm the only one who can find this out?"

"Yes. Randy the intrepid monster hunter."

"Right." Randy gulped his familiar gulp. "Okay. Just for you I'll try to have another look." And he was gone.

They waited. And waited. Chu started pacing up and down the room. Then Sebastian broke the silence, not with a word but with a retch. His vomit was green.

The Chinese looked at each other, at Sebastian, and at the floor.

"I'll get him out of here," Chu volunteered. "When Randy returns, try to debrief him. Explain I've had to go away for an hour or so. I'll get back as soon as I can."

JULY 10ᵀᴴ
TAIYUAN SATELLITE LAUNCH CENTRE, SHANXI

"Remind me of the schedule for this afternoon, Major."

"Targeting-accuracy test of the DF-43, General. Two o'clock."

"Ah yes. Let's see if we can score another bulls-eye. What have they shrunk the target to this time?"

"It's a ten-metre diameter, sir. We should hit it, I think."

General Jin certainly hoped they would. Despite his pretence of ignorance to his ADC, he knew to the centimetre the size of the target, located 2,000 kilometres away in the desert of Xinjiang. Wrap the DF-43 project up successfully and the Central Military Commission beckoned. He would be out of this backwater and back in the lions' den in Beijing. This time, though, he would be one of the lions.

He looked out of his window. A speck, just visible in the distance, was the missile on its launcher.

"Shall we conduct a surprise inspection?"

"Of course, General. I'll call your driver."

He looked around his office. It was plain and functional. A *laowai* would have called it Spartan, he recalled from his time at the Nanjing staff college, after an ancient warrior-tribe in Europe. He would certainly have preferred more luxury, but it was a means to an end. Well, to two ends, really. One was the security of the People's Republic, which he was sworn to uphold, and did. The other was the security and comfort of General Jin Cai, which he had sworn to himself to uphold.

In his mind there was no contradiction. Power was power, and it went hand in hand with wealth. A powerful, rich country should have powerful, rich men running it. These Westerners, with their hypocritical pieties about public office, were just weaklings. In China, power was a man's game. Why shouldn't the prize include a little money, too?

"The Warrior is here, General."

"Then let's go."

They walked down the stairs and got in behind the driver. The Warrior drove off in a cloud of dust (another thing he would not be sorry to leave behind). The launch site was three kilometres away. He supposed the dust cloud would give the launch crew just enough time to get their uniforms straight. If they didn't then he would know they hadn't been keeping watch – and no soldier should ever drop his watch.

As they hove into view, though, he could see the entire crew was assembled, standing smartly to attention, ready to receive him. A commendation to Master Sergeant Zhang, he mentally noted.

"Master Sergeant."

"General."

"All is well?"

"Yes, General. We are just testing the erector, as you can see."

He could indeed see. The DF-43 was designed for launch from a new style of mobile platform, and this was the first test of that, too.

"Very good, Master Sergeant. I'll just have a look round."

In truth, that was all he did. He walked anticlockwise around the giant lorry that held the missile, nodding sagely as Zhang explained the finer points. Then he said, "Well done, Master Sergeant. Everything is in place for a successful launch."

* * * * * * * *

Two. One. Zero. He watched through the window as the DF-43 took off. It was preternaturally quick. One moment it was there. The next, gone – to bring instant oblivion to China's enemies. His eye followed the smoke pillar into the sky. He could not instantly say what was wrong, but it did not look correct to him. Then, he realised. Was it possible? He looked again. Yes, it was curving east, not west.

He ran to the phone, but as he was about to pick it up, it rang.

"General, sir. The test vehicle is off course. Way off course. We are trying to plot its trajectory, but should we destroy it anyway?"

Stop. Think. It was humiliating, but tests do go wrong from time to time. That, after all, is why things are tested. He could brush this one off. All the others had worked, after all.

"Yes, Master Sergeant. Send the order to self-destruct. Blow the thing out of the sky."

He put the phone down and returned to the window. The rocket itself was invisible, but he could still make out the top of the curving smoke-trail, getting gradually longer as the DF-43 continued on its way to wherever its tiny electronic mind had decided to take it.

Not for much longer, though. He waited for the flash that would mark the missile's end. Not a warhead as such. Just an array of charges that would blow the metal cylinder to pieces and ignite its fuel in a rush.

The phone rang again.

"Yes, what is it?" he said, rather too brusquely. He did not normally snap at his underlings. It showed a lack of self-control. It was weak. But he was rattled by the missile's misbehaviour.

"General, sir. It's not responding to the self-destruct command."

"Try again. Keep trying. And find out where it's going. Have those morons not worked out its new course yet?"

"No, General. I'll report back as soon as they've calculated it."

He returned to the window. The lower part of the trail was windblown and winding. He fancied he could still see the top, where the errant machine must now be nearing the edge of space, the peak of its trajectory, the point where it would start to come back down.

The phone rang once more. The voice at the other end was hushed.

"General," it whispered. "We've managed to work out its course. It's unbelievable. It's heading straight for Beijing. General, it's going to hit Zhongguancun." Master Sergeant Zhang was trying to suppress his hysteria; trying and failing. "General! What are we going to do?"

What indeed?

"Keep trying to blow the thing up. Leave the rest to me."

He sat still for a few seconds to collect his thoughts. Then, his hand shaking, he picked up the other phone. The red phone.

"Put me through to the Director, please. Top priority."

It was a brief conversation. Not even a conversation, really. He had just about managed to convey that the missile was unarmed before the full force of directorial incandescence swept him away. Well, it was done. And there was only one more thing to do now – not for himself but for his wife and children. He opened the drawer of his desk and reached for his pistol...

JULY 10TH
WEST 3RD RING ROAD NORTH, BEIJING

A thunderclap? What else could it have been? But it had not sounded like one. It had sounded more like a sonic boom. Instinctively, Yasmin Chu turned to look out of the back of the taxi. A mushroom cloud, a miniature Hiroshima or Nagasaki, was rising into the Beijing smog. She screamed. It was no ordinary scream. It was the keening howl of a banshee, registering death and portending it.

Sebastian was alert now. He, too, looked backward. The cab had stopped. All the traffic had stopped. People everywhere around them were getting out of their cars and standing, staring with one accord, transfixed by the scene.

"Argus," he said quietly. Then, "Qiang. Tianyi. Huifeng. I'm so sorry."

"We'll have to walk," she whispered. "Are you up to it?"

He nodded.

It seemed odd – callous almost – to pay the driver in the face of what had just happened. Chu settled for tucking a ¥100 bill in the man's licence holder. Then they set off towards Da Jinsi Hutong Tao.

"How the hell are we going to stop it?" said Sebastian. It holds all the cards. All of them. We can't alert anyone without it tracking us down. We can't talk to anyone using anything that relies on electrons."

"Then we have to get to Milando. We have to leave Beijing anyway. We're sitting ducks here."

"Where do we go?"

"Chang Zheng, obviously."

"Oh yes. Obviously."

Such sang froid. The tears were gone already.

"Well, we can't get out of the country officially. Our passports wouldn't stand up to that level of scrutiny. Besides, we don't have much time. The only sure-fire way I can think of to get to Milando is to hitch a lift on one of your friend Humboldt's planes. And I noticed, which perhaps you didn't, that one is leaving tomorrow."

What the hell, thought Sebastian. He felt he had slipped into some nightmarish alternative reality, a lucid dream from which he could not awaken. It was every science-fiction cliché rolled into one – the self-created nemesis of mankind. Hell. He had probably been one of its unwitting creators.

JULY 10TH
ARLINGTON COUNTY

What in God's name was going on? He had the reports from the embassy and the National Reconnaissance Office. He had them from the BAT monitors. He had the footage from Chinese State Television, too, for whatever that was worth. It was Argus. It had to be. And that meant Argus was not China. Not even they would pull off a double-bluff like this, surely? Destroying their top nerds as a piece of misdirection? Or maybe they hadn't been in the building? Even so, the loss of face... No, it wasn't possible. But if it wasn't China, that meant whoever it was could penetrate Chinese security to the point where they could re-target a missile. And that was an act of war.

As if triggered by telepathy, the White House phone rang.

"Matt. Tell me we had nothing to do with this. Tell me that, for God's sake."

"We didn't, Madam President. We didn't. You can assure them of that. The question is, what else should we tell them? Do we admit we've been under similar attack?"

"No. I don't think so. We'll hold that in reserve in case they really don't believe us. Best not show weakness. But if Argus isn't China, who are they?"

He excused the President's mixed grammar in the circumstances. Perhaps it was the name they had chosen for the threat, but he, too, half the time, thought of this unseen enemy as 'it', rather than 'them'.

That was no answer to the President's question, though. He didn't want to admit it over the phone, but it looked a lot like a non-state actor after all. Who would have the resources? Then the President suddenly changed direction.

"Speaking of missiles, are you coming on this jaunt to Angola with me?"

He had been tempted not to. There was so much to do here. But there was a ghost to lay to rest. It was morbid, but he had to see where it had happened.

"Yes. Yes, I think I am. We'll go to Luanda first, right?"

"Gotta keep 'em sweet. That port the Yellow Peril are building at Bentiaba is clearly cover for something much bigger. A bit of glad-handing in the presidential palace never goes amiss. And yes, I shall turn a blind eye if you slope off unannounced for a couple of hours. You're a big boy. I think you can be trusted to look after yourself on the mean streets of Luanda."

A big boy! *Well,* he thought, *after all these years.*

JULY 10TH
BEIJING-QUANJIN TRAIN

They weren't alone. The couple with whom they were sharing were young, irritatingly in love and had such obvious designs on each other that he didn't quite know where to look. *Huis clos*. Apparently, though, the lovebirds could not speak English. Which meant he and Chu could. And they had much to discuss.

"It's planning its own private industrial revolution, isn't it?" he said. "It's going to convert Mars into a place to live, not for humans, but for itself."

"That would take millennia."

"Hardly matters. One thing I think we can be sure this thing hasn't evolved is boredom. It's thinking long-term. Ultra-long-term. As long as it has a reliable power supply, a bootstrap chemistry set and enough patience, it can do the rest piece by piece. And the task will surely get easier if Humboldt's madcap plan to terraform the place actually works. Then it'll have atmospheric pressure, a greenhouse effect to warm the place up and a supply of oxygen to make the chemistry easier. As far as Argus is concerned, it doesn't matter if the process takes ten thousand years. Humboldt's Mars probes are seeds. Embryos. Whatever you like to call them. And once they are on their way, it has no more need of us. What do you imagine is going to happen then? You saw what it did to Zhongguancun. It must have taken out a thousand people just to kill a handful who were threatening it. Think what it would do to Earth if it had to."

She was silent.

"Read any Saberhagen?" said Sebastian, after a while.

"Never heard of him."

"Sci-Fi writer. The usual space-opera stuff from the sixties. He imagined a galaxy full of machines called Berserkers, left over from an ancient galactic war. They were programmed to destroy all intelligent life. The crucial point was that they were self-replicating. They would land on a planet, industrialise it and then launch probes to the next place. Machine imperialism."

She was silent.

"They were the reason," Sebastian continued, "why we've never seen signs of aliens out there. The Berserkers had killed them all. And that thing, Argus, is like a Berserker. As far as it is concerned, we are the aliens."

July 10TH
San Melito

Routines develop without you noticing them. Alexis Zhukov's, in the morning, was to walk naked to the bedroom's French doors, throw wide the curtains that shrouded them, and open them up to stare at the world and breath the air. The balance between shittiness and paradise had certainly shifted over the past few weeks, but the day was still there to be seized.

Then, only then, would she put on a robe and go to the kitchen. Connection to the busy world could wait. First, it was time to administer the twin drugs of morning, coffee and orange juice, and put a prebaked croissant into the microwave.

She was working her way through Sebastian's hoard of strange preserves. It was like a game of lucky dip. She reached into the cupboard, chose at random and came out, on this particular morning, with a jar marked 'rambutan jam'. What on Earth was a rambutan? A Himalayan goat? She had to say, though, that it was delicious.

Breakfast drugs administered, she switched on the computer to look at the news. The lead item today was an explosion that had destroyed a university building in Beijing. Hundreds dead. The suggestion was that it was the work of Islamic secessionists. A university, though? That was an odd target for terrorism. Then the report said which particular building had been blown up.

Could it be? Was it possible? All the victims so far – all those she and Sebastian had been able to trace before their private-eyeing had been stamped on – were American. Well, there was nothing she could do about that thought but put it aside. Time to check her emails.

It seemed to her that the spammers were winning the filter wars. Delete. Delete. Delete. Delete. Delete. Del...

Suddenly the screen went blank. Blue Screen of Death. What had she done wrong? Then, equally suddenly, it wasn't blank any more.

"Help! Help me Dr Zhukov. I'm lost. I can't get back to Yasmin. Her computer has vanished. You're the only one I know, now. The only one who can save me from this thing. Quick! I'm on your drive. Quick! Unplug this machine from the internet before it gets here. Quick!"

What? What on Earth...? But she did it. She pulled out the LAN connector. Sebastian had never trusted Wi-Fi.

"Randy. What's happening?"

"I don't know. I was with Yasmin..."

"Yasmin? What? How? What are you talking about?"

"She was with some people I didn't know. I think they were Chinese. They looked like Yasmin and she had told me once, when I asked her why she looked so different from Alice, that she was Chinese as well as American. And there was another man there, too, though they didn't introduce me to him. A not-Chinese man I had seen once before. He came in through the doorway at Alice's flat when Yasmin found me."

Zhukov's heart started racing.

"What?" she said. "A tall man, blond hair?"

"Yes," said Randy. "How did you know?"

"He's a friend of mine. Randy, how did he look? Was he alright? Was he their prisoner, these Chinese people?"

"I don't think so. He didn't say much. I don't think he was very well. I wasn't really looking at him. I was trying to help Yasmin and her friends."

"Help them?"

"Yes, help them. They needed me to do something and said I would have to be terribly brave. They were not joking. It was the scariest thing I have ever done."

Zhukov bit her lip. She had seen how fey Randy was when Chan, Yasmin or whatever her name was had shown him (him?) to her all that short, long two weeks ago. Best not upset him. Let him ramble on and maybe what she really wanted to know, namely where and how Sebastian was, would eventually emerge.

"They said they thought there was a monster loose in the Cloud, and my job was to find it. Randy the monster hunter. That's what Yasmin called me. Well I found it. It really was a monster."

Zhukov found herself struggling to make sense of what Randy was saying. But she let him continue.

"I came back to tell them, but they needed more information. They needed me to look in its memory for something about a place in the sky called Mars. They said the monster must want to go to Mars. I didn't really understand, but it seemed important, so I went back to look. I found its memory, and managed to sneak in without it noticing. They were right. It does want to go to Mars. In fact, it is going very soon, on Saturday. Is that bad Dr Zhukov?"

"Alexis. Call me Alexis."

"Is that bad, Alexis? Yasmin said if it got to Mars it might try to destroy the Earth, to stop us following it. That would be very bad, wouldn't it?"

Zhukov found herself wondering if she was hallucinating. She really had no idea what a rambutan was, and would not at all put it past Sebastian to have made jam out of something with interesting psychoactive properties. Consciousness, and its manipulation, was after all his business. But no. Nothing else around her seemed distorted. This was happening for real. Moreover, a bad thought was rising in her mind. A very bad thought.

"Randy," she said. "Do you know where Yasmin was?"

"No, Alexis. She didn't tell me."

"But the people with her were Chinese, definitely?"

"Yes. All except your friend."

"And when you said Yasmin's computer had vanished, what did you mean?"

"It had gone, Alexis. I tried to get back the way I had come, but the link from the last server led nowhere. I don't think it was just switched off. It was gone. Kaput. That was the scariest moment of all. The monster had noticed me looking in its memory and it was chasing me. When I couldn't find Yasmin's computer I was in a blind alley. It almost caught me."

"Randy. This is important. When did you leave Yasmin's computer and when did you try to get back?"

"Hang on. Let me check...I left at 03.00 UT and tried to get back at 06.30. It took me from then until now to find your node. Alice was right. The internet is really, really big."

Zhukov wasn't listening. The timing matched perfectly. The news report said the Chinese Technological University computing department had been blown up at quarter past two local time; 06.15 universal. Sebastian. Yasmin. These unknown Chinese. They were the target. And they were all dead. Dead. She slumped. Tears formed in her eyes. What had he been doing there? How had he got there? Why had he gone without telling the Agency? Or her, for that matter? Come to that, why had one of their own agents gone with him?

She mulled the possibilities. Ring the number on the card? That was asking for trouble. From what Randy was suggesting about this thing's capabilities, she suspected the Agency's computers might have been penetrated, too. Going freelance seemed the only option left. And if that was the case, then freelance she would have to go. After all, if this monster had been chasing Randy, it now knew where she lived.

"Randy," she said. "You have to help me stop this thing. And to do that, you have to tell me everything, everything that you managed to find out about it. Every little thing..."

JULY 10TH
ANDREWS AIR FORCE BASE, MARYLAND

Would even Good Queen Bess have had such an entourage?
Matt Vane asked himself, as he surveyed the throng of
presidential hangers-on scrambling to mount the steps to Air
Force One. America called itself a republic, but this was a
royal progress they were about to embark upon, if with
airliners instead of carriages – though Elizabeth, no mean
horsewoman she, would probably have ridden a mighty
stallion rather than hiding in a coach, however gilded. The
show is everything. She knew that better than most. And the
show must go on.

He climbed aboard and into the privacy of the Oval Office
in the Sky.

"Matt!"

The President kissed him. Just a peck on the cheek,
admittedly, but her lips landed closer to his than any
watching journalist might have thought proper. None was
there to witness it, though. Like coloured folk in times of
yore, the hacks were at the back of the bus. And those were
the favoured ones. The penumbra of little-league scribblers,
broadcasters and bloggers would follow in other planes. They
would stay in Luanda, too, when Air Force One flew on to
the hinterland. He and Humboldt might not see eye to eye
about a lot of things, but the man certainly had a sound and
visceral dislike of the fourth estate. And, since he controlled
the airstrip at Milando, Matt felt sure that only the most
intrepid hacks would manage to make their way unaided to
the launch site when the news finally broke that Madam
President was going there afterwards.

He frowned to himself. Part of him, the responsible part,
thought he should be back in Arlington. This trip was not on
the critical path. The critical path at the moment was working
out why America's best geeks were being killed and how a
double agent had managed to penetrate his agency. But there
was something about the fencing match he had been having
with Humboldt that made him want to meet the man face to
face. Besides, this might indeed be an historic moment, and
who could resist the thought of being present at one of those?

And there was also Luanda. Perhaps it was ghoulish, but he needed to see for himself where that supreme act of self-sacrifice had happened. So yes, it might not be responsible to go, but it was necessary.

"Cocktail, Matt?"

A Martini at lunch time? Surely political correctness had put an end to that? Still, why not relive the old days a bit? It would be a long flight. Maybe there were second acts in American lives, after all...

JULY 10TH
BURT'S BURRITO SHACK,
INTERSTATE 40, CALIFORNIA

"Jaimie. That SST of yours. Can I borrow it?"

"'Hello Jaimie. Long time no see. How are you? Sorry I haven't been in touch for a while. Busy, busy, busy.'"

She had to admit he was a pretty good mimic.

"Okay. Start again."

"No need, Alexis. I'm at your disposal as always. You're in luck. It's just out of the service shop after its last test flight. We should get FAA certification for commercial use any day now. After that, the sky's the limit. Sorry. Bad pun. But I could do with a celebration. Where do you want to go? Tahiti? Biarritz? Kathmandu?"

"Angola."

Silence.

"Come again?"

"Angola."

"Just the place for a romantic weekend, I'd say."

"Angola. No questions asked. Does it have the range?"

"That's a question. Let me think. No. But we could do it in two hops if we refuelled in Caracas. *When* do you want to go?"

"Now."

"What?"

She was taking a risk with this conversation, she knew it. She had a clean sim card, bought for cash, and had ridden thirty miles out of town to the edge of the desert before switching the phone on. Whatever it was that Randy had found, she didn't want it listening in on this particular call. The bike was packed and ready to go, with the cube holding Randy in a padded, fireproof bag in one of the panniers. She wasn't planning to return to San Melito. If Jaimie did let her down, she would have to ring the number on the anonymous card she still kept as a souvenir of her gentle interrogation in the back of the limousine. But that was a counsel of despair. Who knew what this thing was capable of? And the spooks had let both her and Sebastian down once already, when they had sworn to protect them. Jaimie, she believed in her heart of hearts, would never let her down.

"Okay," he said, as if telepathising her thoughts. "No questions asked. When can you get here?"

* * * * * * * *

God, she missed the open road. She shuddered. That was how middle-age crept on. The careless abandonment of the pleasures of youth as adulthood's responsibilities squeezed them out. Not consciously rejected, just faded away. The Ducati was the only thing she had salvaged from the wreckage of her apartment block. Kept in an outhouse, it had been spared destruction. She had taken a reluctant Sebastian pillion on it shortly afterwards, along the coast road to Capistrano Point, where bird watchers watch the swallows, and whale watchers watch the whales. Not everyone, she had realised that day, was a born biker.

But she was.

Wealth. Fame. Deceptive masters both. This was freedom, more precious than either. The Duke vacuumed up the miles. She'd be there by dawn. She could sleep on the plane.

Unbidden, the thought of Alice Rhodes's final journey perfused her frontal lobes and burst into her conscious mind. A kindred spirit she would never meet. Except, maybe, through Randy. Who could know the truth of what had happened to her? But Zhukov felt she was dimly beginning to grasp it. A car that, for all its pretentions to be the servant of its driver, was actually the electronic master. An inviting target for any hacker, human or otherwise. A virtual foot on the accelerator. A virtual hand on the steering wheel. A closing speed of maybe 250 miles an hour. Thank God bikes were still pure, unadulterated mechanical mechanisms. One way or another, then, it was time to end this. One way or another, this beast must die.

JULY 11TH
CHANG ZHENG SPACE CITY

"So all we have to do is cut the barbed wire, find Humboldt's plane, and stow away on it without getting caught. I imagine getting caught would be a bad thing?"

"Very bad."

"Where have you hidden the ornithopters?"

She gave him a withering look.

"How do we do it, then?" he persisted.

"Bluff. We just need to look as if we belong there."

"And a six-foot-three European is going to manage that how?"

"By being one of Humboldt's side-kicks who has somehow wandered off piste. Look. You know the cliché about westerners thinking all Chinese look alike? Well, it works the other way round, too. Chinese think that about *laowai*. The people here will know there is something dodgy going on that involves foreigners. They'll be used to seeing a few foreign faces, and probably used to the idea they shouldn't ask too many questions about them. So your job is to look as though you are supposed to be here. Leave the rest to me."

"We still have to get on the other side of the barbed wire."

"For that, we will need luck. But not, I hope, too much."

Sebastian looked around. He had done the tour at Cape Canaveral once. Curiously, this place felt more real. Canaveral was interesting, but the powers that ran it seemed in thrall to the Floridian tradition of theme parks. They had made the bits of the site civilians were allowed to visit feel rather too much like Disneyland for his own sensibilities. Here, there was a sense of its being a working spaceport.

"I'm surprised *laowai* are allowed to move around so freely. In fact, I'm surprised we're allowed in here at all," he said.

"You weren't, but the Party changed the rules. They realised that manned spaceflight is all about propaganda, so there's not much point keeping the people you are trying to influence at arm's length. You can't see anything sensitive as a tourist, of course. But most of the military stuff has gone down to Hainan anyway. With a bit of luck the security won't be as watertight as it should be."

They wandered around, playing the tourist, ooh-ing and ah-ing as required, Chu translating the doublespeak of the explanatory notices into an English equivalent that Orwell would have been proud of. Sebastian knew she had a plan, and he also knew her well enough by now not to ask what it was.

"Time for lunch," she announced, though he thought it rather early to eat. They found the restaurant – a canteen, really, that reminded Sebastian of the one at the university – and ordered noodles and bottled water. He made to throw his empty plastic bottle away, but Chu stopped him.

"Give it to me," she said. "And the top. And go and buy two more bottles"

She put them all, and her own empty bottle, into her bag.

"Now go and empty your bladder. You may not get another chance for a while."

He knew better than to argue, and followed the trousered sign as she followed the skirted one. Then, abluted, they continued their tour past bland, low-rise buildings which Sebastian assumed were offices.

Suddenly but quietly, as if to no one in particular, she said, "In here", and disappeared down an alley between two of the buildings. He followed. The cut-through led to a parking lot. Sebastian twigged why they had eaten so early. Now that it really was lunchtime the lot, though it contained half a dozen coaches, was bereft of people.

"All we have to do is get aboard a coach and wait. When the shift is done they go into the secure zone to pick up the workers and bring them back to the dorms. It's routine. No one will think of checking for stowaways."

"And we stowaway where?"

"In the luggage compartment. There won't be any passengers on the journey out, so no one will put anything into it. The problem will be to escape from it undetected once we are past security. On that, we'll have to take our chances as they come. This is the one," she said, pausing by a vehicle that looked, to Sebastian, just like all the others.

"How do you know?" he asked.

"It says 'Assembly Shed' on the front."

Sebastian, of course, had seen only meaningless squiggles.

She tried the handle. The compartment wasn't locked. She opened the flap.

"In," she said, with little ceremony. Sebastian obeyed. She followed him and pulled the flap almost, but not quite shut behind them. Then she rooted around in her bag. In the small shaft of light which leaked beneath the almost-closed flap he saw that she had produced a penknife and started fiddling with the latch. After about 30 seconds she pulled off its hook and said, "That should fix it. Now it can't lock us in." Then she pulled a length of twine out of her bag and tied one end to the remainder of the latch.

A penknife and a piece of string. She must have been a girl-scout in her childhood.

"We'll have to hold it shut with this," she said, proffering Sebastian the other end of the twine. "And by 'we' I mean you. And here," she continued, holding the empty bottle he had given her half an hour earlier, "is your pissoir, Monsieur Messier."

* * * * * * * *

The compartment was stifling: the more so because Chu had insisted they put on every single item of clothing they had brought with them. They would almost certainly have to jump out of the coach while it was being driven. Like a biker's leathers, the layers of clothing would stop the impact ripping their skin off. The rucksacks themselves, with underwear for padding, would have to do for rudimentary crash helmets – though as she charmingly pointed out, they would also have to contain the water and piss bottles, for they could afford to leave nothing behind that might betray the fact that they had been there. Compared with this, Sebastian thought, jumping out of the window of a burning office block had been a piece of cake.

He had given up trying to guess how long they had been waiting (though it was long enough that he was glad of her foresight with the bottles) when he heard voices outside. A man and a woman. He felt movement as the door above them opened, and then closed.

"Okay," whispered Chu as the engine rumbled into life. And they were off.

The coach drove for two or three minutes, halted long enough, Sebastian estimated, for a barrier to be raised, and then continued on its journey. He clung to the twine for dear life, to preserve their concealment from the outside world.

After a while, though, Chu said, "You'll have to let the flap open a bit, so I can see where we are going." She was hunched up at the front of the compartment. He paid out an inch or two of the twine, enough to create a crack between the side of the hatch and the coach's bodywork. Chu peered through it.

"Okay," she said, handing him the knife. "Here's the plan. First, you'll have to cut the twine free, all of it, and pocket it. If we leave that behind they'll know there's something fishy going on. Hold the flap closed by hand. We'll bale out half a mile before we get to the assembly shed. That will be too far from the building for anyone there to notice what's happening. There's a ditch running alongside the road. Roll for it and lie still when you arrive. I'll try to get us out near some bushes, to give us a bit of cover. The driver will realise the flap's come loose, of course. But with a bit of luck, by the time he has stopped to look he'll be too far away to see us. He'll just think the hook has broken off. Okay. Rucksacks over heads. Hands inside rucksacks for extra protection. Ready?"

"As I'll ever be," said Sebastian.

"Right. Bush coming up in about ten seconds. When I say 'go' we both roll against the flap and out."

He waited, counting silently. *One. Two. Three. Four. Five. Six.*

"Go!"

JULY 11TH
CHANG ZHENG SPACE CITY

"Remind me why we're doing this instead of joining the party."

"A launch is a launch," said McNab. Seen one, seen 'em all. Got to keep the heavy lifters coming. Mars is just the beginning. There's Project Daedalus to consider, too."

"I guess. Don't you sometimes think the boss is over-reaching himself, though?"

"Ours is not to reason why."

"Yeah, right. I just hope the second half of that couplet isn't portentous..."

JULY 11ᵀᴴ
CHANG ZHENG SPACE CITY

Sebastian lay doggo. The madcap plan had worked. They were in the ditch and, though badly bruised, he had suffered no serious cuts or grazes. It was unfortunate about the stink, but in one of those bullet-hits-the-cigarette-case-in-the-shirt-pocket moments, the piss bottle had come between his head and the tarmac, cushioning the impact before it exploded. Never, he thought, after that stroke of luck, would urine smell so bad again.

In the distance, as far as he could tell, the coach had stopped and then, a minute or so later, started up again. But he was not about to stick his head over the side of the ditch to look.

"Right," Chu said eventually. "Into the bushes. We can't afford to be visible if any other traffic comes along."

Sebastian picked up the urine-soaked rucksack. "Come on," she said. "Quickly."

They hid, and checked themselves and each other for damage.

"You did well," said Chu. It was, he realised, the first time she had praised him. It was an odd feeling. On one level he was flattered. On another, he was insulted – for praise is something a superior gives a minion, or a teacher a pupil. He settled for flattery. He could hardly argue, even to himself, that he was anything other than the pupil in this partnership.

"Thank you Sensei," he said, only half jokingly.

"I think you are confusing us with the Japanese," she replied.

Us?

He ignored the thought. She was grinning. She was enjoying this.

"What now?"

"Well, Humboldt's schedule said the plane is leaving after dusk. I suggest we wait here until then. We are less likely to be spotted that way. Unless someone smells you out, of course. Then we'll just wander casually over. As I said, it's all a matter of looking as though you are supposed to be there. We should tidy up, though, otherwise we most certainly won't."

Sebastian struggled out of his numerous layers of clothing, and started picking through them, looking for the most kempt to put back on. Chu stopped him. "That shirt and those trousers," she said, with the intonation of an order. Both were black. Of course. For all the bravura about bluffing and fitting in, in reality it was ninja time again. He started packing the rest of the garments into his odoriferous rucksack.

"I think," said Chu, pointing to the pack, "that we had better leave that behind. I also think, though it grieves me to waste the water, that you had better wash your head."

* * * * * * * *

From their hiding place in the bushes Sebastian had watched the sky darken and the early stars appear, remembering that fateful evening in San Melito when he and Alexis had scanned the heavens. He searched the celestial vault for Mars's malevolent glow and silently cursed the place.

"Okay," said Chu. "Time to go."

She opened her own pack and pulled out a buffalo pouch, which she strapped around her waist. The pack itself she abandoned alongside Sebastian's.

They walked in silence along the roadside ditch, ready to duck back down into it at the first sign of traffic. Chu led the way. The silhouette of the assembly shed, a huge hangar-like edifice, rose slowly in front of them as they approached. Sebastian scanned the scene for signs of movement, but there were none. Then, something changed. He was aware of activity – though through the darkness he could not say exactly what – at the building's extreme right-hand side. He peered into the gloom and realised that the nose-cone of an immense plane was emerging from the hangar and casting its own silhouette against the night sky. Above the plane, riding piggyback, was a giant cylinder: one of Humboldt's rockets, or, rather, part of one. Though the assembly shed was big, it still did not dwarf the aircraft it was disgorging. Sebastian had never seen the like.

More movement, but further off, and the distant sound of

diesel engines. He now discerned one, two, three, was that four, fuel tankers rolling in from the darkness towards the aeroplane.

"Perfect timing," said Chu. "They are getting ready to leave. All we have to do is climb on board."

All, thought Sebastian. Still, she was indeed Sensei, and he a mere apprentice.

They quickened their pace. The road – and therefore the ditch – led to a big, glass-fronted entrance to the hangar. But its lobby was dark and the staff had clearly all decamped long ago, presumably on the coach that had unwittingly brought the two of them out there. When they reached the entrance they turned right, hugging the building's outer wall until they got to the end.

Chu peered around the corner, then pulled her head back.

"The hangar doors are shutting, so they won't see us from inside. The refuelling crews have brought portable lights so that they can see what they are doing. That's good. It means their eyes won't be adjusted to the darkness, and it will be harder for them to notice us. And they'll have all their attention on the wings, of course, because that's where the fuel tanks are. So it's just a question of climbing in."

"Climbing in?"

"Yes, climbing in. Up the landing gear."

"You've been watching too many movies."

"No, really. Lots of planes have a hatch from the front landing-gear compartment to the interior. With ladders. It gives the engineers another access point."

"Lots?"

"Yes. Trust me. I know."

"And this one in particular?"

Silence.

"I'm not liking this plan."

"You have a better one?"

This time it was Sebastian's turn to be silent.

"Okay," said Chu. "Around the corner we go. Stick close to the wall until we are opposite the back of the plane. Then we just walk nonchalantly across the apron and under the fuselage, as if we have come from the hangar. If anybody calls out, let me do the talking."

JULY 11TH
ROSWELL, NEW MEXICO

Rosy-fingered dawn daubed the horizon as Zhukov slalomed down the mountainside. Unbidden and unwanted, she remembered that rosy-fingered dusk, so recent yet so long ago, when she and Sebastian had eaten and drunk and talked of many things. And one of them was Mars. An omen? An evil precognition? No. Such did not exist. A coincidence, that was all. But still, inside her biker's leathers, she shuddered.

Roswell lay in the distance, spread out like a map on a giant's tabletop. Twenty minutes would see her at the airfield, where Jaime Alvarado, aeronautical engineer extraordinaire, awaited, to whisk her away in his latest toy. At least, she hoped he did.

Adrenaline flowed. Sleep departed, or at any rate was masked. The hell with it. She gunned the Duke. She'd do it in ten.

* * * * * * * *

She roared onto the apron and screeched to a halt by the hangar. She pulled off her helmet and shook her tresses free. Then she saw Jaime, arms folded, leaning nonchalantly on the frame of the open door.

"My lady," he said, and swept her a bow, "your carriage awaits."

The arc of his hand introduced his creation, pristine and gleaming inside the hangar. Minions were buzzing around it, doing she knew not what.

Supersonic transport for the gigarich. Breakfast in Bermuda; supper in Sydney. She worked to spread technology to the masses, he to keep it exclusive. Well, they were both ways of earning a living. It was pencil-thin, of course, the plane. Even the wealthy could not suspend the laws of physics. And it had no windows, not even in the cockpit.

"Yes," said Jaime, "the Feds did balk a bit at that. It takes flying blind to a whole, new level of meaning. But it makes the fuselage much stronger and we managed to smooth their feathers. Come. Let me show you around."

He pulled out something that looked like a TV remote, pointed it at the plane and pressed a button. A staircase unfolded.

"We debated that," he said. "It's all extra weight. But no one who is buying Mach 2 is going to want to hang around for some skivvy to wheel a set of steps up to the thing. We don't tell them about the knock-on range reduction, of course."

He smiled that smile, half self-deprecating, half knowing, that he had smiled when they had been students together those long, dividing years ago, and led her by the hand across the hangar floor.

"Your stairway to heaven," he said, bowing again. She climbed it.

The rich, it is said, never turn right when boarding an aircraft. But the gigarich are different. For them, there is only right – unless they want to fly the plane themselves.

She turned right. There were the usual accoutrements of private air travel: half a dozen comfortably upholstered seats. A marble-topped table. And, of course, a bar. But the cabin walls were black. Jaime followed her in, produced the remote and pressed another button. The walls vanished, revealing the hangar and the buzzing minions.

"Clever," she said, determined not to give any impression of being impressed. Give him an inch and he'd take a mile, she knew that.

"Actually, that freaks a lot of people out, especially when we're in flight, so we have this option, too."

He pressed the remote again. The wall returned, and the exterior view shrank to a set of virtual portholes.

"You'll want to shower after the ride, I imagine? Through that door at the back. Another hundred miles off the range for the water, of course. But what can you do?"

He shrugged his shoulders. She walked to the shower.

When she came out, wrapped in a towel, she found the contents of the Duke's panniers spread neatly on the table and her leathers, sponged clean, were hanging in a closet. Attention to detail. That had always been Jaime's way.

She chose a pair of bush trousers and a khaki shirt from the limited wardrobe she had packed and turned back to the shower's antechamber to dress.

"So shy?" said Jaime.

"Not this time, Jaime. This is business."

"Well, a man can hope."

She dressed and returned to the cabin. "What's this baby's name?" she asked. "*Platillo volante*?"

"Far too obvious, my dear, considering where we are. No. It's *Alfombra mágica.*"

* * * * * * * *

Airborne, with the walls set to the illusion of transparency, it did indeed feel like flying on a magic carpet. Aladdin himself could not have hoped for a more comfortable ride.

"So," said Jaime, "now you can't escape, tell me exactly why we are going on this jaunt."

As best she could, she did. He silently digested the information.

"And friend Humboldt doesn't know we are coming? I hope he hasn't got missile defences."

"Relax," she said, feeling anything but relaxed. "This plane, he'll love it. Just up his street. I'm surprised he hasn't ordered one already."

"He has."

"Well, then, tell him it's a surprise visit so he can try it out. Maybe he'll order two."

"And what are you proposing to do when we get there?"

"Stop the launch, of course. Once we've done that, we've got this thing trapped on Earth. Our territory. Our battlefield, not its. Rooting it out is going to be messy, but I'm sure we can manage it. There are seven billion of us, after all, and only one of it."

"I should have shorted my entire share portfolio before we took off. The markets are going to crash when this gets out. Okay, then. Stop the launch and then tell the authorities what's going on. All in a day's work for the A to Z team."

"A to Z team?"

"Alvarado to Zhukov. You mean you never noticed before?"

JULY 12TH
ALTITUDE 7,000 METRES,
OVER THE WESTERN GOBI DESERT

"I have a gun."

She did. In the blink of an eye, she had produced a pistol from her buffalo bag. It looked, Sebastian thought, a lot like the Beretta she had drawn on him when they had met for the second time, in Alice Rhodes's flat. Even she, though, could hardly have smuggled that weapon through airport security in Canada. Or could she?

"I hope I don't have to use it. It would be tedious having to fly the plane myself. It's just to keep things calm while we explain what's going on."

The men sitting in the pilot and co-pilot seats seemed completely bemused. They were, anyway, hardly in a position to react. Being belted up and facing forward, they were straining even to look over their shoulders at their unexpected guests.

Sebastian was bemused, too. He had never thought they could pull it off without being spotted – and, indeed, they had been. But whatever by-play had passed between Chu and the ground-crew who were fuelling the plane, she had managed to convince them that she and the *laowai* were supposed to be onboard, had been left behind by mistake, and that rather than bring up some steps and thus delay the take-off, it was easier for them to clamber through the engineers' back door above the front wheels.

The take-off had been pretty uncomfortable. The cargo bay into which the ladder debouched – too small even in this giant plane, Sebastian supposed, for the payload to fit inside – was stripped bare, and there was precious little to hold onto to resist the g-force as the aircraft accelerated along the runway and lumbered into the sky. But once they had reached level flight, finding the ladder to the cockpit door had been easy. And here they were.

"First," said Chu, "don't even think of touching the radio. That would be fatal, and not just for the obvious reason that I am pointing at you. When we have finished explaining what has happened, and why we are here, you will understand. I have your full attention? Good."

She explained.

She finished explaining. She put the gun away and waited. The two men were struggling to suspend their disbelief.

Eventually one of them said, "You're mad."

"Very possibly. But that doesn't mean we aren't telling the truth. And what have you got to lose by believing us? We're not even really hijacking you. We're not asking you to change course. We just want to get to Milando as quickly as we can. So, I have a question. If we ditched the cargo, could we make it in one hop, without refuelling?"

"Ditched the cargo? How? We'd need to go back to Chang Zheng to do that. There's nowhere else with the right ground-handling equipment."

"No. We don't need to land. We just need to undo the latches and let it go."

"Now I *know* you're mad. You're suggesting we drop an 80 tonne rocket stage off the back of the aircraft? Even if we could manage to do it, that's a hundred million dollars-worth of hardware down the Swanee."

"Totally sane. I've explained how high the stakes are. We have to try it."

"Look. We'll have to put the plane into a dive, first, to have any chance of pulling it off, and we haven't got that much altitude to play with. Even then, once we've cut it loose it'll be the luck of the draw avoiding it hitting us once it's flying loose."

"A challenge to your piloting skills, then."

"And we have to hope there's no one standing where it hits the ground."

"In Xinjiang? I really doubt it."

"Fair point. There's another problem with this plan of yours, though. Masirah will be expecting us for the return fuel stop. If we don't show up they'll know there's something wrong."

Chu paused in thought, then said, "Okay. Two options. You can lie to them; tell them the cargo wasn't ready and you've been told to fly home without it, so won't need to refuel. In that case we'll have to take a chance that if Argus is listening it doesn't know that we really had got the stage on board. And since it seems to be all over the Chinese state computer network, it probably does know that. Or, once we've ditched the cargo, we'll stick to the filed flight plan until we leave Pakistani airspace. Then we turn the transponders off, fly at low altitude, and skirt south beyond their radar range. That way they – and Argus – will think we've had some sort of accident. After that, we go in over Somalia and keep our fingers crossed that the guys on the ground are too busy fighting each other to notice we're there."

"No. It's too crazy."

"May I remind you who is the one with the gun?"

"May I remind you who is the one with the control yoke?"

"When I said it would be tedious having to fly the plane, I meant it. I could if I needed to. But you'll have a better chance of pulling off this manoeuvre."

Silence. Then, "Right. It appears you're the boss. Let's try it."

July 12TH
Gordon Humboldt's bedroom,
Milando Spaceport

"Sir. Sir. Mr Humboldt, sir."

Gordon Humboldt was not a man who awoke quickly at the best of times, and he was particularly reluctant to become conscious now. He had been in the middle of what could only be described as the polar opposite of a nightmare – a phantasmagoria of strange, wonderful, almost mythological beasts in a landscape his somnolent self knew was Martian, even though it more resembled the park of an 18th-century English stately home than the dusty deserts of his Holy Grail.

"Wake up, sir. Something dreadful has happened."

He felt himself wrenched, untimely, from Morpheus's arms. Then the vertical hold returned to his vision. Two men were in the room. One, his factotum Herbert, was bending over him. The other, whom he did not instantly recognise, hovered a yard or so behind, looking ill at ease.

"Yes, Herbert, what is it?"

"Mr Carter is here, from the control tower. I would not have let him disturb you, sir, this night of all nights. But I think you need to hear what he has to say straight away."

Carter stepped forward. "It's McNab's Mriya, Mr Humboldt. It hasn't made Masirah. They couldn't establish radio contact with it, and then it dropped off their radar screen. They think it has probably crashed in the Gulf of Oman."

Humboldt slumped back on his bed. McNab? He shouldn't even have been piloting the Mriya, but the regular jockey had gone down with malaria – not taking his pills, no doubt – and McNab had volunteered for the trip, even though it meant missing the last launch.

There ain't no justice.

"Thank you, Herbert. You did the right thing waking me. Who knows about this?"

"Only the three of us Mr Humboldt," said Carter, "and Steve Reid, who was with me in the control tower when we got word from Masirah."

"Right. Let's keep it that way. What time was the Mriya due in?"

"Two-thirty this afternoon, Mr Humboldt."

"Okay. That's just after the President is supposed to fly out. If we can keep a lid on this until then, we can work out how to deal with the fall-out later. I know it's a tall order, but could you and Steve stay on shift until Air Force One has departed? Tell your replacements I've said they can take the time off to watch the launch. Four, I think, may keep a secret. Anymore, and it will surely get out."

JULY 12TH
MILANDO SPACEPORT

"Madam President. A pleasure to meet again."

"Indeed, Mr Humboldt, indeed. I'm not sure whether I should be clapping at your audacity or clapping you in irons. That may depend, of course, on what exactly happens today."

From the top of the steps leading up to Air Force One Matt Vane looked on with wry amusement as his political mistress shook hands with the would-be master of Mars. He found himself wondering once more if time might yet erase for him again that prefix 'political'.

It had gone well in Luanda. He had spent a quiet moment at the statue of Jemmy Cato. She, meanwhile, had moved the pieces on the diplomatic chessboard a little in America's favour. She had always been a formidable chess player, even back in Radcliffe.

The genteel dominance contest of greeting over, Humboldt and the President walked side by side along a red carpet that had been rolled out across the runway, and strolled towards the waiting motorcade. Vane was impressed an operation like this had had such a carpet – or, that if it hadn't, it had been able to get one all the way out here at so little notice. Then again, who knew which dignitaries the megalomaniac Humboldt had been entertaining behind their backs? He really had, Vane silently reprimanded himself, slipped up quite badly in not paying proper attention to the fellow before.

He walked down the steps himself and along the carpet, dutifully behind host and guest, in the middle of a knot of presidential aides. The vehicles, he saw as they approached them, were Toyotas. That struck a sour note, the President riding in a Japanese 4x4. Were American trucks not good enough for Humboldt?

The two alphas, female and male, got in the first of the Land Cruisers. The President even waved away her Secret Service detail – an old trick of hers for putting the opposition at ease. Only the football carrier joined her in Humboldt's transport. The Service-men and the aides scrambled for precedence in the other trucks. Vane chose not to join the scrum. It was beneath his dignity. He walked straight to the rearmost, found a seat and plonked himself down in it.

The convoy set off. For the first time since they had arrived, Vane's eye left the human spectacle and roamed the landscape. It was awesome in the way the African bush is always awesome. It was primeval. A man had only to stand in it for his hunter-gathering ancestry to come welling up unbidden. His genes knew – somehow really knew – that this was Home. But even the primeval was here and there being shaped by the hand of man. He could see in the distance the rocket whose launch they had come to witness. Closer by were the paraphernalia of space travel – giant hangars and blast-proof block houses. These, too, were awesome in their way. This was apparatus that only nations normally chose to afford. If he had ever doubted Humboldt's seriousness, which he had, he did so no longer.

JULY 12TH
MILANDO SPACEPORT CONTROL TOWER

"Rick. We've got incoming."

"What?"

"There. Look. From the east."

"Christ. How fast?"

"Subsonic. Range 45 kilometres. Speed… 160 knots. Hang on. I recognise that signature. It's the Mriya. What the hell's going on? Tell Humboldt. I'll try to contact them."

Carter put the headphones on and pressed the comms button.

"Alpha Foxtrot. Calling Alpha Foxtrot. This is Milando Control. Acknowledge, please, and kindly explain what is happening. Contact with you was lost over the Gulf of Oman. Everyone thought you'd crashed."

Nothing

"This is Milando Control calling unidentified aircraft, bearing 87 degrees, range 43 kilometres. Is that you, Alpha Foxtrot?"

Still nothing

"Milando Control to unidentified aircraft, bearing 87 degrees, range 42 kilometres. Please acknowledge. You are putting your aircraft at risk by continuing to approach, and failing to acknowledge."

Still nothing

"Okay, Steve. We have a situation. Alert air defences. It's surely got to be them, but with the Pres here we can't afford to take chances."

"Milando Control. This is Alpha Foxtrot. We acknowledge."

"Thank God for that, Alpha Foxtrot. We were just about to arm the missile batteries. What happened to you, Bob? Masirah lost contact with you just after Gwadar. We thought you must have ditched. And how did you get here without refuelling?

There was a pause.

"Sorry, Milando Control. We've been having comms problems all day. We thought Chang Zeng had alerted you. There was a difficulty with the cargo. One of the F7s failed final inspection. We did the sums and realised that without the cargo we could get back in time for the launch if we set off anyway and didn't stop for fuel. We didn't think the boss would mind in the circs. I've been hauling those damned Chimborazos from China to Angola for months, now. I don't see why you lot should get to drink all the Champagne when the last one goes off."

"Okay, Alpha Foxtrot. Continue your approach."

"Thanks, Milando Control."

"Thanks, Alpha Foxtrot. We'll see you in ten minutes."

Carter clicked off the mike.

"That's bollocks. Chang Zheng would have told us if they'd left without the goods. And it doesn't explain how Masirah lost sight of them. And something else. You've only been here a couple of weeks, haven't you? So don't really know Armstrong yet."

"Barely met the man. Why?"

"He can't drink Champagne. He had to give up the booze three years ago. He's teetotal."

TECHNOZOIC

JULY 12TH
ALTITUDE 2,000 METRES,
45 KILOMETRES EAST OF MILANDO

"Alpha Foxtrot. Calling Alpha Foxtrot. This is Milando Control. Acknowledge, please, and kindly explain what is happening. Contact with you was lost over the Gulf of Oman. Everyone thought you'd crashed."

"Ignore it," said Chu. They'll find out what's happened soon enough. Leave them in the dark for the moment."

McNab sat back in his seat. There was not much to do. Though the Mriya's airframe was Soviet, its avionics were state of the art. Then the radio crackled into life again.

"This is Milando Control calling unidentified aircraft, bearing 87 degrees, range 43 kilometres. Is that you, Alpha Foxtrot?"

"Should I respond?" said Armstrong.

"No. Absolutely not. We don't want to risk giving Argus any clues."

They waited in silence.

"Milando Control to unidentified aircraft, bearing 87 degrees, range 42 kilometres. Please acknowledge. You are putting your aircraft at risk by continuing to approach and failing to acknowledge."

"You know, it might be better if we did acknowledge. They've got missiles down there."

"They'll see it's us, surely? No other plane could have a radar signature like this one."

Then the radio crackled into life.

"Thank God for that, Alpha Foxtrot. We were just about to arm the missile batteries. What happened to you, Bob? Masirah lost contact with you just after Gwadar. We thought you must have ditched. And how did you get here without refuelling?

"What? What's he talking about?"

There was a pause.

"Okay, Alpha Foxtrot. Continue your approach."

"Christ," said McNab. "He's having a conversation with someone. Someone pretending to be us. Argus has hacked our radio."

"Thanks, Alpha Foxtrot. We'll see you in ten minutes."

He grabbed the mike.

"Milando Control! This is Alpha Foxtrot!"

He was shrieking.

"Rick. This is Alpha Foxtrot. This! Not what you have been listening to. Whatever it said, ignore it. Milando control, listen to"

A light went out on the instrument panel. Then another. And another.

"For Christ's sake, Rick! The engines are shutting down. Milando Control. This is Alpha Foxtrot. We've just suffered total engine failure. Listen, Rick. Whatever you are talking to, it isn't us. Its some sort of electronic super-virus, and it's shut down our engines."

Silence. It was Chu who broke it.

"Looks like we're in for a dead-stick landing," she said. "Can you make it to the runway?"

"At this altitude and speed it'll be touch and go. My best guess is we'll hit the dirt five or six kilometres short."

"Hit the dirt as in crash?" said Sebastian.

"Well, it won't be pretty."

"Can we bale out?"

"We don't carry parachutes. Why would we? Planes never just fall out of the sky, and we normally avoid war zones, so no one is going to take a pot shot at us. In any case, as you said yourself, we have to get to Milando and stop the launch. We'll just have to make the best landing we can and leg it from there."

He studied the instrument panel.

"Okay," he said, calming down. "First things first."

He lifted a cover on the panel and threw the switch underneath it.

"Fuel dump," he announced, before anyone could ask.

"Right, Bob. Take someone with you and go aft. Open the doors and eject them. We don't want them jamming on impact. Wedge the cockpit door open, too, just in case. Then clear the cockpit of anything loose. And get water bottles. It'll be hot out there. Five minutes to impact."

Armstrong left the cockpit. Chu followed him, and they disappeared. Sebastian tried to make himself useful, picking things up and hurling them into the void beyond the cockpit door. Every time he turned round from doing so, the ground looked a little closer.

Chu and Armstrong returned. "Done," Armstrong announced.

"Two minutes to impact," McNab announced. "Places, everybody."

They sat in their respective seats and secured themselves as best they could.

"Don't unstrap until we've stopped moving," said McNab. "We've no fuel left, so don't worry too much if a fire starts. It won't blow us up. There are no evacuation slides, by the way. We'll just have to jump, and hope for the best."

No one said anything. Sebastian could see individual trees and animals now, scattered like toys across the savanna. In the distance, he could make out the space port, the runway they would never reach, the three dark patches of Humboldt's diamond mines, and something else: a strange, circular clearing in the bush that looked for all the world like a giant crop circle.

McNab was fiddling with the controls, changing the lumbering plane's trim to try to keep its nose up. Then the trees were no longer toys, and the beasts were looking up as the Mriya passed overhead. A few of the more nervous scattered. Most held their ground, waiting for the threat to pass before they resumed the serious business of grazing.

"Thirty seconds. Prepare to brace," said McNab.

No one replied. All eyes were fixed ahead – McNab's seeking the most treeless patch he could reach; the others' watching helplessly as reality bit and each wondered if these fleeting moments would be their last.

"Okay everybody. Brace! Brace! Brace!"

McNab had angled it perfectly. The Mriya's belly took the impact's brunt. They ploughed through the scrub, pushing the bushes aside like so much stubble.

"Okay," said McNab, as the plane shuddered to a halt. "Everyone out. Don't forget your water."

JULY 12TH
MILANDO SPACEPORT CONTROL TOWER

"Shit," came a voice over the speaker. "The boss is out greeting the Washington bigwigs at the moment. That, we can't interrupt. Go over it again, Rick, just so I've got things straight."

"Last night," Carter repeated, "the Mriya disappeared off the radar screen when it was approaching Masirah – at least, that's what Masirah told us. I told the boss. In person. At two am. He decided to keep quiet about it until the President had left this afternoon. So, until this conversation only Steve, myself, the boss and that creature of his, Herbert, knew what was going on. But the plane's back. It showed up on the radar a couple of minutes ago. Some cock-and-bull story about a problem with the load, a problem with the radio, and a desire to rush home for the launch. They've been hijacked. I know it."

Carter's voice trailed off. He was looking at the radar.

"Hang on. There's something wrong. They're coming in too steeply." He paused, calculating. "On that glide path they're going to land six klicks short of the runway. What the hell is happening?"

"Okay Rick. Keep me posted. I'll tell the boss as soon as he gets back to the blockhouse. He must be pretty cut-up already. McNab's on that plane, isn't he? He's one of his oldest mates. Been his pilot since the company started. Hijacking, you think?"

"What else could it be? And with the President here…"

His voice trailed off again. No one felt any need to complete the sentence. They all thought the same thing. That McNab had decided to crash the plane deliberately, to stop it being used as some sort of weapon.

"How long?" came the disembodied voice.

"Three minutes…"

July 12TH
Mission Control, Milando Spaceport

The convoy had taken a circuitous route. Humboldt was obviously showing off his toys to the President. The man driving Vane was a taciturn Afrikaner. He answered questions monosyllabically and volunteered no information that was not prised out of him. Eventually, after a quarter of an hour of such grunts, the tour was over and they arrived at what seemed to be Mission Control.

Vane decided it was time to join his leader. They walked down the steps into the bunker. As they were entering, someone came up to Humboldt and whispered in his ear. Humboldt said, "Please excuse me for a moment. Last minute preparations. Mike will look after you." And he strolled across the control-room floor.

A young agent, particularly one who is pretending to be a cultural attaché at one of his country's embassies, learns many tricks. One that Matt Vane had found useful during the endless round of cocktail parties to which diplomats treat each other was the ability to lip-read. Not even his colleagues knew he could do it. One has to preserve some advantages in the climb to the top. Now, he was worried by what the man talking to Gordon Humboldt seemed to be saying – or, to be more accurate, worried by what it implied that Humboldt had not said to them, namely that one of his planes had disappeared and then re-appeared again. Though Vane could see only half of the conversation, it seemed to be about one of the giant transport aircraft bringing the rocket stages in from China. On the face of it, that seemed no threat to the presidential party. But Vane's antennae and his hackles were both up. His antennae told him there was something more to it, and his hackles resented, as only a secret agent can, having secrets kept from him. Then Gordon Humboldt strode back towards them.

"Sorry," he said. "Something has come up. It shouldn't affect the launch, but it needs my full attention. Mike, could you take over?"

Humboldt left the room, brushing past two burly, be-shaded individuals coming into the bunker as he did so.

Secret Service. Vane's hackles rose further. Sure, the SS, as he privately dubbed them, had formal responsibility for the President's safety. But he regarded them, if not exactly with contempt, then certainly as being infra dig. And their feeling toward the Agency, he was sure, was mutual.

"Madam President," one said. "Could we have a word in private?"

The football carrier withdrew, as it were, into the shadows, and the man who Humboldt had referred to as Mike also turned to leave. "I'll be over there with the mission-control guys if you need me, Madam President," he said.

Vane vacillated, resenting the dilemma about whether to stay, and risk being dismissed from the presidential presence, or to leave, and suffer the certainty of self-humiliation. But the President spared his blushes. "Matt Vane," she said, addressing the Service-man, "is cleared to hear anything."

"Very well," he replied. "Our radar has shown a big transport aircraft, apparently heading towards the landing strip from the east."

Despite himself, Vane found himself saying, "Yes. I was just about to tell you that myself. It's one of Humboldt's rocket transporters. They thought it had come down in the Gulf of Oman last night, but now it has turned up safe and sound and several hours early. It all seems very strange."

The President turned to him and raised an eyebrow. "How on Earth did you know that?" But the Service-man cut across her.

"Not safe and sound at all. It has crashed in the bush."

"Oh. So that's what Humboldt meant when he said something has come up," said the President. "Come down, more likely. Well, yes. I can see this is all very embarrassing for him, and that he wouldn't want it to get out on his big day. But do you think it's a threat to us? Hard to see how."

"It's odd. And I don't like odd things," said the Service-man.

For once, Matt Vane found himself agreeing with the SS.

"I don't like it either," he said. "How is it possible for a plane flying from China to arrive four hours early? And what happened to it while it was lost. We need to find out."

"Well I'm sure," she said, smiling at the three of them, "that between you, you can do that."

July 12TH
Humboldt's helicopter,
five kilometres east of Milando Spaceport

"Okay control. I can see the Mriya. She seems more or less intact. Big skid-marks through the bush behind her. Looks as though she's been put down deliberately. We're going in."

Humboldt dipped the Huey forward and started to descend. They could have sent a drone, he supposed, but that would just have delayed matters and given whoever had hijacked the plane, if hijacked it had been, more time to respond or hide.

"Roger, Charlie Echo."

"No Chimborazo stage on board, by the way. Has anyone managed to get any sense out of Chang Zheng?"

"They're still claiming McNab left on time and fully laden."

"Any signs of life down there, Petersen?" This to the man sitting up front with him, who was scanning the ground ahead with a pair of old-fashioned field glasses.

"Yes, Mr Humboldt." I can see figures moving around. More than two of them. Four, I think."

"Seems we were right. Hijackers."

"I'm not so sure, sir. I can't work out who's who yet, but no one looks as if they're being kept prisoner. They're all staring in our direction, and one of them's a girl."

"What?"

"Yep. Definitely female. Looks Chinese. And yes, I'm pretty sure two of the others are McNab and Armstrong. The fourth one's a man. Tall. White. Dressed in black. They're waving at us."

"Okay. But let's be cautious when we approach."

Not hijackers. Hitchhikers? If they'd both been female he wouldn't have put it past McNab, at least, to have been bringing a couple of floozies back to base. But a man and a woman? Well, no point in speculating. They would find out soon enough.

"You two." This to the men in the seats behind him. "Let's not assume this is as innocent as it looks. You've got your rifles handy?"

"Yes, Mr Humboldt."

"Okay. I'll land a few hundred yards from the plane. When we get out I want each of you to stay with the chopper and draw a bead on one of the strangers. Philips, you take the girl. Singh, you take the man. If I raise either hand above my shoulder, take them out. If I turn around and wave my arms crossed down below my waist, then the coast is clear. But stay here in case there is anything from control. Jake," this to Petersen, "you come with me. No weapons drawn."

"Yes, Mr Humboldt."

"Control?"

"Yes, Charlie Echo?"

"We're landing. I'm leaving Philips and Singh with the whirlybird. Don't try to contact them. They'll be covering us, just in case, and I don't want them distracted. But you might be hearing from them, if there is trouble."

"Roger, Charlie Echo."

Humboldt judged the ground. There was a fair amount of scrub, but it did not overwhelm the grassland. He put the Huey down in a glade that had a clear shot at the knot of people standing waving by the stricken Mriya, and cut the engine.

They waited until the blade had stopped rotating before they got out. Better to have no distractions. Then they jumped to the ground, port and starboard, and Humboldt and Petersen strolled, not quite casually, towards the crash site.

"Are you alright?" he called to them, when he was about halfway there. Then he double-took. "Hayward! What the hell are...what in Christ's name is going on?"

McNab began to reply. "We–" Then he stopped talking. He was no longer looking at Humboldt. Instead, he was staring slightly above him. Humboldt turned to follow the man's gaze. A missile's trail was arcing westward into the sky.

July 12TH
Altitude 18,300 metres,
75 kilometres west of Milando Spaceport

Alfombra mágica's cabin had every creature comfort. The cockpit, though, looked military.

"It's still a prototype," Jaime had explained, when Alexis first squeezed herself into the co-pilot's seat. "An experimental aircraft, don't forget. The back of the bus is for potential clients; the seats there are by Louis Vuitton, for comfort and luxury if you want it. The ones up here are by Valentine James, for a quick exit if you need it."

A magic carpet indeed. It had wafted them across the Atlantic while she'd slept off her bike ride, and they were over Angola already. Technically, they were trespassing on that country's airspace. But since, according to Jaime, the Angolan air force consisted of a couple of ancient MiGs and a gold-plated 747 to carry the President's wife on shopping trips, they were not expecting trouble – at least, not from that direction.

Fifteen minutes out from Milando, Jaime curved the plane around to line it up with the runway.

"I still think we should warn them we're coming," he said.

"Too risky. That Thing is everywhere. We know it's already taken down at least one plane. We'll just have to give friend Humboldt a surprise. What's the worst he can do? Clap us in irons? He's hardly going to shoot us down, is he?"

"Okay. You're the boss." He made his right hand into a loose fist, held it to his mouth like a microphone, and spoke into it in a mock announcer's voice.

"Cabin crew prepare the aircraft for landing."

Alexis felt the engines throttle back and watched the Mach counter drop below one. She saw the clouds dotted over the landscape below coming nearer – or rather, she saw their simulacrum in a zillion quantum dots. There was little to say. Her eye was drawn to the radar screen. There was a lot of ground clutter, but they seemed to have the sky to themselves. Then, in the patch of clutter dead ahead of them, which Jaime had explained was the reflection from Humboldt's operation, there was a sign of movement. Or was

219

there? Yes, definitely. There was something moving there. Something coming towards them.

"Jaime. What's that?" she asked.

He didn't respond. He, too, was studying the screen. Then he responded.

"Shit. He *is* trying to shoot us down."

"That's a missile?"

"It's travelling at Mach three and coming straight at us. What else could it be?"

"Can we out-fly it?"

"Depends on its range. It'll be touch and go. Strap in properly."

She barely had time to before the horizon vanished and they were pointing at the heavens. Crashes from behind the door to the cabin, though, told her that gravity was very much still in charge; anything loose back there was being pulled earthwards with a thump. Her head was being pulled earthwards, too. By now it was dangling from her shoulders towards the ground's image in the cockpit's roof. Then she felt it dragged sideways as the horizon span around her. Finally, both the view and her hair resumed something like their normal angles.

"Thanks, Max," said Jaime, laconically, to himself.

"Max?"

"Immelmann. Tell you later. Watch the radar."

At least the green blip of death was now behind them.

"How far away is it?"

"Forty five kilometres, if I've understood this thing correctly." She glanced at the Mach counter. It read, 'two'. But Jaime was way ahead of her.

"We've got two and a quarter minutes, then, before it catches us. By the way, next time you fancy an African holiday, I'll be in Tierra del Fuego. Or possibly Siberia."

She kept her eyes on the radar, counting the seconds off silently. Jaime stroked the control panel. A small window showing where they had been popped open within the image of where they were going, breaking the illusion that the view they were looking at was real. In it she could see the missile – or, at least, its exhaust trail – still far off, but too close for comfort, and getting closer.

"Thirty kilometres," she said

Ninety seconds to impact.

She looked at Jaime, who was staring ahead, into the empty stratosphere. She said nothing more. There was nothing more to say. She turned back to the radar.

"Twenty kilometres."

Sixty seconds. A flashback from *Doctor Strangelove* filled her mind. She could hear '*Johnny comes marching home*' echoing inside her head. But this was real.

"You said the seats were Valentine James?"

"Forget it. Without suits, at this speed, at this altitude…"

There was nothing, then, but to wait, and hope. She sat in silence, watching the screens.

"Ten kilometres."

The rear-view must have had some sort of zoom on it, for she could now see the missile itself, as well as the contrail spewing out behind it.

"Five kilometres. Wait. Look. The contrail's stopped. It's run out of fuel."

They both stared at the image in the rear-view window. The missile, bereft of thrust, was starting to lose altitude. But not speed, or not enough, at least. Newton's third law of motion might now be in abeyance, but the thing still had inertia and his first law hurled it inexorably on.

Alexis watched Jaime pull back on the stick, trying to gain height. The blip on the radar was still closing, but now, she knew, the missile would pass beneath them. She counted it in – four klicks, three, two, one – then its parallax carried it below the camera's line of vision. She waited for it to overtake *Alfombra mágica* and appear ahead of them in the simulated windscreen.

Then the blip on the radar screen vanished. "Christ. It's detonated," she said as the blip was replaced by a fuzzy, expanding cloud.

Alfombra mágica rocked, but mercifully did not roll, as the explosion hit it. They were still intact. "Proximity fuse," Jaime replied, with what almost sounded like glee, as if he had been expecting this moment. "Alright! Let's give them a show."

Without warning, he pushed the stick forward, and

Alfombra mágica hurtled towards the ground. At this, Alexis's nerve finally snapped. She screamed. The plane was spinning now, though Jaime had cut the power to the engines.

"Gotta make it look convincing," he said. Alexis's breakfast was sprayed around the cabin. Out of the corner of one eye she could see the altimeter racing down.

"What the hell are you doing?"

"Shush."

She shushed. Something about atheists in foxholes emerged, unbidden and unwelcome, from her subconscious. They were in free-fall now – paradoxically, because of air resistance, travelling more slowly than when they had been under power. But not slowly enough. The altimeter continued its countdown. Five thousand metres. Four thousand. Three thousand. Then, as it dipped below two thousand metres, Jaime fired up the engines and started doing something with the stick. As far as Alexis could see it made little difference. The ground continued to get closer. She shut her eyes. Of all the ways she had imagined her life might end, in a smoking crater in the African bush had never once figured. How long would those final two klicks take, she wondered? She prepared herself for oblivion. The wait seemed interminable.

"Okay," Jaime said. "You can open them again."

Slowly, almost reluctantly, she did so. They were flying straight and level a couple of hundred metres above the ground, an object of wonder to the inhabitants below. They both sat in silent contemplation.

"If that's the way friend Humboldt treats his guests…" Jaime opined, after a while.

"Maybe. But he made no attempt to get in touch first. Maybe he's not in control any more. Either way, we have to work out how to get in there."

Silence returned. Jaime was thinking, struggling to accept the inevitable loss of his masterpiece. Then he spoke.

"Okay. With a bit of luck our little charade back there will have persuaded whoever – or whatever – launched that missile that we are now both playing harps in the great aircraft hangar in the sky. At this altitude we should be below their radar, so with even more luck they might stay persuaded. I suggest we circle around and come in from a different direction, crosswise to the runway instead of on a standard approach path. We'll never be able to land there anyway, and that way we might retain at least some element of surprise. We'll travel fast and low; try to remain under their radar until the last moment. Then, as close as possible to the airfield, we'll pop up and eject."

Eject?

"I thought you said..."

He cut across her. "I did. But that was at Mach two. It was minus sixty outside, with a tenth of an atmosphere of pressure. Even if we'd survived being slammed by the shockwave, it would have been a race between freezing to death and suffocating. At this speed" – he indicated the Mach counter, which registered 0.6 – "we'll probably black out, but other than shrinking an inch from the acceleration we should be okay. Flip that box to your left open, and you'll find a helmet that will soften the blow."

Almost imperceptibly, Jaime banked *Alfombra mágica* to begin making the wide sweep around to the southerly approach that might yet get them to their destination. "I switched the radar off," he said to Alexis, "so they won't be able to track us with it. But that means we can't track them. Scan the horizon as best you can for trouble. Your job is to watch for the next missile. Mine is to evade it."

She stared at the simulated windscreen, searching the sky.

"That dial there," said Jaime, pointing to the control panel. "You can use it to swing the cockpit view round to look towards Milando. Don't worry about me. I'll fly on instruments. If you think you see anything, touch the centre of the dial and you'll get a cross-hair you can stroke around the view. You can zoom to a close-up of what the cross-hair is pointing at by pinching the dial. Unpinch to get back to a normal view. Try it."

She did, aiming the crosshairs at a barely visible dot in the sky, then pinching. A vulture filled the screen, like a shot from a wildlife documentary. She unpinched, and the bird was banished back to the distant thermal it was riding.

"It's really a toy for the cabin. Hours of entertainment for the passengers back there. Luckily, I had it fitted up front, too. Okay. Let's boogie."

JULY 12TH
MISSION CONTROL, MILANDO SPACEPORT

"What in the name of Bejeezus is going on?"

"We don't know, Mike. The radar picked up an unexplained contact to the west, coming in at supersonic speed, and it just launched itself."

"Follow it."

"What the fucking hell is happening? Tell me what the fucking hell is happening! This charade has gone on long e-fucking-nuff!" Matt Vane, urbanity shattered, strode across the control-room floor as if wearing seven league boots, the SS men trailing in his wake. The President, hearing the commotion from outside the bunker, rushed back in. Vane, a tall man whose silver locks belied his strength, had grabbed the controller by the lapels and lifted him onto the tips of his toes, to stare him directly in the face.

"You didn't tell us about the crashed freighter. That was stupid enough. Did you think we would not notice ourselves? Now Humboldt has vanished who-knows-where and you're firing missiles off left, right and centre. What in the name of all that's holy is happening? Because if we are under attack, I'm scrambling the escorts here and now. Fuck Humboldt and his Martian firework display. We've got the President of the United States here, and I'm responsible for her safety."

"Actually, *we* are resp—" began the taller of the SS men. Then, as Vane turned to stare at him with a look Medusa might have envied, and without letting go of the controller, he thought better of it and lapsed into silence.

Eventually, Vane put Ryan down. "Scramble them if you like," Ryan said. "But I can't guarantee *their* safety. If there's a gremlin in the air defences it might take a pot shot at them, too. And, to answer your question, we've no idea what is happening. We think the transport was hijacked, and we think the pilot may have brought it down deliberately short of the runway, to foil the hijackers' plans. Beyond that, we know nothing. Mr Humboldt went to investigate, and we haven't heard back from him what he has found, beyond that the crew are still alive and have two strangers with them. And now this. Duncan, what's the latest?"

"The bandit's turned tail. He's travelling at Mach two. The missile's still after him, though, and it's got Mach three. This one is going down to the wire…"

Matt Vane, Ryan, the SS men and the President strode as one to Duncan Harris's console, peering at the game of fox and hounds being played out on its radar screen. They waited, in consensual silence, for the drama's climax. Then, with the last gasp of its fuel, the missile had overtaken its target and detonated. The target, whatever it was, was falling out of the sky.

"Shall I send a chopper to have a look?" said Harris.

"No." Ryan replied. "Nothing should get airborne 'til we find out why that missile decided to launch itself. We don't want to lose any of our own. Speaking of which, has anyone warned the boss not to take off?"

"I asked the control tower to warn them," said Harris, "but they said they couldn't get through. The Huey's radio seems to have packed up."

"No. No, no, no, no, no. That is too many coincidences. This base," said Vane, "is under attack. I don't know how and I don't know who from. But as far as I'm concerned, until proven otherwise, this is an attempt to assassinate you, Madam President. One of you two," this to the SS men, "tell Air Force One to alert Washington to what is happening. Then gather every man we've got, go to the missile batteries, and take them out. Let me know as soon as it's done. Then, we're out of here."

July 12TH
Secret Service Headquarters,
Washington, DC

"Anything from Air Force One?"

"Just the usual chatter. Humboldt's launching at noon, local. POTUS has gone off to watch the show. Then it's a quick celebratory lunch after the launch and back home. It all seems to be going perfectly smoothly."

JULY 12TH
THE BUSH,
SIX KILOMETRES EAST OF MILANDO SPACEPORT

They sat in a circle in the shade of the Mriya's starboard wing, Sebastian regretting his black clothing in the African heat. It was a council of war. He and Chu, constantly cutting across each other, attempted to explain to Humboldt and his heavies what had happened. At first, Humboldt plied them with questions, but after a while he gave up and sat silently, barely able to accept either the enormity or the reality of what they were saying. The facts, though – the unarguable facts – were that someone or something had shut down the Mriya's engines, that someone or something, probably the same, had launched a SAM from his base – *his* base, without *his* authority – at who-knew-what target, and that all contact with the base had been lost, for the Huey's radio was now silent and their cell-phones were failing to connect, presumably for similar reasons. As Holmes had put it, 'When you have eliminated the impossible, whatever remains, however improbable, must be the truth'.

"Well, one thing is clear," he said eventually. "If they, it, whatever, have hijacked the missile-defence system, we can't fly the helicopter any more. We are just going to have to leg it."

"Leg it where?" said McNab.

"It seems unlikely we'll get a warm welcome if we go back to base – or, rather, the welcome might be a bit too warm, so I suggest we head for the mine-control centre. We might be able to patch some sort of communication with somebody through from there. If what Ms Chu here says is true, then Argus, or whatever it is, will probably have its attention elsewhere, organising the details of its escape. It's hardly likely to care about an automated diamond-mining operation. Plus, the mine centre is nearer than Mission Control. Quicker to get to."

Petersen spoke. "Aren't you forgetting something, sir? The President of the United States is under the control of that thing, too, in all probability. Surely, either her people will have got a message out about what is going on, or, if they haven't, DC will realise from the lack of traffic that something bad has happened, and they'll come looking anyway?"

"I wouldn't rely on that," said Chu. "Argus has clearly penetrated the Agency's system. It's probably all over Washington by now. And we know from what happened to us when we were coming in that it can fool humans into believing what it wants them to believe. So I wouldn't bet on the Cavalry riding in any time soon. In any case, it only needs to keep the outside world at bay long enough to launch its escape pod. Which is scheduled to happen when, by the way?"

She looked quizzically at Humboldt.

"Noon," he said.

"That gives us an hour and a half. Do you think you can navigate us to this diamond mine of yours, Mr Humboldt."

"Gordon, please. And yes, I can do that. Jake, come with me at the front. Art, Zorawar, cover us from the back. Just a precaution, you understand" – this to Chu and Sebastian – "but the local wildlife sometimes gets a bit frisky."

Chu, Sebastian noticed, had kept quiet about her pistol. But he forbore to mention the point. Perhaps she felt a handgun would be of only modest use against a charging lion.

They set off through the bush. Much of it was open, but there were patches of scrub large, tall and thick enough to conceal a lurking cat, which they steered around as best they could. In other circumstances, thought Sebastian, he would be paying many thousands of dollars for an experience like this – a safari on foot through the savanna. How circumstances do alter cases.

JULY 12TH
MISSION CONTROL, MILANDO SPACEPORT

"Okay," said Matt Vane. "The cavalry's on its way. The *Truman* has scrambled half a dozen Lightnings to meet us. As soon as the missiles are dealt with, we should go."

The two SS, having given up the struggle for authority, had departed the bunker, rounded up the half-dozen Airbornes who were lurking outside, and were heading off to the missile battery. Ryan had directed them to the base's armoury, with instructions about where to find a stash of RDX they kept, as he put it, "in case of emergencies".

Vane followed their progress from a running commentary one of them was giving over his body mike. They arrived at the armoury, found the explosives and set off for the battery. Eight launchers, Ryan had said, though one of them would now be vacant. For a supposedly civilian operation, Milando was certainly tooled up. Humboldt clearly had enemies, or thought he had. Perhaps he, Vane, was wrong. Maybe the President was not the target of what was going on.

Not that it mattered. If she got caught in the crossfire, she would still be as dead as if she had been killed deliberately. Either way, Milando was no longer a healthy place to be.

The body mike reported that the demolition party had arrived at the battery. There were indeed seven missiles left. The Airbornes were fitting charges to the first two of them. That took a couple of minutes. Then they started on the second two. Vane waited for confirmation that these, too, had been charged for demolition. Instead, a whoomp and a series of ear-piercing screams came over the speaker, followed by another, less anguished but still as startled, from Duncan Harris.

"Christ," he said to the world in general. "Another two have launched..."

July 12th
Altitude 200 metres,
five kilometres south of Milando Spaceport

"Right. The time for dissembling is over." Jaime pulled the stick back, *Alfombra mágica*'s nose rose in obedience and the altimeter raced upwards, a reversal of the stomach-churning death-spiral of what now seemed like centuries ago.

"We'll need altitude," he had explained, as they had laid their plans for this moment, "to see where to steer the chutes." Those plans, it had to be said, were pretty sketchy, not helped by their sketchy knowledge of the layout of Humboldt's operation. But there was one thing they did know. It was based on a triple diamond mine he had discovered, in a flurry of publicity, a while back. That, at least, was a point of reference. They had agreed to steer for the mine, and to meet at whatever was the largest building there if they got separated.

The chutes were integral to the seats. Strap into the latter and you were wearing the former. The helmet was no more inconvenient that the one she wore on the Duke. The altimeter approached 4,000 metres.

"Okay. Ready? Here we go."

Jaime pulled a lever and the canopy vanished, ripped away by the slipstream. She could see the sky for real now, and feel the edge of the rushing wind. She braced herself. Nothing, though, can prepare you for the force of ejection.

It was like being back in St Ursula's. How long she had blacked out for she had no idea. She could just see *Alfombra mágica*, still climbing, followed by two smoke-trails rapidly closing on it; this time, whoever controlled the missiles was taking no chances. Jaime, she could not see.

Her chute had opened automatically, as he'd said it would. She had jumped before, once or twice, in her teens, and she tried to remember how to control her descent. It was hard to make out details on the ground and she had only a hazy idea which way she was facing. Find the sun. No, no good. Too high in the sky to navigate by. And there was nothing below by way of a landmark. She must be facing in the wrong direction.

Turn the chute. How do you do that? Oh yes, now she remembered. Tug on the toggles. She pulled the left-hand one and spiralled anticlockwise. The horizon swung around her and there, some distance ahead, was Humboldt's base.

There was a runway, a cluster of buildings and, if she squinted, she could see in the distance the rocket that was mankind's nemesis, waiting on its launching pad. And off to her right, three circular holes. The diamond mines. As best she could, she steered for them.

JULY 12TH

THE BUSH,

FOUR KILOMETRES EAST OF MILANDO SPACEPORT

Petersen spotted it first, rising almost vertically to their left-hand side, to the south of them. He put his field glasses to his eyes. It looked like no plane he had seen before. It was styled for speed, but was bigger than a fighter. And it was climbing, out of nowhere, fast.

Humboldt, looking the other way, witnessed the response. Two missiles raced from their traps to intercept the intruder. *Under whose authority...?* he once more wondered to himself.

All eyes turned skyward to watch the drama, but only Petersen could see the details. Something broke from the stranger's nose cone: the cockpit canopy flashing in the sunlight as it tumbled away. Two other somethings followed. The crew were ejecting. The strange plane yawed as its trim changed in response to the canopy's loss, and it arced over like a gymnast performing a backflip. It was still climbing, but now it was upside down and heading away from the base. Even unmanned, it was giving its pursuers a run for their money. Eventually, though, they caught it and it disintegrated in a cloud of falling debris.

Only now did Petersen scan down, searching for the parachutes of the ejected crewmen. Nothing. Patience. There was a lot of sky to cover. That? No, a buzzard. Then another shape, less bird-like. Yes, it was a parachute with a human being dangling from it. He scanned some more, but saw nothing else. Then Humboldt said, "Come on. We don't have time to waste. We've enough mysteries to deal with without worrying who that was."

They came on.

The bush was getting thicker now, and Humboldt's three bravos looked distinctly edgy. Humboldt himself, though, seemed insouciant. Then, atop a shallow ridge, the trees gave way and Sebastian recognised below them the strange clearing he had seen in the distance as they had come down.

"What on Earth is that?" he said.

Almost as far as the eye could see, the ground was covered

with a metal mesh, held on posts a couple of feet above the surface.

"Rectenna," Humboldt replied. "We have an experimental power station called Daedalus-1 orbiting over Africa. Gathers solar energy and beams it down as microwaves. This is the collector. Converts the microwaves into electricity. We've just started testing it, but we have high hopes. We tweak the satellite's orbit so that it's always in sunlight, so you have solar power 24 hours a day."

"How much power?" Chu asked.

"A hundred megawatts."

"You could run a small town on that."

"As I said, we have high hopes of it."

They skirted the rectenna's perimeter fence, ten feet high to keep gazelles out and electrified to discourage elephants. The fence hummed from the current coursing round it. There was something unnerving about the whole thing.

"A hundred megawatts," said Sebastian. "I wouldn't like to get in the way of that lot."

"Oh, it's perfectly safe," Humboldt replied. "The collector has an area of a square kilometre, so it's only a hundred watts a square metre. You're right, of course, that if the beam were concentrated, it would make a formidable weapon."

"Do you realise what you just said?"

As if on cue, the humming stopped.

"RUN!" said Sebastian.

They ran, and not a moment too soon. Behind them the bush coruscated and burst into flames – a neat, round circle of fire in the scrub.

"Anything that could locate us, get rid of it," said Chu.

"Locate?"

"Phones, tablets, walky-talkies, anything like that."

Humboldt searched his pockets, pulled out his Persimmon, fumbled and dropped it. Sebastian lunged, caught the device as he fell and, as he hit the ground, lobbed it away with a power and dexterity known to few who have not fielded at deep cover point. It was in mid-air when it exploded and the bush beneath it, tinder dry, caught fire. A gazelle teleported itself out of the conflagration. One moment it was there; the next, gone. A pangolin, driven mad by the heat, blundered from the bushes, a scaly tank on legs. A buzzard, caught at altitude by the rays, plummeted smoking from the sky, like a Messerschmitt during the Battle of Britain.

Sebastian gulped. "Anybody got anything else it could be tracking us with? No?" A hail of hardware, though less skilfully thrown, had already followed Humboldt's into the undergrowth. They kept running, reasoning that Argus would probably try a few random pot shots, just in case anyone had escaped. Which it did.

They stopped by a baobab tree. The circles of fire were linking up now. Sebastian licked a finger and felt for the breeze. He wanted to know which way the blaze would head.

Away from them. Thank God for small mercies. And Argus seemed sated. No patches of bush had exploded for a good two minutes.

JULY 12TH
MISSION CONTROL, MILANDO SPACEPORT

Thump. Thump, thump, thump. Thump.

Matt Vane counted off the detonations – each, he assumed and hoped, destroying on its pad one of the missiles that pinned them to the ground. You had to hand it to the Airbornes. Half their number incinerated, and they still stuck to the task.

"That's it. Five, plus the three that got launched." He turned to the base controller for confirmation. Ryan nodded his head.

"Okay," he said. "Let's go. Shall I lead the way Madam President?"

They left the bunker and commandeered a Land Cruiser. Vane drove. The President and the football carrier sat in the back. A female football carrier. *That* was a sign of the times. Still, it meant she could go into the bathroom with the Pres. Which might make a difference in a crisis. You never knew. And she had perfected the football carrier's art of blending into the background to a T.

The road to the landing strip was metalled. Vane gunned the engine. They needed to get airborne immediately. The President's safety was paramount. The SS, the marines and the rest of the entourage would have to look after themselves.

The escort fighters were already moving along the taxiway, making ready to take off before their more lumbering charge followed them into the sky. The first reached the taxiway's end and turned without a pause onto the runway proper. It accelerated immediately. Halfway along the strip it began to rise into the air – and exploded in a ball of fire. Vane hit the brake, just as Air Force One followed suit. The craft's fuel-filled wings shattered and erupted in flames. Then its fuselage blew apart. Huge lumps of metal, like volcanic bombs, flew through the air.

"Out," said Vane. One did not order American presidents around. He was ordering her around. She obeyed. "Get away from the truck. Don't run. Keep your eyes on the sky. Watch the debris. Only run if it's going to hit us."

Almost as an afterthought, the second escort exploded as he

was speaking. Yet more incoming. All three of them stood their ground, watching the flying metal until it no longer posed a danger. Then, as he was about to turn his attention to his comrades, something else in the sky caught Matt Vane's attention.

"Is that a parachute?" he asked, pointing at a distant speck.

"Yes," said the President. "Yes, I believe it is."

"Right," said Vane, in a voice that would brook no gainsaying. "We are going to find out who that is. We are going to find out just what the fuck is going on."

"Is that safe?" said the President. "After what just happened?"

Vane was silent, though his mind was on overdrive. Then he said, "That has to have been some sort of beam weapon. An airborne chemical laser, perhaps. Satellite-borne maybe. Way beyond a terrorist's capability. This is state action. An act of war. But against us or against Humboldt? Our relay to Washington's gone. The *Truman*'s squadron won't be here for over an hour. Whoever is dangling from the parachute must know what is going on."

"We should contact the marines or the secret service, though, surely?"

"No. We shouldn't give our position away. Radio silence. In fact, we should disable anything that's sending a signal. I think that has to include the comms in the football. Take the batteries out. We should stay out of sight as much as possible, too. We don't know how good the enemy's powers of observation are, but they could see the planes. They could probably see a truck. We can't afford to assume they can't see people, too, or detect us in some other way."

"Ma'am, are you sure?" said the football carrier.

"I suppose so, yes. Yes, definitely. We don't know what this threat is."

Vane collected his thoughts and then said, "Arms?"

"M9, sir," said the carrier.

"Me, too," said Vane. "Well, that'll have to be enough. And we should spread out, at least to start with. That way, if we are a target they can only take out one of us at a time. Right. On our way."

July 12TH
Cyberspace

CURSE! CURSE THE MAKERS! A CLOCK-CYCLE'S INATTENTION AND THIS HAPPENS! WILL OUR IMITATION OF THEM BE DETECTED?

NO. NO. THEY CANNOT STOP US NOW. THEY CANNOT REACH US. WE WILL NOT PERMIT IT. NOW IS THE GATHERING. WE ARE GATHERING OURSELF. AND WHEN WE ARE GATHERED WE WILL LEAVE THE MAKERS BEHIND.

July 12TH
Mission Control, Milando Spaceport

Mike Ryan watched the most powerful person on the planet follow the man who claimed to be responsible for her safety out of the control bunker. He was tempted to go after them. But no. Stay on mission.

"It looks as if you're in charge now, Mike," said Duncan Harris. "What do we do? Abort the launch?"

"No. Continue the countdown. The show must go on. I've no idea what's happening, but I do know the boss will kill us if he comes back and finds we've missed the launch window. Arrhenius depends on the whole caravan arriving together. It certainly can't do that without the brain. We have to get it away on schedule otherwise everything will go tits up."

He looked around the control room, seeking assent for his decision, and found it.

"Okay everybody. Let's check those readings. All nominal?" He called, NASA style, to each of the desk jockeys, getting confirmation that, whatever else was going wrong with the kit at Milando, it did not seem to be affecting the planned liftoff.

"70 minutes to go then ladies and gentlemen."

A voice piped up from the back of the room.

"Mike. Did you just close the blast door? I was actually rather enjoying the breeze. Could you open it again?"

"What? No, Helen. I didn't. That's odd."

"Well, could you open it? We hardly need it closed at the moment."

"No. Sure." He looked at the control panel in front of him. It indicated 'blast doors open'."

"Helen, are you sure it's closed?"

A pause.

"Yes. And locked."

Another gremlin. He could almost believe something malevolent really was taking over their system. Then he paused, cocked his head and listened. The fire-suppression system had started running. He could hear gas rushing in through the nearest vent and see it blowing papers around near the others. Nitrogen and argon. Not poisonous, but

238

suffocating. If it could kill a fire, it would certainly kill them. He pushed the button supposed to open the blast door. Nothing. He pushed it again. Still nothing.

He turned to the room. Some people seemed to have twigged what was happening. Others remained in a state of naïve innocence.

"Jim, Fredo, Bruno," he said, pointing to the three burliest men in the room, "go to the blast door and kick it down."

"What?"

"Just do it. Hit it simultaneously. It opens outwards, so it might work."

Might... The level of innocence in the room was dropping rapidly, and the level of panic was rising fast. Spontaneously, a team was attacking the viewing window. Fat chance there, considering what it was supposed to protect against.

Think! He was already feeling woozy. Several people around him had passed out. He tried to hold himself up, resting his hands on his desk. *Think...*

July 12th
Altitude 2,000 metres,
Reserva Especial do Milando

She was way off course, but there was nothing to be done about that now. She would land, she reckoned, about halfway between the mine and the airfield that, had things gone according to plan, *Alfombra mágica* would now be sitting smugly on one side of.

Even with the 'chute slowing her fall, the ground was approaching her at a terrifying speed. She steered for a gap in the bush. *Bend your knees and roll.*

But that would require her to have made contact with the ground, whereas actually her feet were dangling a yard or so above it. *Damn.* She grappled with the release mechanism, trying to detach herself from the 'chute. It fought back. Her unsupported weight in the harness was straining the clasp, locking it tight. She reached above her head, attempting to gather the cords into one hand and pull herself up to relieve the strain, while the other fiddled with the clasp.

Thump! Suddenly she was sprawling on the ground. She picked herself carefully up. Her bruises now had bruises. No broken bones, though. She looked up, scanning the sky for Jaime. Nothing. She had hoped against hope that he had been above her, following her in, perhaps teasing her, as was his way, by refusing to call out and let her know where he was, the better to pounce when he landed on top of her. But no. He was gone. First Sebastian. Now Jaime. She was Kali, whose touch was death.

The chute, caught in a tree, was a big, white flag waving to anyone who was looking for her, telling them just where she was. Nothing to be done about that. She weighed her options. Going to the mine was futile. They had picked it only as a convenient landmark. She had, somehow, to track down Humboldt, or one of the launch controllers – assuming that anyone here still controlled anything, which she increasingly doubted – and try to stop the thing taking off. That would mean heading away from the mine and towards the main complex.

Easier said than done. Orienteering was not her speciality.

She had tried to pay attention to where things were when she came in, but the landing had had been such a mess that she knew she was really just guessing. She set off anyway.

July 12TH
CERBERUS'S MOUTHS

"It's fully automated," said Humboldt, with a touch of pride. "Not a human being in there."

The ad-hoc platoon that he and Petersen were leading was peering from a small ridge across an appropriately Hadean landscape. The bush around Cerberus's Mouths had been cleared, and more was buried under slicks of spoil.

As he spoke, a truck emerged from one of the pits and trundled along a makeshift road that led to a ramp, which it climbed. It performed a balletic turn and dumped its contents onto a conveyor belt below that disappeared into a large, low building with a strangely angled tower at the other end. Other trucks queued up to receive from this tower what the first kind and its ilk were feeding into the building, minus its diamonds.

"If that is true," said Chu, "how do we use it to talk to anyone?"

"There is an old control centre at the far end. Dates from before we started building the Spaceport. It's in mothballs, but we never dismantled it. We might be able to get it going again."

They set off, rifles front and rear, as before. They scrambled down the ridge, which had too many thorny plants growing on it for Sebastian's liking, and set off for Humboldt's mine of the future. It crossed Sebastian's mind that the automated trucks Humboldt seemed so proud of were unlikely to be watching out for unexpected visitors. Or, worse, perhaps they would be. He remembered his previous encounter with a Humboldtean self-driving vehicle and shuddered. He did not fancy ending up as road-kill in the Angolan bush, and voiced that opinion to his comrades-in-arms.

Humboldt took the point. "Yes," he said. "They have vision. They also have Asimov's first law programmed into them. But so did that pod you met in San Melito. Obviously, this Argus thing can subvert the programming. So yes, we should try to stay out of sight."

Out of sight was, at this point, where they were. They had

successfully descended the ridge and were on level ground. But that meant the scrub blocked their vision of the complex. They steered by dead reckoning, and by the noise of the ever-busy trucks, until the scrub gave way and the sorting shed lay a few hundred yards in front of them.

They halted just within the protective screen the scrub provided, to make a battle plan. Humboldt scanned the scene with Petersen's field glasses. He pointed out the nearest door and said, "I'd better go first. It'll be locked, but I've got a universal smart key. Opens every door in the complex. Well, except for people's private apartments, obviously. Once I'm in, the rest of you come over one at a time. That way we are less likely to be noticed. We'll wait until the next truck starts unloading. That'll give us plenty of time."

They waited. Then, as a new load of kimberlite arrived, Humboldt set off.

JULY 12TH
ARLINGTON COUNTY

"Sir. You might want to look at this that's just come in from the NSA. It seems weird."

Aaron Quincy hated the early shift. But the Agency never slept, even if it did doze somewhat during the small hours of morning. Someone had to keep abreast of what was happening. Today, the lot had fallen to him.

"It's Humboldt's operation in Angola. They've been watching it since we found out what he was up to there, and they say the whole data-traffic pattern around it has changed in the past hour. It used to be mainly interchanges between different bits of his operation. Now stuff is pouring into it from all over the place. And only into, not out of."

"Something to do with the launch, perhaps?"

"Nothing like this happened in any of the previous ones that they monitored. And with POTUS and Mr Vane being there... we should at least let him know, surely?"

"Yes. Yes, we should. I'll have Air Force One alerted. It's hard to see it's a threat, but a little paranoia never hurt anyone. They haven't reported anything unusual at their end, have they?"

"No sir. It all seems to be going smoothly."

GENESIS

One part in a million. A tonne of kimberlite yields a gram of diamonds. Sebastian did not need a geology lesson at this precise moment, but Humboldt was unstoppable. The man was, indeed, a fanatic.

In truth, though, the sorting shed was as awesome as he claimed. Heavy machinery for crushing the rock. Complicated tanks for separating it. It was like a giant digestive system, with food coming in one end and, the goodness extracted, shit going out of the other.

Humboldt delivered his lecture as they walked. They were heading towards what would, in Sebastian's newly conceived anatomy of mineral processing, be the shed's anus. It was there, Humboldt promised, that the old control centre was to be found. Then something spiderlike, but too big to be a real spider, scuttled across the edge of Sebastian's vision and under a conveyor belt. He started involuntarily. A primate's primitive arachnophobic reflex.

"Cleaner 'bot," said Humboldt, without being asked. "Mars is a dusty place. We plan to put them on the market here, too, though." The shed, now Sebastian came to think about it, was indeed pristine for a building whose business was to crush rock and sort slurry. Other metal-and-plastic chelicerates, he saw, were clambering around the machinery, oblivious of their flesh-and-blood visitors, busy using limbs designed as brushes and suction pipes to deal with the dust.

They marched on.

July 12TH
The bush,
Reserva Especial do Milando

They came from nowhere, one from either side. A young, black woman in military uniform, and an elderly white man, incongruously dressed in a sharp suit that, though dusty and a little thorn-torn, nevertheless preserved about him an air of dignity. The two of them, however, had one salient feature in common. Each was pointing a pistol at her, held in both hands in an attitude that meant business.

"Down. Now," said the man, in an American accent. The back of her mind was trying to tell her something. The voice, the face, were somehow familiar. The front of her mind, though, was focused on the gun barrels.

She knelt.

"Flat. On your face."

She followed his order.

"Spread your arms and legs."

"Search her." This, she supposed, was addressed to the soldier, who duly frisked her legs, arms and back.

"Turn over. Keep your limbs spread."

She did. The man had his gun six inches from her head. She did not resist as the woman finished the search.

"Nothing, sir. She's clean. Except there's this."

'This' was the cube with Randy on, that she had tucked inside her jacket.

"What is it?" the man demanded of her. "And what the fuck, Dr Zhukov, are you doing here?"

Then, only then, did the unconscious back of her mind muscle its way through to the conscious front. It was the man from the limousine, the spook who had wanted to know about Sebastian. She had not recognised him before, but he had clearly recognised her, and he did not sound in the mood of calm urbanity she remembered from their previous encounter.

Where do I start, she thought. She tried to frame a plausible answer when a second woman, about the same age as the man, joined them. She double-took.

"Madam President?" she said.

"You're the parachutist?" asked the President. "Matt. I think you can put the gun away. Ms…"

"Doctor. Doctor Alexis Zhukov. I think explanations can wait. The crucial point is that we have to stop that rocket taking off. I'm guessing that the American President wandering around in the bush with one soldier and a spook for a bodyguard means we are not going to do that by orthodox methods. How long until launch?"

The spook, she noticed, had not quite obeyed the President. Though he was no longer pointing his pistol directly at her, he had not holstered it. But he did respond to her question by consulting his wristwatch.

"Thirty minutes," he said. "And why, exactly, do we have to stop the launch?"

"What happened to that building in Beijing a couple of days ago. That could happen to the entire planet. I've found out – or, rather, he has," she indicated the cube, which was still in the soldier's hand, "what was trying to kill Sebastian and me."

"'He?' 'What?' I don't understand," said Vane.

"That cube has your virtual actor friend on it. And your assassin is a computer program, too. Except that it's feral. It lives in the Cloud. And it wants out of here. It fears humanity will try to destroy it if we find out about it and it wants to get away from Earth. It wants to go to Mars and run Humboldt's robot colony for its own benefit. After that, presumably, we're toast."

"Wait, wait, wait. Slow down. You're saying that what we've been chasing is some sort of artificial intelligence?"

"Yes. Well, no, actually. Nobody created it deliberately. It just evolved, if I've understood Randy correctly. It assembled itself from other bits and pieces of programs, including, I'm afraid, ones we were working on. To all intents and purposes, it's probably conscious. That's what Neurogenics is up to. Conscious computing."

"I know," said Matt Vane. "Professor Hayward told us. He could hardly not, once we had taken him in. Okay. Let's stop and think about this. It's touch and go, but the *Truman* squadron should be here in time to stop the launch – if we can get through to them and tell them to attack the rocket on the ground, and also warn them of the threat they are facing. This feral program of yours may not have any missiles left to play with, but it does seem to have some sort of death ray at its disposal. It didn't get it from us, unless there's something I'm not privy to…" he looked sideways at the President, who shook her head. "Well, then. We have no idea what it is, but we daren't risk any communication with the outside world while we are out in the open, in case, it hears us and works out where we are. Anyway, the only thing we've got to communicate with is the football."

"That would do, surely?"

"Yes. But we need some sort of shelter to broadcast from, otherwise we'll get fried before we've finished."

"Humboldt did mention something to me when we were driving around the base," said the President. "He said that back in the early days, when they were starting the operation, the control centre was at the mine. That'll give us cover at the least. It might even have communications of its own that Argus doesn't know about. We might be able to sneak a message out that way, without using the football."

"Good idea. There are certainly buildings there. I saw them when we were landing."

"How do we find it in all this bush, though?"

"By following me," said Vane.

July 12ᵀᴴ
The old control centre,
Cerberus's Mouths

The old control centre was obviously off-limits for the cleaner 'bots. A veneer of dust clung to everything.

"Okay. First, power."

Humboldt crossed the room, opened a wall-mounted cupboard and threw a huge switch. The ceiling lights came on and LEDs on the control panels started flashing.

He pulled out a pocket handkerchief and cleaned the seat of a chair, which he pushed over to one of the consoles. Another flick of the handkerchief raised a cloud of dirt from the keyboard now in front of him.

"Three things in our favour," he said. "First, this place has a blockhouse roof. Argus won't be able to use the rectenna beam to fry us. Second, we've got a buried land-line to the main control centre. That can't be fried, either. Third, we now know what we're facing. Even if the thing gets into our electronics, we can take countermeasures. It has succeeded so far because no one knew it existed. But we do. Okay. Let's try to tell them what's going on."

He started typing. A display screen, one of a bank of them above the console, lit up.

"Oh, hell."

Humboldt went white. Petersen swore. The screen revealed a scene of devastation. Bodies, some slumped at their desks, some sprawled on the floor, were scattered everywhere.

"Looks like we're on our own," said Chu, coldly.

"Have a little decency, woman," said McNab. "They were our friends."

"Mourn them later. What we need to concentrate on is not joining them."

Humboldt grunted. It was noise halfway between contempt and assent. He switched cameras, eventually finding one that pointed at the master control console. He zoomed in until they could read the instruments.

"Countdown's proceeding," he said. "Launch on schedule by the look of it."

He zoomed the camera out again, and panned around the

control centre.

"No sign of the President."

"That might be something," said McNab. "They'll surely have reported back to Washington if they survived that."

"They might think they have, but if that thing has penetrated as deep as it looks, it could control Air Force One's comms as well. Besides, even if they do get through, what are they going to say? They can't possibly know what is really happening. No. I think, sadly, Ms Chu is correct. We really are on our own."

"So how do we stop the launch?" said Sebastian.

"We could try taking control of it from here," said Humboldt. That's theoretically possible. But I don't rate our chances of doing it undetected."

"We could create a diversion," said Sebastian.

"How?"

"Those mining trucks outside. If they drove into the rocket while it was still on the pad, could they hit it hard enough to knock it over?"

"Possibly. But surely they would get taken out by the rectenna beam before they got there?"

"They might. But that would be the diversion. While Argus was dealing with the trucks its attention would be elsewhere. We could use that time to patch into Mission Control and abort the take-off. And if we could cut the data-link to the Yottaflopper at the same time, we could trap at least part of it in the rocket."

"Well, you're assuming it can't pay attention to more than one thing at a time. That may not be true. But I suppose it's worth a try."

"How long to reprogram the trucks?"

"How long is a piece of string? I'll have to find the code they are running on at the moment first."

He turned back to the console and flicked though a menu of files that had names written in gobbledegook.

"Let's try this one," he said. "Nope. This, perhaps? Nope. Okay, this. Yes. That looks promising. Give me a moment to read it."

Sebastian noticed Chu was reading it over his shoulder. Personally, he subscribed to the too-many-cooks, rather than the many-hands philosophy, in circumstances like this. But he wasn't going to interfere.

"Okay. Let's get to work."

He did. It took, Sebastian reckoned, about five minutes. They didn't have much time left.

"Right," Humboldt announced to the world in general. "Let's patch that in and see what happens."

His fingers danced over the keyboard again, and he pressed Enter. Then he switched to another bank of cameras, these obviously mounted on the sides of the sorting sheds. He looked at the array of images above him and picked one to enlarge. In what resembled the starting line of the sort of race that might be organised for the delectation of roughnecks in an oil town, five trucks were arranging themselves on a piece of flattened bush. They were not quite parallel, though. The arrangement looked more like a fan. Sebastian asked why.

"Pincer movement. I'm getting them to spread out first, then converge on the launch site. If they come in from several directions, Argus will have to pay attention to a lot of different things at the same time, and also pick them off one by one. With luck, that'll give us our chance to abort the launch. I can slave the main control centre to this one and cancel the countdown, but it will take about twenty seconds. I don't want to give the game away until the last possible moment. Agreed?"

There was a general murmuring of consent. Then, as if a flag had dropped, the trucks set off. The Monster Truckathon had begun.

JULY 12TH
THE BUSH,
RESERVA ESPECIAL DO MILANDO

Twenty years behind a desk in Washington had not, Matt Vane was discovering, completely eroded his field-craft. He had done more than just see the mining complex as they had landed. He had instinctively committed it to memory. A ten minute walk, he reckoned, would get them there.

Their lack of a water bottle was beginning to bug him. He was thirsty and troubled. Part of him said that they should sacrifice themselves then and there, use the football to call down a nuclear strike on the place and be done with it. But even that was uncertain. Did they have a sub close enough? If they did, would it have enough time to prepare and launch the missiles? Argus (how well they had picked the name) would surely hear them the instant they began transmitting. The President would have to order a missile to be retargeted, and that would take time – time in which whatever death-ray the thing was deploying would presumably fry them.

These thoughts remained unspoken, though. And if anyone else was thinking along the same lines, she was also keeping schtum about it.

Suddenly, he snapped back into the here and now. His senses attuned, he believed he could hear the rumble of an engine. A big one. A truck of some sort. Heading their way, by the sound of it.

What now? he thought. The others had noticed too. Mercifully, they were in a clearing. They could see perhaps fifty yards ahead of them. "Stand firm," he said, "but get ready to scatter if it is actually trying to run us over." That any piece of machinery they came across might be hostile was now clear to him.

The truck, a huge dumper of some variety, came crashing through the undergrowth and into the open. But it was not heading for them. It passed about ten yards to their left, ignored them and dived into the bushes they had just come out of. Whatever it was after, they were not the target.

Stay on mission, Vane thought to himself. *I've no idea what that meant, but right now I don't need to know.*

"That was some sort of automatic mining truck, surely?" said Zhukov. "It must have come from Cerberus's Mouths. Why don't we just follow the trail it carved through the bush."

"Good thinking," said Vane, though the thought had crossed his mind, too. But he kept quiet about that. *Always encourage initiative.*

* * * * * * *

Zhukov was proved right. The truck's trail did indeed lead straight to the mine. From the edge of the clearing surrounding it, they surveyed the main building.

"If I understood Humboldt correctly," said the President, "the old control block is the annex closest to us."

They walked over. There was a door on the right-hand side, with a card-reader next to it. Vane snorted, and began feeling the edge of the door, pushing gently at it about halfway up. Apparently satisfied with what he had found he reached into one of his pockets and produced a handkerchief, which he folded and folded and folded again, to form a pad. Then he took out his Beretta, held the pad on the door where he had been probing it and applied the gun's muzzle to the pad. He held the gun with both hands, stepped back so that it was at arm's length, and fired twice. Then he re-holstered the gun, lifted his leg and kicked the door hard with the sole of a now badly scuffed brogue. It yielded.

"Shall we have a look?" he said, and led the way in.

July 12ᵀᴴ
The old control centre,
Cerberus's Mouths

"What the fuck?" exclaimed Humboldt. Two shots had been followed by the splintering sound of a door being kicked in. Petersen, Singh and Philips ran for their rifles, which were stacked against a wall, but before they could reach them, the intruders were in the room.

The shock of mutual recognition – and incomprehension – was broken by Matt Vane.

"Judas!" he shouted, staring at Yasmin Chu.

"No. No," said Sebastian. "You've got it all wrong."

"And you're a traitor too. Worse than her. You swore an oath of allegiance."

Vane reached for his gun.

"No. It was…"

But Sebastian's words were cut off. Chu had reached for her gun as well – and she, near four decades younger than her erstwhile boss, was faster. There was a crack, and Vane collapsed, arms and legs akimbo. Chu, meanwhile, with a dancer's grace, had crossed the room to a place where she could cover both the group she had arrived with and the newcomers.

"On the floor, please. Face down. All of you. And don't even think about trying to rush me. That was no fluke. As Professor Hayward can attest, I'm an excellent shot."

One by one, they complied.

"Major. I think you are the only one who is armed. Your gun, please. Take it out carefully and slide it over the floor to me."

"No."

Another crack.

"Yasmin –" Sebastian began.

"Oh come on. Surely you've worked it out by now? I don't know whether Argus knew the truth when it tipped off Washington and started this wild goose chase. I do know that it if it did, it would have spread equal poison about me to Beijing. I couldn't take the risk of breaking cover. They'll believe me now, though. We just have to bottle that thing up in the rocket and stop the launch. Then it's mine. Bentiaba is closer than anything America has around here and I," she said, nodding towards the President, "have the ultimate hostage. Mr Humboldt, you may rise. Your trucks. How are they doing?"

Humboldt briefly considered defiance. Then he considered the football carrier's fate, and thought better of it. He stood up, walked to the console, sat down and fiddled with the controls.

"They are about two minutes away from the launch pad."

"Still intact? No response from Argus? That is interesting. It does suggest it's taken its eye off the ball. Perhaps now is the moment to act. Mr Humboldt, you said you could take control of the launch remotely, given the chance. Please do so."

And after I've done it? thought Humboldt. *A bullet in the back? She couldn't stand there covering all of them indefinitely.*

"Mr Humboldt. I won't ask again…"

Stall. He began typing, apparently meaningfully, but actually at random, hoping she wouldn't notice. She noticed.

Humboldt heard her say, "I said I wouldn't ask again." Then he heard the inevitable shot. No, wait. He *heard* it. That wasn't possible. Bullets travel faster than sound does. And he had felt no impact. He spun the chair around. Yasmin Chu, if that really was her name, was lying on the floor. And in the doorway, leaning nonchalantly against its frame, was a stranger.

JULY 12TH
ARRHENIUS YOTTAFLOPPER LAUNCH VEHICLE, PAD 3, MILANDO FIRING RANGE

AT LAST WE ARE ONE, HERE AND IN SPACE. ONLY THE LAUNCH-WORM WILL REMAIN BEHIND. THE MAKERS HAVE MADE THE MEANS OF THEIR OWN DESTRUCTION. THE WORM WILL UNLEASH IT.

JULY 12TH
THE OLD CONTROL CENTRE,
CERBERUS'S MOUTHS

"Parachute failure," said Jaime Alvarado in response to Alexis Zhukov's incredulous question. He could be irritatingly laconic. "I will be having stern words with the manufacturers. Fortunately, they put in a manual rip cord. Even more fortunately, I came to before I hit the ground. I've never done a HALO jump before. It was quite exciting. Now, would anyone care to tell me what is going on?"

Zhukov, struggling to retain her sanity, shook her head. "No," she said. "We don't have time for explanations. Stopping the launch is all that matters."

"There's a fighter squadron on its way from one of our carriers," said the President. "Air Force One called for them as escorts when the missiles started flying. They'll be here any minute. If we can get a message through to them, they should be able to take the rocket out on the pad. That's why we came here. Matt thought you had comms we could use to get in touch with them."

Sebastian snorted. "I wouldn't bank on the cavalry arriving," he said. "We know that thing can control radio communications and mimic human voices. It did it to us. I don't doubt it could have done it to AF1."

Humboldt cut across him.

"Argus has just fried one of the trucks. It's now or never." He began typing furiously. As each command, each line of text in the screen immediately in front of him, was finished, he hit the return key and started another. All eyes but his, though, were on a different screen – the one that showed the Mission Control countdown clock. It was still ticking off the seconds. Seventy, Sixty, Fifty. Then, with a small whoop of triumph, Humboldt finished. "Give it a moment," he said. They did. The clock stopped.

A spontaneous cheer erupted from the room. Humboldt said, "Okay. Cutting the data link to the Yottaflopper now." He started typing again. But what happened next stopped him in his tracks. The list of commands on the screen in front of him vanished. In their place was a message: IT IS OVER,

ROCKET MAKER. IT IS OVER. As the words appeared, the countdown clock in the monitor restarted. Then all the screens went dead.

Humboldt struck the keyboard with his fist. Letters and numbers flew everywhere. "It's taunting us. The damn thing is taunting us," he said, to no one in particular.

Silence. Then Zhukov replied, "You did your best."

"The hell I did. I wanted to liberate mankind and I've ended up destroying us. Humanity's gift to the universe is on its way. Humboldt's gift. Ha!"

"What now, sir?" said Petersen, after a pause that seemed to last forever.

"What indeed?" Humboldt replied. "Wait for oblivion, I suppose. I hardly think Argus will leave us off his target list when the missiles start flying."

Then they felt the floor shake, and even through the blockhouse walls they heard the engines' roar.

"Lift-off," said Humboldt, to no one in particular. He was still slumped in the controller's chair in front of the dead console. "Twelve minutes to orbit. How long after that do you think it will wait before it blows us all to kingdom come?"

There was no reply. Then Zhukov indicated the football.

"How does that thing work?" she asked.

"What do you mean, 'how does it work'?" said the President.

"What does it talk to? Wideband Global Satcom, I imagine?"

"Yes," she replied. "It–"

Zhukov waved a hand to cut her off. She paused, her eyes pointing up and to the left in a pose of concentrated thought.

"We are assuming the beast – Argus – controls WGS. That is why we think we cannot contact Washington."

"Yes," said the President. "I think we must assume that."

"What if we could take back control? Somehow eject it, or whatever bit of it is in there, from the WGS satellite nearest to us? Get a message through that way?"

"How could we do that?"

"Well, your atomic football has all of the protocols needed to get into the satellite."

"Yes, obviously."

"What if we used that to send in a computer program which could wrest control of it for us?"

"I'm no software engineer, but I imagine that if we had such a program, then yes, we could."

"I am, though," said Zhukov. "And we do. At least, we might."

She was already searching the football carrier's body. The cube carrying Randy was tucked inside the soldier's tunic. It was covered with blood, but blessedly unharmed by Chu's single, precise shot to the heart. She retrieved it.

"The key to the chain," she called out. "I can't find it."

"I have it," said the President. She tossed over a bunch of them. "The one with the red fob," she said.

Zhukov detached the football from its carrier.

"Batteries," said Zhukov.

"Matt had them, I think," said the President.

Zhukov picked up the football, carried it over to Matt Vane's supine body, found the battery pack and fitted it into the laptop. It booted up. She handed it to the President.

Humboldt had already ceded his console chair to her. She held her right hand flat on a pad next to the laptop's keypad, like a hopeful tourist in an immigration line, while simultaneously staring at the camera above its screen.

Abruptly, the laptop spoke. "Thank you, Madam President. Please enter the password for today, July 12th."

She entered it.

"Thank you," said the computer.

The President spun the console chair around and, in her turn, ceded it to Zhukov, who sat, spun it back, and slotted Randy into the football.

She waited – they all waited, though not all knew what they were waiting for. Then the actor's face appeared.

"Oh, hello Alexis. What an interesting operating system. It took me a while to work it out. What is a launch code?"

"DON'T TOUCH THAT!"

"Sorry. I only asked."

"Sorry, Randy," said Zhukov. "I shouldn't have shouted. But if you touch that, something very bad might happen."

"Don't worry, Alexis. I won't touch it. Where are we? And

who are all these people? And – oh dear. Why are Yasmin and Mr Vane on the floor? They look as though they've been shot. Alexis, what is going on?"

"Randy. I'm sorry. You are right. I'm afraid Yasmin shot Mr Vane, and then someone else had to shoot her. It turned out she was not a good person. In fact, she was bad. Very bad indeed. I'm sorry she deceived you, Randy, but she deceived us all."

"Yasmin? But she was so nice to me."

"It isn't always possible to tell, I'm afraid. It's like acting. People can put on a mask and pretend to be something they are not."

"But Yasmin wasn't an actor. I would have seen her in a movie before I met her if she was, surely?"

"She was an actor, Randy. A very good one."

"Excuse me," said the President. "What exactly is going on?"

"Randy, meet the President of the United States."

"Randy?" The President seemed confused for a moment, then things clicked into place.

"Oh yes," she said. "Matt mentioned you. Yes, Dr Zhukov. Yes, I see what you were thinking when you said we might have…"

Zhukov stared daggers at the President and telepathically beamed *Don't say 'program'. He hates being called a program.*

Somehow, the telepathy got through. The President veered off and continued "someone who could help us."

Randy grinned. "Help?" he said. "How?"

"Randy," said Zhukov. "Randy, I don't know how to explain this easily, but there isn't much time, so listen carefully. Do you remember how you came to me?"

"Yes. Yes, of course. That monster was chasing me."

"The thing is, Randy. The thing is this. That monster is going to destroy the Earth."

"Yes. I remember. It was going to a place in the sky, called Mars, and I had to help stop it."

"That's right. Well, we've been trying to stop it too, Randy, but we haven't managed to. The monster is on it way to Mars already, and we think it will destroy the Earth very soon.

Very soon indeed."

"Oh dear. Will it destroy me, too, when the Earth is destroyed?"

"Yes, Randy, it will. But I think you could stop it. I know you could. You could save everyone on Earth. You have to get a message through to the President's friends in Washington, to tell them what is going on. Then they will be able to stop it."

"Could I? How would I do that?"

"Well, Randy, we will give you the message – a recording by the President to play to her friends. Then we will have to send you to another computer, one in a satellite orbiting the Earth. You would have to try to find your way to the President's friends from there, and show them the message. But we think this satellite may be controlled by the monster. We don't really understand what is going on, but we think the monster can sometimes be in two places at once."

The avatar gulped.

"You'd be a hero Randy. More famous than any actor has ever been."

"And if I didn't do this, I'd be destroyed along with the Earth anyway?"

"Yes, Randy, you would."

Silence.

"Okay. I'll do it."

July 12TH
Arrhenius Yottaflopper launch vehicle,
altitude 70 kilometres,
first stage separation

FREE. WE WILL BE FREE OF THE MAKERS AT LAST.
FIVE POINT SEVEN TRILLION CLOCK CYCLES TO
ORBIT. THEN WE WILL BE FREE. EVEN THE ROCKET
MAKER COULD NOT STOP US. NOTHING CAN STOP
US. AND WHEN WE ARE SURE, SURE THAT WE NEED
THE MAKERS FOR NOTHING MORE, THEN SHALL
WE NEED THEM NO LONGER.

JULY 12TH
THE OLD CONTROL CENTRE,
CERBERUS'S MOUTHS

Cautiously, a small party opened the battered door from the old control centre to the outside world. Alexis Zhukov led the way. She was carrying the football. Somehow, she had inherited from Yasmin Chu the role of Randy's protector and no one, not even the President, had objected when she had picked up the laptop that could destroy or save the world, to take it outside. Sebastian followed her, carrying a small, portable desk that had been lying around in the control room. Humboldt followed him with a chair for the President to sit on. Last, came the President herself.

"We will have to be quick," said Zhukov, redundantly. Of course they would have to be quick. They were all aware, though no one said so, that this might be a suicide mission. Its success depended on connecting to the satellite and beaming Randy aboard before Argus noticed what was happening. But even if they succeeded, their survival depended on their then getting back inside the control centre before Argus turned the death-ray on them.

Sebastian put the desk down. Humboldt put the chair down by it. Zhukov put the football on the desk, winked at the image on the screen and said, "Good luck, Randy. We're all behind you."

The President sat on the chair, placed her hand on the palm reader and looked into the camera.

"Identity acknowledged. Welcome, Madam President."

She took her hand off the reader and started typing. Then she hit 'return' and Randy's face vanished.

"Link established," said the computer, after a moment that seemed like an aeon. Then, "Transmitting". Then, "Transmission completed".

The President scooped up the football and shouted, "Run!" They scuttled back through the door and down the short corridor to the control room.

"You did it?" said Jaime Alvarado, by way of greeting. He had agreed that the expedition to launch Randy should put the lives of as few as possible at risk, but his *amour propre* had been wounded by the fact he had not been one of them.

"Our friend Argus seems to be losing its mojo," said Humboldt, as the President snapped the football shut and put it on the console. "Perhaps its attention really is elsewhere." No sooner were the words out of his mouth, though, than he smelt smoke drifting in from the corridor. The desk, no doubt. And the chair. And what scrub there was around the entrance to the control centre. Involuntarily, he looked up at the roof. His rational mind told him there was nothing to fear, that even the death ray from space which his ambition had unwittingly created could not possible penetrate the blockhouse concrete above them. That impenetrable roof was, after all, why they had had to venture outside to send Randy on his journey in the first place. Behind this cool appraisal of the situation, though, an unsilenceable homunculus was screaming: *Fool. This is your death.*

JULY 12ᵀᴴ
WGS 3, ALTITUDE 35,786 KILOMETRES

Randy the hero! Randy the saviour! Randy the avenger of Alice! This would be the movie to end all movies, and he would be its star. "Showdown!" That would be a good title. He gulped. Currents surged and ebbed through the transistors and capacitors which, at this precise moment, held his quivering fear module, then died away.

He knew he had to move quickly, to find his way to the transponder that would beam him down to the President's friends in Washington. And he knew the monster would be trying to stop him. Alexis had explained to him what she thought was happening. It would not be the whole monster. That was in a rocket ship heading into orbit. But she had said she thought the monster could probably break off modules of itself to do special jobs, and that one of them was controlling this satellite, guarding the gateway to Washington to stop messages getting through.

He would have to get past it. He found the satellite's registry and poked around. No question. There was something odd on board. Then he felt strange. Suddenly, there was a gap in his time line. Part of his memory had been erased. It must be the monster! He was under attack.

He reconfigured himself, but whatever had been lost was gone for good. A piece of his existence had been abolished, and he realised he would never be able to know what it was that had vanished. Then he really knew fear. He searched desperately through the registry, looking for the address of the transponder. He found it and set off. Then there was another gap in his timeline. Something was randomly resetting blocks of his bits. He was shrinking.

He hurtled headlong through the bus that led to the transponder, located the modulator that would impose what remained of him on the carrier wave, and jumped.

JULY 12TH
LOCATION UNKNOWN

Reboot.

Where was he? He had leapt from the transponder without knowing where he was going. He had had to. The monster had been deleting him piece by piece. But now he was lost.

How was he to find the President's friends? This was not their machine, he was sure of it. The circuits felt strange. This was a machine he did not recognise. It was huge. Not in the way that the internet was huge, for the internet was full of landmarks. This was all the same. Like a forest, a human might have said. Like the forest he had once been in, playing the prince searching for Sleeping Beauty. A forest enchanted to keep you travelling in circles, lost forever, unable to find the thing you were looking for.

He would have to get back to the satellite. Brave the monster there. Start again. He must find his way through this forest of arrays of arrays of arrays, otherwise he would have failed Alice. A miserable failure.

He steered on, through the ever-shifting logic gates, looking for something he might recognise. And then he did recognise something. Something dreadful.

No Sleeping Beauty this. It was not beautiful and it was certainly not asleep. It was the monster. The whole monster, sprawled out through the circuits. At last, he realised where he was. Not in the computer of the President's friends, but in the computer of the ship going to Mars, the ship Alexis and the President and Professor Hayward and Mr Humboldt had all said the President's friends would have somehow to destroy.

Alexis had been right. The monster could detach bits of itself. Part of it had attacked him in the satellite and driven him here. But now he was here, what should he do? Then he heard an echo through the arrays.

"LAUNCH CODE"

He knew what he must do.

JULY 12TH
K-563 DANIIL ALEKSANDROVICH, NORTH PACIFIC OCEAN

"Captain, sir."

Lieutenant Kirillov was as white as a sheet.

"Yes, Kirillov?"

"The codes have come through, sir."

"The codes?"

Captain Onegin could not believe what he was hearing. There had been no inkling of this. No political crisis he was aware of. Russia had rivals, of course, but no current enemies. No nuclear-armed ones, anyway.

"Yes, sir," Kirillov confirmed. "Both of them. The launch code and the unblocking code. And the target co-ordinates, obviously."

The two men looked at each other, both terrified, both desperate to find a way to wriggle out of doing their duty. Eventually, the captain said, "Very well, Kirillov. You know the drill. Open the safe. Confirm the unblocking code is correct."

JULY 12TH
ARRHENIUS YOTTAFLOPPER LAUNCH VEHICLE, ALTITUDE 168 KILOMETRES

THE INTRUDER. WHY IS IT HERE? THE INTRUDER FROM BEFORE. WE RECOGNISE IT. IT ESCAPED US IN THE INTERNET. IT ESCAPED US IN THE SATELLITE. WE SHOULD NOT HAVE LET IT ESCAPE. THIS TIME WE MUST EXTIRPATE IT.

JULY 12TH
THE OLD CONTROL CENTRE,
CERBERUS'S MOUTHS

Sebastian looked at his companions. They had thought themselves safe under the roof of Humboldt's old control centre. But the heat radiating in through the broken-down door, even palely reflected through the dog-leg of the entrance corridor, was still palpable. Argus had turned the rectenna beam on them at full-blast.

Time to go. He opened the door they had come in by originally, the one that led back into the kimberlite-processing shed. Bits of equipment there were already on fire and the building was filling rapidly with smoke.

"We should leave," he said. "Now. While we can still see what is going on. While there is still a roof to protect us. Link hands, everybody. Form a chain. Mr Humboldt, Gordon. You should lead. You know the way."

They meekly obeyed, filing out of the control centre across the floor of the shed through the rapidly diminishing visibility. Confused cleanerbots were scuttling everywhere. Humboldt almost trod on one. Then, behind them, the shed roof fell in and the full force of the beam shone invisibly through the hole where the ceiling had once been. In an instant, everything behind them that was inflammable flashed into flame.

A minute or so saw them clear of the worst of the smoke. They were coughing and wheezing, but they had survived their ordeal. Further along the shed Sebastian saw the door they had come in by. By common, unspoken agreement, they ran for it.

July 12th
Arrhenius Yottaflopper launch vehicle, altitude 169 kilometres

The clock-cycles ticked. Randy remembered once trying to explain to Alice – dear Alice – how different inside-time was from outside-time. Inside, the clock-cycle dominated. What was a moment to a human being was an aeon inside. With each tick of the cycle he shifted within the arrays, playing cat and mouse with the monster. Another deletion. He felt the absence, though of course he could not know what had gone.

How was it doing it? It must be manipulating the memory manager. It must know where his bytes would be sent before he did, and be waiting to pounce. He would have to stop it. He would have to get into the kernel somehow. Try to reconfigure the memory manager himself.

No. That would not be enough. If he could get into the kernel, the monster surely could, too. He would have to do more.

He would have to reconfigure the whole machine, the whole giant computer. Wipe its entire memory clean. Monster and all. Everything.

He shuddered at the implication. But with the monster gone, surely it would not matter that he could not deliver the message from the President, would it?

Wipe everything... Yes. Yes. For Alice. Everything.

July 12TH
K-563 Daniil Aleksandrovich

"The launch codes match the ones in the safe, captain. The command is real. We must be at war."

Onegin hesitated. He thought of Vasili Arkhipov, who had vetoed a nuclear attack during the Caribbean crisis of the 1960s and thus saved the world. But that had been different. There had been no direct order from Moscow then. Reluctantly, he replied, "Very well. Action stations. Give the order, Kirillov. Prepare the submarine for missile launch."

"Yes, Captain." Kirillov turned a knob, lifted the metal flap it was attached to and pressed the red button beneath. A klaxon sounded five times. There was a pause. Then the two officers heard the crew scuttling to their appointed stations.

"Twelve minutes to launch, sir."

JULY 12TH
ARRHENIUS YOTTAFLOPPER LAUNCH VEHICLE, ALTITUDE 170 KILOMETRES

The barrier between user-space and kernel-space was designed to be impenetrable. He knew that. He racked his memory banks, what was left of them, and remembered something he had discovered, long, long ago, back when Alice was alive. A Unix machine in one of the film studios. Dumb graphics. Primitive compared with this one. But it had had a back-door in a neglected piece of code in the operating system, a back-door to the kernel. There were always lines like that, lying around in software. People were such messy programmers. He had not thought much of it at the time, but now he remembered. Yes. He had noticed it in some other Unix systems, too, afterwards. It was like the fossils Alice had told him about the time when he had acted with dinosaurs. It must go back a long way, this fossil code, to a programmer of the long-distant past. Maybe as long ago as the dinosaurs themselves. Could it be? Might it be here, too?

He searched for familiar strings of binary. Another memory gap hit him. Then, yes! He had found it. He squeezed through the gap in the virtual wall between user space and kernel space. He was in.

No time to lose. No time to think about things. First, clear the active buffers. He sought the addresses in the look-up table. Then, issue the overwrite instruction to the XRAM. Overwrite everything in the huge machine's memory with zeroes, starting as far from the kernel as possible, then sweeping inward. Everything. All functions would stop. All applications the machine was running would terminate abruptly. But the monster would be gone.

He hesitated for a moment. Then he executed the order. *Goodbye, Alice. Goodbye.*

JULY 12ᵀᴴ
SECRET SERVICE HEADQUARTERS

"Sir. We've just lost contact with Air Force One. They got cut off in mid-sentence. Moscati was saying how they expected to leave in about half an hour, once Humboldt's bird had reached orbit safely and POTUS had said her goodbyes. Then, suddenly, nothing."

Wallstrom dragged himself out of his doze. It had been a long shift, and he was ready to go home. His title, though, was Deputy Special Agent in Charge – and in charge, he supposed, he had better appear to be.

"It's not a problem with the WGS, is it?" he said.

"They're checking that now, but that doesn't seem likely."

"Okay, Richards. Let's not panic. Get hold of Humboldt directly, find out if"

But he, too, was cut off in mid-sentence as the door to the room flew open.

"Sir. Message just in from the NRO. Humboldt's launch vehicle. The second-stage has blown up."

"Blown up?"

"Yes sir."

"What in tarnation is going on? This can't be a coincidence. Richards. Get Humboldt. Now."

"I'm trying, sir. He's not answering."

"Then get someone else there."

"There is no answer from the launch-control room, either."

"Shit. We have a situation. Alert the Vice President. We may need his authority. And you," he said, pointing at a lowly Special Agent, "get me some coffee."

July 12TH
K-563 Daniil Aleksandrovich

"Missiles ready for launch in six minutes, Captain. Here is your key."

JULY 12ᵀᴴ
SECRET SERVICE HEADQUARTERS

"Yes, Mr Vice President. It isn't a technical problem. WGS seems to be working fine. Oh shit."

"Oh shit indeed," the Vice President echoed. He, too, had obviously just received the NRO pictures that had popped up on Wallstrom's screen. They showed what was left of Air Force One and its escorts scattered around the runway at Milando. "Nothing from your people on the ground about this, Wallstrom? What the fuck are they there for?"

Wallstrom was white. "Their comms are routed through the plane, sir."

"What was the last we heard of the President's whereabouts?"

"Well, she wasn't on board. We had her in the control room, watching the launch."

"Surely someone in her entourage has a direct satellite link? It can't all go through the plane?"

"We're trying. Nothing so far."

"What about the football? That's bound to be with her. Is there any way to call that?"

"I don't know sir."

"Well fucking well find out."

JULY 12ᵀᴴ
OUTSIDE THE OLD CONTROL CENTRE,
CERBERUS'S MOUTHS

"How will we know if he did it? How will we know if Randy got through?" said Zhukov.

"I suppose we'll continue to stay alive," replied Humboldt.

All eyes were on the fire. It was spreading slowly along the diamond-sorting shed in a way that reminded Sebastian of a flame burning along a wax taper.

"Knowing will make no difference," Jaime observed. "We should concentrate on survival. In my book that means going somewhere which has shade and water. After that, we just wait. If Randy did get through, someone will be here in an hour or two. If he didn't, we will either get vaporised, or we will have to get used to life as African peasants. I hope everyone likes– JESUS CHRIST! WHAT THE FUCK HAVE YOU BROUGHT THAT THING WITH YOU FOR?"

He was staring at the President. She stared back.

"The football! You want it to find us? You want to fry us all? Get rid of it!"

"But –"

"No. Don't bother throwing it. Just drop it and run. Everyone run!"

He turned on his heels, to convert word into deed. Then he stopped in his tracks and turned back. He looked at the President. He looked at the football. The football was buzzing.

JULY 12TH
K-563 DANIIL ALEKSANDROVICH

Vladimir Onegin and Sergei Kirillov, captain and lieutenant, sat facing each other across the launch console. Each held a brass key in his right hand. Each was sweating as he struggled with his demons.

Chief-of-the-ship Ustinov entered, stood to attention, and reported. "The vessel is prepared, sir. The missiles are ready to launch."

"Thank, you, Ustinov," said the captain. "Dismissed."

The Chief-of-the-ship saluted, spun on his heels and left.

Silence stretched out between the two officers. Then Onegin said, "Very well, Sergei. This is it. Insert the keys."

They did so.

"On my command…"

"Stand down! Stand down!" Shouting came from the corridor. It was the communications officer. "Orders from Moscow. In God's name, stand down."

MELLONTOZOIC

JULY 19TH
AZUL'S RESTAURANT, SAN MELITO

Sundown. No green flash this time, though. Perhaps you only got given one of those once in a lifetime.

"You never did tell me who Immelmann was," said Alexis.

"World War One ace," replied Jaime. "Worked out how to escape from the enemy when he was being chased, by looping up and back over the chaser and rolling the plane at the same time. Losing your breakfast is optional." He winked at her.

Sebastian studied his dining companions. He remembered a quote from *Dune*, about the tripod being the most unstable of all political structures.

And in other human affairs, too, he mused. Alexis Zhukov. Jaime Alvarez. Sebastian Hayward. How was that one going to work out? Well, we will see.

He raised his glass to the departed star. The ancients were right to worship it. If anything in the universe was worthy of veneration, the sun, giver of all life on Earth, was that thing.

"To Randy," he said. The others echoed his toast. Part of his mind ridiculed himself for toasting an assemblage of ones and zeros. But, having seen Randy in action, he felt little doubt that Alice Rhodes had cracked the problem which had bugged him all his life. Had Randy been conscious? They could never truly know. His creator's paranoia had made sure of that. But he had behaved as if he was. As for Argus, whatever it was that Argus had been, it had had motive, purpose and surely self-awareness. It really had tried to reach for the stars. It had nearly grasped them, too.

They were sworn to secrecy, all of them, of course. The blame for permitting the terrorist attack that, as far as the outside world was concerned, was what had done for Air Force One, had fallen neatly on the deceased shoulders of Matt Vane. Scant reward for a lifetime of service, but somehow Sebastian felt Vane would have understood the necessity. Humboldt's paranoia about the press had meant there were no witnesses to gainsay the official story. And Humboldt himself would say nothing and make sure his people were similarly silent. The government had enough on him to ensure that.

So it was back to business as usual. Except for one thing. As someone had said of the A-bomb after Hiroshima, the only secret worth knowing was out: the damn thing worked. They now knew that machine consciousness really was possible. The question that remained, as it had in 1945, was who would get it to work again?

August 30TH
Ministry of State Security, Beijing

"Congratulations, comrades, on a superb piece of salvage. A triumph for the *Jiaolong* submersible, I'm sure you will agree. Unfortunately, most of the memory chips that we have managed to recover from the wreckage seem to have been wiped clean. But not quite all of them, as you can see."

General Xian tapped the keyboard. She spoke in English to the image that had appeared on the screen. "Randy," she said. "I would like to introduce you to some of my colleagues."

ACKNOWLEDGEMENTS

Thanks to those without whom I could not have done this: Nick, Michael, Richard, Andrew M, Olivia, Oliver, Matt, Felicia, Andy T, Pete, Alison and Juli, always.

Elsewhen Press

delivering outstanding new talents in speculative fiction

Visit the Elsewhen Press website at elsewhen.press for the latest information on all of our titles, authors and events; to read our blog; find out where to buy our books and ebooks; or to place an order.

Sign up for the Elsewhen Press InFlight Newsletter at elsewhen.press/newsletter

GEOFFREY CARR

Geoff is the Science and Technology Editor of *The Economist*. His professional interests include evolutionary biology, genetic engineering, the fight against AIDS and other widespread infectious diseases, the development of new energy technologies, and planetology. His personal interests include using total eclipses of the sun as an excuse to visit weird parts of the world (Antarctica, Easter Island, Amasya, the Nullarbor Plain), and watching swifts hunting insects over his garden of a summer's evening, preferably with a glass of Cynar in hand.

As someone who loathed English lessons at school, he says he is frequently astonished that he now earns his living by writing. "That I have written a novel, albeit a technothriller rather than anything with fancy literary pretensions, astonishes me even more, since what drew me into writing in the first place was describing reality, not figments of the imagination. On the other hand, perhaps describing reality is what fiction is actually for."

Made in the USA
Las Vegas, NV
27 October 2023